Guillermo Romano

****

Beneath the canopy of the rainforest, at the base of a tamarind tree, is an entrance to a Cenote, one of a series of intricate underground cave systems and well entrances found in the Mayan Peninsula. Mayans used Cenotes as wells for collected rainwater, but also as portals to the underworld; many served as religious sacrifice pits. The complex tamarind root system, resting on huge polished boulders, camouflages the opening, but in an instant, the dark orifice transforms into a light well. Most observers would perceive only a reflection of sunlight from rainwater collected on leaves. But there is no sunlight reaching this far down into the jungle – only that strange glare. The trained eye, however, will see the sign of an entrance to an underground passage to another world.

Underground, away from the entrance, is a partially lighted, vaulted glass-like vault chamber. It is the size of a basketball court or a high school gym, but with a circular base and a polished, hemispherical ceiling with a small shy hole at the apex, no more than a meter wide. At the far side of the chamber was the source of the light, a bright object that defeated the darkness with flickers of intense light. The light carries unevenly through the vault until, reaching the center, it vanishes as it moves up. The luminous effect is amplified by the shallow, still, mirror-like water flooding the floor of the chamber.

Suddenly the peace is broken by the sound of moving water. Ripples distort the light, creating jagged water reflections on the cave vault. A tired breathing accompanies the sound of water displaced by slow steps. On the top of a perfectly polished cube stone is a hand sized quartz-like crystal. Although amorphous in shape it is of good appearance: balanced, proportionate, almost artistic. The crystal

1

emanates light in slow pulses. The wrinkled and shaking hands of an old man gently touch the crystal's surface, the tips of rough fingers slide along its sculpted sides. Then, in a final gesture, the old man grasps the whole crystal with an agonizing pain, as if he were clinging to his last breaths of air, his last shimmers of hope.

The Call

Concentrated on a breathing meditation, a man jogs along a forest trail, until the sound of breaking branches breaks the silence. While the breathing and running steps had provided a rhythmical background noise, this sudden sound awakened Serge from his thoughts. Many times he had drifted away in this moving meditation, escaping from the present, longing for the past, and wondering about an uncertain future.

He was starting his daily routine a bit earlier but like all mornings, rain or shine, it started with a free-weight calisthenics warm-up, followed by a long run. The quiet forest trial had a wet surface on a dark soil background, and was covered in places with fallen old leaves, small branches, woodchips and bark. Underneath his moving feet Serge saw a moving pattern of greens, ochre, yellows and browns that resembled the design of a modern office carpet, moving in the opposite direction. Already his clothes were damp with sweat and dew from hanging leaves; he could hear drops of a residual rain falling on his shoulders, at times synchronizing with his breathing.

"One-two, breathe in, one-two, breathe out, one-two, breathe in, one-two, breathe out. . . ."

He repeated the words in his mind, as if falling into a meditation, one he enjoyed on his long, solitary runs close to nature.

Without thinking he said out loud: "Steph... where are you?"

There was no answer to the same old question he repeated whenever faced with an uncertain time in his life. "Help me find my way..."

Serge felt that things around his life were, if not in disarray, at least not in the right place. He had lost his wife – his best friend – six years ago, sixteen years after their marriage and as they were into their best "growing together" years. She had left him early but at least with the greatest gift of all: a now twenty year-old, bright young man, their son, Max.

Stephanie had died of a sudden, undetected aneurism. One day she complained about a terrible headache; she fell unconscious and never awoke again. It was right after Max's fourteenth birthday and before a long-awaited family trip to an archeological find in the jungles of Belize and Guatemala, south of the Yucatan peninsula, where Stephanie was researching lost Mayan cities. Stephanie had been exploring the Mayan jungles in search of traces of a lost nomadic culture. Although referenced in some glyphs of the Mayan Codices, there were no references to this culture in modern history, which made a mystery to be researched. Some scholars credited these people as founders of some of the classic Mesoamerican cultures. It was understood they had stopped being nomadic but no one knew where they established their residence. The puzzle was not why they vanished, but where they settled and where their wisdom came from, as their influence was felt throughout Mesoamerica. This work had exposed Stephanie to long travel and research hours, and hard, stressful negotiations for grants and funding, but her efforts paid off and she had been awarded significant contributions that allowed her to continue her work.

Although proud of her achievements and promising future and that she was strong and fit, Serge knew that she was reaching some kind of limit. She had started to complain of blinding migraines, dizziness and lack of strength. Hard work was getting to her, and Serge wanted her to spend time for herself. Her drive and passion were so strong, though, she could not find a way to stop when she felt she was getting close to getting an answer.

To Serge's heart, her sudden departure was an irreparable tragedy, one that even after six years felt like it had been yesterday.

Serge had no other family he could relate to. Years had passed since his father declared him dead. Words spoken in impulse were fueled by manipulation and lies by his father's wife, his stepmother. Taking advantage of his father's early Alzheimer's, she convinced him to take Serge out of his will and give everything to her two daughters, his stepsisters. They did not complain at the injustice, even though he had stood by them and helped them all through their lives. Both turned their backs on him after the one-sided effort by his stepmother to control his father's estate.

For more than 20 years he had had a close relationship with his father, but living away for the last six years in combination with the early Alzheimer's, had made things more difficult. The sisters represented a part of Serge early teen life. Being fifteen years older than them allowed him to teach them many things, from their early steps to, homework, to advice with boyfriends. All that was gone now.

After being apart for so long and with so much at stake he decided not to fight for anything; he thought it was not worth it, for Max and for him. This detachment was used by his stepmother as a selfish expression of an ungrateful son towards his ill father, one with no loyalty to his family or a giving father. Serge understood her struggle to control his father's estate. The promise of a hefty inheritance to both sisters and an assured future was more valuable than blood or half-blood. Both girls sided with their mother, confirming any slander, believing every lie his stepmother created to get him out of the picture. While Serge treasured his father's memory and example, he wished for a chance to see him again, but they had refused him several times. The last time they saw each other there had been a painful goodbye where his father declared that he had died, that Serge was no longer his son. He had walked away, preferring to remember his father as the man he had been, knowing that in the end, he had inherited the best gifts from his father: his generous heart and his solid integrity. That day, the last time he saw his father had departed with a hug and kiss and never looked back.

Stephanie's parents, although close to his son Max, had distanced themselves from Serge after their daughter's death. He had thought that those sixteen years since marriage, and the previous seven dating, would have given him the chance to be part of her family, a part of them. But according to a brief talk with a family friend, they thought he could have done something more to prevent their daughter's death; that he had not made any effort to treat her, and even less to save her. At times Serge blamed himself for the same reason, adding to an unnecessary guilt. With regards to his in-laws relationship, he knew that people can tolerate their own kin's weaknesses but can't ever forget others' mistakes.

In the past few years and with all these events, Serge's belief system had been shaken to the ground. While he was spiritually hungry, he lacked the faith to follow any religion. He preferred to believe in a God with whom he could have a personal relationship, no intermediaries. He was always full of questions for a non-responsive God, at least as measured in human terms. He was not sure anymore where his faith rested but he trusted the values of a partial, self-taught Judeo-Christian religion and the moral values taught by his father during his early upbringing. A year after Stephanie's death, Serge lost his business to corruption and bureaucracy. He had spent years building a client base, a name and a professional practice, but in his last venture a corrupt official with a greedy pocket had partnered with one of his competitors. He lost a big contract and with that assumed a huge debt that eventually forced him to close his office and shut his practice for a while. The calculated gamble of not playing with the system did not pay out. With Stephanie gone, he simply had lost his motivation. He decided to move away for a year, to take a sabbatical with Max and try to "find his way".

His son was turning into a man, still young but definitely independent. While Serge felt his work raising Max had been good, he knew deep inside that not having a mother meant not developing certain parts of his life. Max resembled his mother so much that Serge knew that whatever he did would reflect his own limitations and weaknesses.

*   *   *

"One-two, breathe out, one-two, breathe in, one-two, breathe out, one-two breathe in...." He had fallen again into the breathing rhythm that took him out of this world and into the deep thought-daydream state he enjoyed so much while exercising.

It was 9:53 AM on the deserted trail, every "real" person and "successful" professional were already working on their real lives or personal business. Worthy, self-respecting men and women were productive and able to hold a job on their own. Serge was beating himself up once again: if it was not a matter of luck, if we are supposed to produce our own path and if we are responsible for our own lives, why he was here at this moment, this time? Why, at this point in life, was he was still not going anywhere, the choices made not taking him anywhere? A real mid-age crisis.

With his extensive experience and varied training and education, Serge was perceived as either "overqualified" for the positions he sought, or that he was way late on the job track for someone in his generation. Over and over in his head he played the same words he used in job interviews, phone calls and meetings: "Just exploit me. I just need a chance to prove myself and earn your trust." With no potential work in the near future, with responsibilities to fulfill, he felt more tired, feeling that he could not take it any longer. Although he felt desperate, he continued moving on, "something will come," he repeated and kept on going.

It had been three weeks since he had been "replaced" at the temporary job he got at a nursery. He had been in charge of basic operations, deliveries and quality control. In the last seven months he had learned innumerable names of plants, ground covers, grasses. He had made connections with other nurseries in different areas of the region that had direct sales to the public. He had made friends with most of the Spanish-speaking work crew, most of them illegal immigrants but tireless, hardworking and jovial people.

The nursery was located on the area plateau, 35 acres of open, flat rich land irrigated by a passing river. It was surrounded by a driving range, two wineries, and a seasonal Christmas tree lot. At the back were a total of 22 divided lots with different plants; there were 15 greenhouses constructed of aluminum pipe, with integrated irrigation, concrete landings and clear, hand-cut translucent plastic that kept temperatures warm throughout the year. This allowed the nursery to operate even through the slow, colder months of winter. The seasonal nature of the business started in late winter with the harvesting of plants in greenhouses, through the early part of fall, when planting ended and basic clean-up occurred in the regional landscapes.

The nursery job was something Serge accepted as a temporary gig, well-below his professional pay grade, "Until times and the economy rebounds," he repeated to himself. Being a nursery manager, although far from his professional background, kept him busy and, to his pleasant surprise, motivated. He had learned a lot about landscape architecture, the region's weather and, yes, plants. All his days started at 6:30 AM with a tight, busy schedule that involved two shifts of plant collection and general operations, and late evenings doing invoices and verifying quality control for customer's orders and next day's deliveries.

After the first few days he found that he liked the job. Most of the time he was outside in the fields, getting his hands dirty in black soil, learning names of plants, packaging, inventorying, printing labels, supervising teams. He was being paid, well, not an architect's wages, but considering the promised bonuses and salary adjustments (if he worked there the full season), then it would be a fair salary, enough to make his worldly payments. The most important aspect was the sense of feeling useful, being active, especially after a long, dry period of job search.

Late one afternoon, close to end of the hardest period of the season, the nursery owner called him on the radio, looking for him. Serge was inside greenhouse No. 5, driving a forklift in reverse, moving out a collection of empty wood crates and planks used to collect plants from the field. His face, full of sweat and dirt, resembled a camouflaged hunter at the end of the hunting season. He was joking with the packing crew in Spanish about how his newly-acquired calloused hands would not be able to make any more drawings in his sketchbook.

The call came with a sounding crack and beep; he was summoned to the main office for a business update. "Serge, Serge, please report to Andrei A S A P at the main office."
Ernesto, one of the most experienced job captains in the packing crew, warned Serge with a wide smile "Sounds like trouble...." Serge parked the forklift at the greenhouse entrance, leaving the rest of the clean-up to Ernesto and his crew. He climbed onto one of the cross-country bicycles the nursery made available to employees, to get to the office faster.

"Seems pretty urgent. Slack! Slack!" Ernesto mimicked with hand movements the action of a whip, giving Serge a hard time.

"Then I should not make 'el jefe wait," he replied, looking back to his friend with a smile.

The main office was in an old, 1910's home turned family business some 60 years prior. What probably had started as a hobby for the current owner's grandfather was now a full-time nursery operation that distributed groundcovers to most of the wholesale nurseries in the region. As Serge entered the office he took off his working gloves and left his walkie-talkie in its charging base. He saluted the receptionist in military style, a kind of informal ritual they had.

Joan had been a reservist with the National Guard and had served in the Iraq war. She loved to wear green camo fatigues regardless of the season or fashion trends. Smiling and friendly, Joan had always responded to the salute with "Hola de nuevo" spoken in her best

Spanish accent, a reply that corresponded to Serge's background. Today, however, the salute was greeted with a nod and a somber pale expression.

Serge climbed the stairs up to the first floor, where the owner's office was. As Serge knocked on the door he looked to his left at the wall, not knowing that this was to be the last time he would see the old photographs hanging there, of a time long gone from this valley he had grown to love so much. The old sepia images depicted a simpler life, a time where there were no boundaries, no regulations, no limits. Serge's announcement of his presence was met with a "come in". Andrei was a second-generation German immigrant in his late thirties. He was 5'6" tall, in good shape, with a head shaved bald and an obsession for woolen plaid lumberjack shirts and tight jeans. While always respectful, Andrei had never opened himself to friendship or camaraderie; all conversations with him were purely business and straight to the point. Serge appreciated this as he thought he knew what to expect, where he was standing, but what followed the formal greeting was a complete surprise.

"I'm sorry, but the company cannot risk losing you in the future for another, more lucrative job offer that you might get... and we must let you go." Andrei paused for only a second and without waiting for Serge to speak added," I hope you can understand."

Serge was silent, trying to figure out if he should sit down, ask "why" or simply walk out. He did not wait for the silence to become awkward. When he had his architecture business, Serge had himself been in the nursery owner's position. He simply replied, "I guess you have to do what you have to do."

He looked straight to Andrei's eyes and extended his hand, looking for a business-like handshake, the same as had been enough when Serge had received the job offer seven months before.

"Whatever is convenient to you and your business. I really appreciated the opportunity and the experience. I'll talk with Sally in accounting to finalize my hours and will return your equipment to Joan."

Serge went down to the basement to his office, dusted off his clothes, picked up his personal things, and walked to his car. He decided not to walk to the fields, to say goodbye to the crew and the rest of the staff. There would have been many questions he did not have answers for. The next day Sally gave him a call to verify his last working hours and to see if he wanted to pick up the check or get it by mail. Serge preferred the later. She expressed that she was sorry and told him a few details he was not aware of. He found that he had been replaced by someone with an horticulture background, a much younger woman willing to do his work for half the money he had been promised and without the bonuses. Apparently Andrei liked bargains; there was no argument there.

It had not been the best time for this to happen, still Serge had no grudge against the nursery…. It was the first time he had ever been fired from a job.

Out of the darkness a female hand touches a crystal, though this one is not shining like the other one. The female hand raises it and gently places it in an old man's hands, the same scarred hand that was touching the flickering crystal. The transfer of the crystal is felt as ceremony, formal, full of symbolism and ritual. The rotation of the crystal to an empty base might mean something important, but as the crystal touches the base, there is no light emanating from it. The old man's hands hold and shake the base, as if pleading for the crystal to shine. The crystal remains unchanged; the old man's hands hold the base with strength until their knuckles turn white. The soft female hands take both of his hands with gentleness and pull them away from the base. The dim light remains in the cave, the flickering continues.

11

The Past

The last five years had been very unpredictable, with most of what G's life had been disappearing gradually and this had major effects. At age 45, he found himself living a life that was completely different from what he envisioned it would be. There was a certain disappointment with not being able to live and achieve his dreams, but this was balanced by a deep satisfaction for what he had achieved with what life has given him, without quitting.

Serge was an architect with a master's degree in environmental design. He had complemented his career with studies in archeology, art and volunteer work for accessibility guidelines advocacy. He had also spent three years after high school as a volunteer private with the armed forces, working in disaster relief and damage evaluation. He combined this experience with intensive military training from the sergeant in charge of his unit, as a gesture of his intent to be integrated with the squad he was part of during any deployments in or outside the country. His duty had been continuous only during the first year; he had been a reservist in the following years.

These experiences gave him the opportunity to see and understand the world from a different perspective. He was once deployed in a rescue and recovery relief effort after a major earthquake in Central America. The experience left him humble and touched, not only by the might and power of nature but also by the wide range of responses from people to these events. Upon his return he related the experience to his father: it had been very difficult for him to bear the suffering and pain of so many people while seeing the opportunism of those who stole and profited from others' misery. Their rescue efforts during the first days, assessing damage and distributing relief supplies during the daytime, had been tainted by security patrols and riot control during the evenings. It was hard to be part of a rescue and relief team that had to bear arms for its own safety. Serge and his father had talked about the limitations of the human condition, about growing through adversity and experiences.

All in all, Serge reflected, he had had a good life, perhaps restless, searching, not always good but never bad.

He recalled the many conversations with his father about youthful impetus, fast decisions, easy assessments without merit; how maturity, integrity, becoming a man, was a matter of experience and growing up.

"Son ..." His father used to start the conversation like this, with a pause, when he saw Serge thinking. "You know? You should not worry ... youth is a sickness that is cured with time."

Serge had always wondered if he would ever want to be cured, if he would grow old and become a relic that never changes, a stiff tree trunk that breaks at the first sign of a storm. He had seen many people lose their sense of wonder and desire to live. He wanted to preserve the same curiosity, tolerance and integrity he had been taught by his father, and hoped that at the end it would help him to become a better man throughout his life.

"One-two, breathe out, one-two, breathe in, one-two, breathe out, one-two breathe in ..."

Serge ran on, immersed in the events of the past couple of years. Work, family, friends, places lived, things lost, things learned...."It has been a fascinating journey, interesting" he told himself. He did not like to complain, but he questioned whether if sometimes in our lives, we find ourselves in a place because of lack of determination or lack of luck? A negative attitude, or a willingness to compromise and adapt to changing times? Was he becoming a stiff tree?

"How are we suppose to understand the difference between what is our responsibility and what is beyond our control?" He just did not know. As he ran he noticed a bend in the trail he had not seen

13

before: he was way deep into the forest. The canopy of the trees excluded almost all of the daylight and the trail had grown narrower. His shoulders brushed the wet vegetation on both sides of the trail. Water now dripped directly into his t-shirt. He felt cold, which brought him back from his thoughts and into reality. He stopped, breathing deeply in and out a couple of times; he placed his hands on his waist and then his knees, listened to the sound that silence made when no one was around. He looked ahead and back along the trail, looked around for any sign of movement or source of sound among the closed vegetation. For a moment he felt that he was part of the forest, part of something larger than himself, something that gave him a strange sense of meaning, as if he had been there before or were supposed to be there now. It was a strange sensation, one he had never felt before but which did not feel alien to him. The feeling had lasted only an instant but it left a deep mark on Serge's memory. He knew it was something important, it felt like a call, or an undeniable "déjà vu." He had been there before... or he would be there again. He saw a small shine from one of the dark but strong bases of the surrounding evergreen trees. He was surprised: there was no sunshine, not this deep into the forest; it had been a brief flicker of light, as if bouncing off water on green leaves. He felt something. It was as if he had been lost for so long and then found. He smiled to himself. Whatever it was... or is... it felt good, even spiritual.

"Like Max says – yikes!" He spoke to himself the word that his son used to exclaim when surprised, that was like an epiphany, he thought, or was it a serendipitous moment? I need to check my dictionary. Serge laughed. He looked again, trying to see if he could locate the source of the light, but he could not see anything. A drop of water fell on his forehead. It was cold and bounced down to his left hand; he checked his watch. It was time to go back home, have a shower, go for a bite, check the classifieds for jobs, check his e-mail for any messages... start his day.

"Best of luck there, Serge."

After a brief pause he turned around to go back. He smiled, somehow he knew the way back.

Later that day he was at his favorite local coffee shop. "Vic's" was one of those small cafes that existed before lattes were hip and coffee became a drink for yuppies. The space was an old 1930's house converted to a family restaurant. Half of it was empty and rarely used. The owner had closed the restaurant business years ago after his wife passed away. He was hoping to lease it to an adventurous entrepreneur who could partner with his small coffee shop business. Vic was a quiet and friendly man in his late sixties, with long gray air, a distinctive goatee, dressed as always in denim overalls.

"Hey, Serge, good morning!" shouted Vic from behind the counter, wearing a big smile and handing a coffee cup to one of his customers. "What can I give you today?"
"Hey Vic!" he replied, "Same as always please"
Serge settled himself and browsed through the front page of the classifieds. It had been a while since he had stopped looking for professional positions that matched his qualifications. While he was tired of being "overqualified" for a job opening, he did not mind being considered "underpaid" if at least that meant being active, if it allowed him to work and show who he was. In any case, the market was very slow, all of the firms he had visited had turned into "one-man-show" firms: the economy was not doing any favors to anyone.

Although a very sociable person, his networking skills in the past few years had suffered significantly. Serge had always been a loner by nature but an extrovert by heart. He could easily mingle with people in any setting but always looked for activities where he could find solitude. On one of his latest dates, three years after Stephanie died, his date mentioned to him that it was funny she could not figure him out.

During his early professional years he was awarded some of the highest recognitions for his studies and work. He had been highly recommended by teachers, and later on by his employers, who had often expressed regret at his departure.

Serge's younger life had been a common one, a typical lower-middle class boy raised by a single dad. Although sociable, he would seldom share with anyone what clicked in his heart or mind. Still, he was considered by many as "their best friend," someone who was reliable and responsible. Serge was also a rebel of sorts. He encouraged people to question authority, test the establishment, and at times break the rules. He had never belonged to any professional associations or organized groups. He questioned the intentions of many, looked for hidden agendas or means to serve self-interests. He could go on justifying this perspective by simply saying that he was just a man of small needs.

In the café, Serge drank water from a plastic cup with lid and a straw. The cold water reminded him of his earlier run as it went down his throat and chilled him. He had spent the last hour looking for any opportunity in the professional section, by type, by location, by name. He had marked just a few announcements but as he closed and folded the paper he noticed a small short posting:

House Hold Manager
Live in board and room plus excellent compensation. Must be family oriented, responsible, well-educated. If interested call this number. References required.

The number had a 206 code, which meant it was a Seattle area number. He became curious. Surrounding this advertisement was a series of others dedicated to nursing, baby-sitting and care-giving. He felt a bit disappointed but decided that, in any case, it was work and as before with the plant nursery, it could be a nice surprise. He decided to give it a try and marked the advertisement with his yellow highlighter.

Once he got home he dialed the phone number and waited for an answer. As with many other classifieds, the response would be either a recorded job description or an answering machine. He was now used to the drill and had rehearsed a two-sentence message that explained he was interested, provided his name and phone number, and ended with a "please call at your earliest convenience" punch line. But this time it was different. A receptionist with a very clear voice answered the phone. By the sound of her voice it was evident that his was not the first call and definitely would not be the last one. Her voice sounded tired yet professional. This took Serge by surprise, and he had to call upon his improvisational skills and his best English. He wanted to leave a good impression. In a very polite and friendly way, he introduced himself and indicated his interest in the advertisement. The lady asked for his phone number and general info, said he would be contacted later that day.

"Just the same, as always, they'll call... Yeah right." He set down his cell phone, feeling a little disappointed. He had been through this before: he could just as well not expect a call. If they had noticed his Spanish accent, they might picture him according to any foreign stereotype and eliminate him in the first run. Serge moved on to the other advertisements he had marked. Restaurants, sales, administration.... Why he could not find something related to design? Where were his friends and connections? With his qualifications, how was it that it was still so hard to get a job? He was a good, honest, hard-working young professional, wasn't he? He had been fired only from the nursery, just four months ago "... fired... why? Am I not good enough? What am I doing wrong? Should I change the resume for the fiftieth time?"

Serge realized he was beating himself up again and stopped there. He would find something soon....

Later that day, while he was folding his son's laundry, the phone rang. The voice was that of an articulate gentleman, conducting follow-up interviews for the household manager job. Serge was grateful for the call and his tone of voice probably helped to erase the possible boredom of the gentleman's previous calls. Serge made a brief comment about this to him and both had a short laugh that eased the tension of the call. The caller told Serge his name was Ben Stafford and that he had a few questions for him. The next 45 minutes went really fast. The interview questions were hidden in a casual conversation, mostly aimed at revealing the interviewed person's personality and principles. Serge never felt interviewed; it was more like a conversation with a friend, an up-date on the lives of two friends separated by distance and time.

"So tell me Serge " asked Ben Stafford, "how long have you been looking for a job?"

 "About four months, almost five." Serge hesitated as he answered truthfully. Would it show desperation or would it show boredom, laziness? He had decided to be truthful, no appearances and no games. He had learned many times before that the best way to act was natural, to be true to himself, even though many times truth was not what the interviewers were hoping to hear. "One day it might make a difference," Serge had thought, and until then there was nothing to lose.

 "Five loooong months," he repeated.

"That bad?" was Ben's reply,

"Yes, but never a minute of regret. I have also enjoyed this time."

"Is that so? What have you been doing?"

"Well... I have been busy reading, sketching, looking for work, meeting people, spending time with my kid, playing, doing exercise. I guess the hardest part relates to self-respect and feeling unproductive, but once you understand that it is not personal, you get by. Something worthy will come... I feel positive about it."

After a brief pause, Serge added, "I have also spent time in the park, laying on the grass, watching birds and leaves go by, listening to kids playing on swings, couples having conversations, taking long walks... I have taken that time too. My last work was really unrelated to my professional experience, but I enjoyed it deeply and I learned a lot. I guess that what I'm trying to tell you is that as I look back at it all, I make the most of any situation. I simply don't have any regrets."

The interviewer was apparently surprised by the candor with which Serge had been talking. He kept asking him questions about other jobs and experiences and came then to the final and most important question: why had Serge applied for this work?

"Serge, I guess you might have guessed that this question was coming, and I will appreciate your honesty. Why are you applying for this work, why do you think you are capable of doing it? After all, your experience at the nursery was good – you knew that eventually you were going to move on. If it were up to me I would have done the same as they did."

Serge had known the question was coming, and he knew he had to really make Ben understand where he was standing. "Yes," he replied, "I knew that if you were thorough you were going to ask me about this." Serge actually appreciated these questions; it spoke well about the people who were interviewing him.

"All I can say is that I know life works in very funny and strange ways, and although I honestly don't see a relation to my past professional experience, I'm willing to give it a try. All jobs will teach you something, all of them deserve respect. I am willing to try anything. I am hungry in many ways; I have things to prove to myself. I know that if given the chance I will do an excellent job. That if the employer is good and treats me with dignity and honesty, the work by itself will be rewarding, well worth it.

"My Dad once told me that I could be anything I wanted and that eventually he would respect any choice I made. 'Son,' he said, 'You can be anything you want. 'If you want to be a shoe maker, go for it. Just make sure that you should be the best damn shoe maker there is.' Any work is noble as long as it is an honest job, as long as you are true to yourself and as long as it leaves you with a smile at the end of the day.

"So, Ben," Serge concluded, "I believe that I need to be active. I'm willing to do anything to get an honest job and keep it, even if it is far from my professional field, because I know that above being an architect I am a man. And beyond any training, one works with his beliefs and heart and experience, and with that you can do anything. I do not lack ambition and I am not a lost cause. I acknowledge that even the strangest roads might take us to a good experience, and with that we become who we are, not only what we know."

Serge went quiet, hesitant to add to his response. He could hear Ben writing, taking some final notes. Throughout the conversation Ben had made few responses, murmuring "hmmm," "ok," and "go on," encouraging him to continue with his responses. , Now done speaking, Serge took some air. Finally, Ben broke the silence.

"What you said is a bit profound for a simple job like this, but it sounds pretty honest to me. I assume you don't want to say anything more…? Listen." he continued, "What are you doing tomorrow between ten AM and noon?"

Serge said smilingly, "Well, according to my busy schedule… let's see… ten AM… and noon… mmmmm… I guess I have an opening. I can squeeze you in between those hours for a quick meeting. It seems like tomorrow might be your lucky day. I can actually make it, let's say... ten AM?"

Ben let a small laugh out before agreeing. "I have you then for ten AM tomorrow morning, ok? This is the address...."

Serge took note of the downtown address, asked Ben for a few landmarks and major intersections. " Is there anything else to bring besides my resume?"

"Just an open mind." Ben spoke with the assurance of someone who knew what he was talking about.

"Great," said Serge, "I'll see you tomorrow at ten."

"Thank you, Serge. Until then...."

"Thank you for your call and your time. It was an interesting conversation. See you tomorrow." Serge hung-up the phone. He continued folding clothes but now he was smiling. It had been a long time since he felt this way" That is what I call an interview!" he said to himself, recalling the way the conversation had evolved. How different and natural it had gone. It felt good.

"Hold it, Serge" he reminded himself, "don't get your hopes too high. Remember how easy it is to fall from these dreams. So let's not build any high expectations, just take it as it comes, what they say here... 'let's play it by ear,' I'll do that then."

Later, he sat on his desk and stared out the window. Out of the pocket of his shirt he took out a small velvet pouch and opened it. After finding what he was looking for, he took it out: a small washed penny held by two of his fingers. He rubbed gently it in his hand and closed his eyes... a tear emerged.

"A lucky penny, among so many others…. This is a keeper." The words echoed in his mind. He smiled with the memory of that first date, the penny at the bottom of the beer glass…. Serge recalled one of the first dates with Stephanie. They have met at a small Italian restaurant, an easy date to know more about each other in a casual and easy way. Their date had gone well, they shared a good conversation over pizza and a pale amber beer. As Serge made a final toss for the evening he emptied the beer glass expecting to see Stephanie through the bottom of the glass. But a round object obstructed his view, surprised. He moved the glass away from his face and noticed that it was a coin. He thought that probably it had stuck to the bottom of the beer mug, as any paper glass holder. He reached down to the outside of the glass to remove the coin but was unable to do it. Perplexed he looked again and noticed the coin was inside. Meanwhile Stephanie had witness Serge's confusion and expressions, and start laughing.

"Any problems?" she asked him mischievously

"There is a penny on my beer!" making a funny face without knowing what to do.

"What?" replied Stephanie from the other side of the table reaching out for the glass.

Serge, extended his arm passing the glass to her, their hands touched casually, sending the same electric rush that he had felt the day when they met, Serge knew how attracted he was to her.

She reached out inside the glass, took the penny with her gentle fingers and as she pulled out, she kissed with her lips.

"There… I guess if there is such a thing as copper poison we both now have it"

And gave the coin back to Serge, who had his hand open.

"That's a keeper, a lucky penny"

Serge opened his eyes and looked out at clouds moving gently towards the east.

"Help me find my way, Steph." Serge spoke the words to the air.

During the past years he had come to realize that one should not expect anything from anyone. Expectations for ideas or for people were always too high and too hard to swallow when they failed, which happened most of the time. This was something that had become natural to Serge. "Most of us don't even know what we want, so why should I expect from the rest what I am not even sure about, myself?" So it became a simple way to look at life. Take it one day at a time and smile and be there, present at all times.

Serge's son arrived home later that day from summer school. He was earning future credits for college. Max was twenty, athletic, clean cut and conservative but very distinctive. He was Serge's greatest friend and fan. Father and son were very similar yet, diametrically different. Max shared Serge's way of thinking; his values and simplicity towards life, all passed to him by the everyday example, of a normal upbringing, but he had his own personality and more so, Stephanie's Nature. They had become one another's sole motivation to go on, ever since they had been alone on this journey without wife and mother. Many days had passed since their last argument about having a room cleaned up or something stored away in its proper place. Their relationship was always more important than those things, things that were not important or that could be changed. Besides, as Max always said: there would always be a chance to get those things right.

In time, Max had grown to be a very responsible young man. As a teenager he had always shown a very responsible and polite manner, but never losing his spontaneous character and independence.

Max arrived that day from summer school with a heavy expression on his face, overwhelmed by all the homework he had ahead in his day. But he knew it was just a few more days, and besides, he could always count on Dad's help. After the term ended, he was leaving for a vacation with friends, and would then visit his mother's family. Then it would be to Arizona for college. Max had just been awarded a full sports and cultural scholarship and was waiting for the experience with anticipation. He hated leaving his Dad behind but they both knew it was something special to be done, his studies and his dreams: his new life.

Max was going to major in anthropology and Indian studies. Native American cultures of the past were a passion passed to him by his mother. His character and easy-going manner were other gifts mostly inherited from his mom, a very special woman. He was deeply interested with this heritage that had been passed to him as if by osmosis, always wanting to cultivate and extend it more. Many times he thought that pursuing this career would be like blending and complementing his parent's work, since anthropology was one of those disciplines that were interdisciplinary by nature. He could combine the architecture and art expression of each culture that related to his father's interests, with the rich cultural and human aspect so loved by his mother.

A responsible, athletic and busy kid…. Serge was very proud – one way or another, Stephanie and him had raised a good boy, a good young man.

Stephanie

Max's mother had provided the balance in his early years. While his father was the disciplinarian and role model, his Mother was the gentle and loving figure that provided care, pampering and many times spontaneous indulgences.

That part of the past had ended six years earlier, but was always present. He missed his mother and all those "what could have been" but he knew that they were gone forever. Max had no reason to think on them other than for the comfort of knowing that it had been great, that it could have been greater.

Her name was Stephanie. She was a very talented and wonderful woman. An anthropologist, she was dedicated to the study and care of indigenous people and their ancient cultures. She respected diversity, difference and heritage. She always saw the good in people. She filled Max with stories of traditions: how the stars were created when the coyote ran away from the heavens with the gods' corn; how the crow saved coyote after he freed the six sisters (Pleiades) from the gods' realm; how landscape was made after the gods chased men; how the gods created men and women from clay, and gave them places that centuries ago were natural gardens of heaven and now were urban metropolis ...

Max always loved to hear those stories. Even Serge took the time to sit by Max's bed, holding Steph's hand and listening to wonderful stories of places and civilizations gone. She had stopped her studies when Max was born, and took more than six months to breast-feed and care for him. Both parents shared in his upbringing and although they were only in their early twenties, they had a natural way of teaching and nurturing in this little person a sense of belonging and security. Their home was a place where Max could grow by playing, discovering and understanding his limits, as well as his responsibilities. At home there were always corners decorated in with some of the most unique pieces from Stephanie's collections. There were photographs of places and faces. There were objects of virtue, each with a symbolic meaning, yet an elegant simplicity. There were items of historical interest, mundane as a vase, a plate, or a clay flute in the shape of a bird. The richness of each piece came from the fact that they had been touched by the ancient hands of a man or a woman.

There was also a picture of Serge barefooted in some remote village by a river. He was holding his feet with both hands as to rub the pain away and by his side a triumphant Stephanie with both arms above her shoulders with a face of victory. Max loved to hear the two versions of story, Stephanie had beaten Serge on a run as he could not take the pain that the sand and rocks of the river bank gave him, he had jumped in pain instead of running. Stephanie had endured the run without complaints. After this run she earned the nickname of "Flat Foot" and in return Stephanie awarded Serge with the "Princess feet" nickname, something he did not enjoy that much.

When Stephanie died, she left Max the legacy of a wonderful character and the gift with people. She had been open and sociable and someone who made Serge a better man. With her, Serge could be anywhere without feeling that he did not belong. She was the kind of person who could relate to anyone and start a conversation on the simplest of pretexts. She had an amazing gift with people, always smiling, happy and content. If she had a past with pain or baggage as a burden, it never showed; it was left in her past. She was spontaneous, open, and enjoyed fully what she had.

Her death had come too sudden. They have been married for 16 years, Max was only fourteen years old. She complained of a headache during dinner one evening, perhaps it was the hot weather, excessive work in the field or school responsibilities. Serge made sure she rested, gave her something for the pain, and took care of Max's activities for the evening. Later that night she was feeling better, and she and Serge sat on the back terrace, watching the mountains and starry sky. They held their hands as two teenagers and remained quiet for a long time. They went to bed around eleven, kissed as always, joked about something trivial, and slept together for the last time. The next morning Serge woke up early, trying to be as quiet as he could. He went for his early run and returned at 7:10 a.m. He was surprised to find the house quiet. By this time Steph would have already taken a shower and awakened Max for school. Serge went up to his room and found her sleeping with a peaceful smile. He kissed her on the forehead, she was cold … Stunned and muttering, he tried to wake her up, pleaded with her to wake up. With tears in his eyes, he tried to give CPR, he tried to cover her and warm her, he looked for a pulse, breathing, anything. He called 911 for help then held her in his arms until the coroner came to take her away. She was only 39 … From that point, everything went too fast. The doctor said she had suffered a fulminating aneurism, probably a genetic defect in her brain. She had died sleeping and in peace, he assured them, she had not suffered at all … She was gone.

For Max and Serge her sudden departure was a terrible loss, a turning point in their lives. . They had made so many plans together, there were trips waiting to be taken, graduations to attend, dreams to fulfill. Serge comforted his son, told him that it was sad but not a tragedy: they never had to see her consumed by sickness, and her memory would never be stained. She was and always would be a beautiful smiling soft spoken woman; Always willing to help, loving, professional, dedicated and smart.

Her death sealed the ultimate bond between father and son. They became the best of friends and knew they would always have in common her memory and her gifts.

Serge and Steph met at the premiere of the first Star Wars movie in 1977, while both were students at the University of Arizona. Steph had gone to the theater with her sister and her sister's boyfriend; they had been waiting for the premiere for weeks and had arrived early for the show. The theater was packed with people by the time Serge arrived, and he barely managed to get a ticket. There were few good seats left, but Serge noticed one at the back of the theater in the middle of the seating area, between a slender female figure and a huge young guy. It was the menacing expression on the overweight man's face that made people avoid that seat, and also the thought that it might be very uncomfortable to sit by his huge side. Serge did not mind the inconvenience and wanted to see the movie. There were still couples and friends exchanging places and walking up and down to find a spot. But Serge was alone and that gave him the advantage: he took the seat. He asked the two ladies at the end of the theater if the empty seat by them was taken, and they both replied with smiles that it was free. Serge smiled back and slide between the rows of seats until he was able to sit by Steph's side. The overweight young man gave Serge a rude look, but Serge smiled in response and told him that it was crazy outside, that he sure was smart for getting that seat he was using. He thanked him for keeping the empty seat open for him. The man frowned, then smiled politely and adjusted himself in his seat. Serge sat down and observed the chaos around him. Fifteen minutes still to go and the theater was packed to its limits. Some people were already seating in the corridors. The showing was oversold and any fire marshal would have had the theater closed at this point.

Serge turned to his other side and was greeted by a feminine smile. He soon forgot the presence of the overweight guy and leaned towards the slender figure on his right. As always, Serge was carrying his sketch book and a small text book for one of his classes, "The Mayan Belief System", he opened it and started reading. Just a couple of minutes later, from the corner of his eyes he noticed that the only two people in the theater who were reading in the dim light were him and her. She was reading a book about native languages in the Sonoran desert. Because he knew a few of the terms, and with his Spanish, he was able to read the title at the top of one of the pages.
"I hope you don't think I am rude…" he asked her and paused "Is that a good read?"

"Oh no problem" she replied, surprised but pleased. "Yes I've just started reading it. I want to learn Spanish and the ancient dialects, which fascinate me. Pronunciation and grammar are very complicated, but I'm amazed at the similarities I've found to other languages."

They had begun a casual conversation based on the books that each other was reading. Serge' was a third year architecture student and had taken a class on architecture, history and belief systems of cultures from the American continent. Stephanie was a second year student in the College of Anthropology and the daughter of a prominent University researcher. This enabled both of them to share an engaging conversation before the start of the movie

"I noticed that we are the only two persons reading in this theater and I was curious, because of all the places we could have ended up sitting, we ended being together."

"Yes, I noticed that, too. What are you reading?"

"'The Mayan Belief System.' It was actually reading material for a class I took last year, but I liked it so much that I wanted to read more. It explains how the architecture of the Mayan cities reflected their belief system. It was compared to the Native American 'kivas' where the underworld is linked to the world and then to the heavens. Very impressive,"

"Are you an anthropology student?"

"No, architecture. Third year, here at the U."
I'm also a student here, but in anthropology ... We might have shared a few classes, in fact I might have seen you before."

"You think so?" was Serge's response. "I would have never forgotten your face ..." He blushed when he realized what he had just said. "I'm sorry," he added.

"No problem. That was actually a nice compliment. A very used line, but nice anyway."

Serge was embarrassed and Steph noticed his nervousness, as if he had done something he regretted.

"My name is Stephanie, by the way. Nice to meet you."

Serge was more embarrassed now. How could he have been so rude as to not properly introduce himself?! "I am Serge. Gosh, sorry again, you sure know how to disarm a man, just with your eyes and your name!"

She laughed naturally and smiled, patting and placing her hand on his arm to let him know it was ok. "You're not telling me you feel intimidated, are you?" Her eyes and smile had a quizzically gentle expression.

At her touch, Serge felt an electricity rush going through his arm, and the more she talked the more beautiful she was and even if it was dim light he could see her eyes and long hair – she was beautiful. "No, no, not at all. I ..." There was another flush of blood to his face and he hoped that the poor light in the theater would hide his expression and embarrassment. Stephanie smiled back. She removed her hand from his arm but patted him as she did, as if to say, "Lighten up, Serge, I like you."

She spoke. "I know, you seem like a very mature and harmless man." Her expression softened the moment and they both laughed. Shoulder to shoulder they watched the movie, exchanging a few glances. What began as a casual conversation had become a normal exchange of words among friends, even during the movie, and they smiled together at R2's sounds and Cheewie's groans. More than once they agreed that the sets and special effects were amazing, and that it was a movie worth waiting for.

The movie ended and the viewers were all standing up, but Serge could not make up his mind or find the courage to say something. He had been so close to this beautiful woman, had seen her eyes so close ... Steph was just about to leave with her sister and friend; it was taking them some time to gather all their belongings. Serge took a chance and told her that he had had a great time that he would like to see her again. "Would you like to go out some time?' he asked her out of the blue.

Steph smiled back. She was pleased that he had asked. It seemed that she was waiting for him to ask but, if he did not, there was nothing she could do. Maybe he did not like her that much after all and it had been only a good time at the movies. Steph's sister asked if she was alright – she and her boyfriend had thought that perhaps "this guy" was bothering Steph. But to their surprise and delight, her sister, who had always been shy and reserved with boys, was asking them for a few minutes alone to say goodbye to the stranger. They agreed and left for the theater lobby. Steph opened up her backpack and took out a card, upon which she wrote her telephone number.

"I can't go with you right now, since my sister invited me and they're going to give me a ride back home, but I'll be delighted to go out with you another day, if you want." Steph turned and saw Serge's expression change, from shyness, to fear of rejection, to eagerness to go out that same night, to resignation but delight to get her phone number. He agreed and promised to call her. They walked together to the lobby, where Steph's sister was waiting for her. Serge and Steph exchanged glances one last time.

"I had a wonderful time," she said.

"Me, too. It was a great movie, and your company made it a hundred times better."

"Thank you!" Steph replied with some embarrassment.

31

Her sister and friend had heard his comment. They appreciated that Serge had been respectful enough to say hello to them, and were also curious how it was that Steph was able to interact with this stranger as if it they had been together all along.

The movie theater was almost empty. Already the personnel were cleaning the auditorium for the next presentation and a crowd of viewers was already in line outside, eager to come in. The overweight young man came out of the restroom and saw Serge standing in the lobby, looking outside to the crowd. Little did he know that Serge was following Steph with his eyes until he lost her among all the heads, jackets and caps.

"Pretty amazing, huh?" The young man said

"Yes, she is..." was Serge's automatic response. He imagined that all around him were watching Steph and seeing how incredible she was in his eyes.

Serge went home to his room. Against the advice of his roommate and best friend Al Gadgett, he called Steph to tell her he had a great time and to be sure she got home safe. "Serge, c'mon, man! She already knows, she gave you her phone number, remember? Don't call her, she'll think she's got you by the balls!"

The voice on the other side of the phone was surprised but pleased. "Thank you for calling. I got home alright, and I also had a wonderful time."

They talked through some of the movie's scenes, then Serge asked her what her sister had said about the whole evening. "She said that it was pretty wild, how I was with you as if we were already dating each other. She even got a little mad and jealous, because during the whole movie I was talking with you and never paid any attention to her!"

They laughed, and Serge felt a certain pride, flattered by the comment. Before saying good night, Serge told her that he was going to call her tomorrow to set a time for their date.

"Hey, I would really like to see you again. Does next week sound too soon for you?" he asked.

" No, sounds great, I'll really look forward to that."

"What about tomorrow, then?" Serge could see Al's eyes roll. He could not believe how his best friend was making a fool of himself, and by making faces and waving his arms, he was telling Serge he was lost, doomed and desperate.

"Tomorrow? ..." Steph was saying, but Serge interrupted. "If it is too soon I can wait, it's ok, I understand."

"You don't wait for answers, do you?" she said with a smile. "I can do it tomorrow, although Friday night would be better since I don't have any classes on Saturday."

"Well, we'll go out again on Friday, now that you have asked me out. I'll call you tomorrow to set the time, and unless you have a better idea, we can meet at this small Italian café I know. It is near the Old Town area. They serve exotic pizzas and have a great view of the mountains."

"That sounds great. I'll wait for your call tomorrow. Thank you."

"Good night, Stephanie, and thank you."

"Good night, Serge. Talk to you soon."

Al found Serge's expression hilarious. He was as if in a dream. "Look at you, Serge! You have this stupid face, you remind me of the stare of cows on the prairie, just looking out to the horizon without anything on their minds but a full belly."

"What? Huh?" was Serge's response.

"Man, you are screwed! Goodbye to Serge! Ladies and gentlemen, the bells are calling; this man has fallen for a girl he just met at a movie!"

"Gadgett... Shut up, idiot that is not true."

"Yeah, right, you should see your face." Al was making funny faces and held his hands to his cheeks as he mimicked Serge's voice: "Would tomorrow night be ok for you? I mean, I don't want to push you, but I am desperate to see you again.'" "She's got you without you even noticing it!"

Serge could not hold his laughter and amusement – was it really so obvious? He had never fallen for a girl like this before. He once or twice had thought he was in love but this time it felt ... different.

"Well, she is very attractive, you know?" was his justification. "And the sound of her laugh and the look in her eyes can really take your breath away. She ... she ... What can I say ... she is perfect!"

Al approached Serge and embraced him by his shoulders. "Man, you do not need to explain to me. I have never seen you like this before. You're acting like a teenager after seeing the girl of his dreams." Al wore an expression of resignation but there was a tone of goodwill in his voice.

"I sure would like to feel that way, just once. I've never taken anything serious in my life. I mean, to be in love ..." There was a brief pause, then he added, "You said she has a sister, didn't you?"

"Yeah," Serge replied "But she's got a boyfriend and they looked good together"

"Hey, I'm not jealous. No problem – she can bring him, too!"

"Fool"

"Yeah, look who's talking, the ladies' man."

They both laughed. The night had come to an end; the two friends finished what they were doing and prepared for the next day. Serge lay on his bed, excited. Already in his head were a thousand ideas and dreams. He was glad he had taken the chance to telephone Stephanie. He was curious how everything had come to be that way. He had never been happy about attending a full theater, but had never before had such a good time watching a movie.

"'Night, man." he told Al, almost asleep.

"See you tomorrow, lover boy."

On the following evening, Serge arrived early at the Italian restaurant, and seated himself at the bar. Already there was movement in the place; several girls among the patrons gazed at Serge with interest. He had come well-dressed, wanting to make his best second "first impression". It was now a few minutes past the arranged hour and Steph had not arrived. Serge became restless, already wondering if she was going to show up. He repeatedly checked the entrance and his watch. He looked at the television above the bar to get the latest sports up-dates, but was not interested. He folded napkins, twisted a straw from his glass of water, scribbled in the sketchbook he had brought to share a few drawings and notes with Stephanie.

The restaurant door opened and an older couple came in, then in succession a family, a young couple, four friends loudly discussing

35

something about work and a possible conflict with a professor that made no sense to Serge. Fifteen minutes past the hour and Serge was beginning to worry: what if she did not show up?

From his seat at the bar near the entrance, Serge could observe the entire restaurant. The bar had a panoramic mirror at its back, a background for the bottles and display cases. On a shelf at the top of the bar were olive oil bottles of many sizes and shapes, filled with spices and seeds, peppers and vegetables. The colors of the bottles matched the rustic look of the place and complemented the orange-yellow washed finish of the walls. Elsewhere along the bar, bottles of wine and memorabilia from Italy hung or rested on carved wooden shelves. It looked handsome and friendly, elegant and clean.

From the corner of his eye, Serge spotted a group of three attractive girls looking his way; he could see them looking at him in the mirror. They laughed and acted casually, but definitely were making sure they were noticed. Serge could not tell if they were making fun of him or if they were wondering why he had not made any move towards them. He was nervous ... maybe anxious. This was not his ground; he seldom went out on dates and had he been spending the evening alone he would have been in another place. He worried that he would be left standing, or hung like one of the decorations on the restaurant walls.

Serge lost his concentration for a moment, then felt his heart sink as the clock on the bar marked half-past the hour. He looked down, gathered his stuff and was almost ready to leave when he felt a soft hand in his shoulder. When he turned around he saw looking back at him the most amazing green eyes, in an apologetic face that said everything he needed to know. She was here.

"You weren't going to go, right?" said Steph.

"Uh ... no ... I ..."

She stopped him there. "I'm sorry for being this late. I left on time after classes but my sister offered, insisted really, on giving me a ride here, she and her boyfriend. I told them it wasn't necessary but they wanted to be sure I was safe. We had to wait for Jim ... there they are."

"No problem," Serge replied, following Steph's eyes as she turned towards the door and waved at them.

"Do they intend to join us?" he asked.

"No way! They have plans and besides, this is our first date, isn't it?" She blushed at saying it so excitedly.

"Yes, it is." Serge replied. How nicely the words came from her mouth! "Our first date," he repeated to himself. He smiled.

"It is good to know they care for you. I could be a serial killer, you know."

"You seem like a very dangerous man, Serge."

The hostess came to ask them if they were ready for their reserved table. They moved through the restaurant, Serge following behind Stephanie, and he noticed that her hair looked a little different from yesterday, long and straight, very soft and bouncing on her shoulders. He checked her back and legs, then felt embarrassed as a woman at a nearby table noticed what he was doing. He just smiled politely with guilt in his face, and the woman smiled back in approval.

At the back of the restaurant, close to the windows and upon a low platform were several booths with tables. The walls were treated with a texturized paint in bright reds, yellows and ochres. Hanging from the walls were framed Italian newspapers, photographs, paintings and memorabilia. It looked busy, but elegant and very unique. The detail and variety helped diners break the ice with casual conversation in an informal setting. Serge followed the scent of Steph's sweet perfume to their table, and waited for her to be seated. Again he found himself checking her legs and waist, the roundness of her breasts, her soft hands with nails perfectly cut. These were working, busy hands yet so feminine. She wore a curious, bug-like amulet on the left side of her sweater, and a pair of silver earrings of an ancient-looking craft design. She looked incredible.

Steph sat comfortably as Serge took her coat and hung it by the side of the booth, then seated himself across the table from her.

"This is a nice place. Do you come here often?" asked Steph.

"Not really," he said." It has been a while since I was here last."

"You must tell that to all of your dates."

"No way! Actually, I used to work here, on the late shift. Since they did not want any more servers, or the servers were only the "good looking" types, I had to settle for the hasher position, you know, the ones that clean after everyone has left. So I cleaned the pantry, washed plates and mopped the place once everyone had left."

"That's a lot of work!"

"Not really. I was supposed to arrive at six PM, but I would arrive around 5:10, right after classes. I helped with food preparation, arranging the tables, and anything else that was needed. Then I'd get my dinner, which was the best part. I usually got the freshest and largest portions ... I'm a big eater." He winked at her in a naughty way. "Then I'd help the cook in the kitchen —they have great chefs, by the way. I chopped onions, prepared lettuce for salads, arranged shrimps on a plate, and filled glasses with ice water at the server stations ...."

"All that before your shift?"

"Yeah. Take the garbage out, check the pantry for supplies, take notes and wait. But I quickly took care of all that and decided to help elsewhere, to keep myself busy. I learned how to wash dishes in a huge Hobart machine; the secret was to keep the water temperature above 120'F ... First thing the health inspector checks when he was in, was the water temperature. You see, dishes are cleaned by the water temperature and some soap. The water itself is constantly recycled."

"You mean the water they used to clean this glass? ..."

"Yes, it is the same used to clean all of the dishes through the night, well, unless there have been many plates in use, when two Hobarts start running. But basically, yes, that is the way. It is actually very clean."

"I never thought it would be that way. Do they ever hand wash dishes?"

"Some, depending on the case, but in general, everything goes to the Hobart. Get a dirty plate, scrape to the waste disposal, rinse, rack, Hobart, and "bing," they are out and hot. Then to the shelves for storage or another round of service."

"And all that was not in your shift duties?"

"No, my responsibilities started when kitchen started to close. No more orders and then I'd help Marco with the grills. After that, trash, broom and mop were my domain." He smiled as if with pride. "I was the best mopper that has ever been."

Serge continued his story. "I would finish around eleven o'clock. Somewhere around nine, the staff began to take turns to eat – that is why I enjoyed my early dinner, alone, no rush and all is fresh." He winked again. "By ten o'clock everyone was usually gone, except the owner and two of the cooks. They checked numbers, inventories, the works, and I'd be mopping the kitchen and dining area, taking garbage out. I'd usually stop two or three times in the pantry for a snack, take a couple of oranges for home, then clean my mop and bucket and close the back door around eleven. Then I'd go home to do school work, or go to the studio at school."

"Do you ever sleep at all?"

"Oh yes, I do … sometimes four hours in a day!"

"And how about having fun… you ever go to parties?" Stephanie asked
"Oh yes, I do go to parties" he told her, "If I go to a party I'll be the first one on the dance floor, singing out and moving to the beat of the music, and I'd also be the last one on the dance floor… now if given a choice, I'm sure I'd rather go for a quiet hike or a long camping trip"

"Sounds familiar… my choice too" Stephanie added

Serge was curious and she noticed his expression.
"I meant, the choice of a hike vs. a party… I'm not a good dancer!"

Serge smiled at her, "I bet you are" Was his immediate reply. "But yes, if you give me a choice, I'll be like one of those bumper stickers that reads: 'I'd rather be SCUBA diving.'"

They continued talking the whole evening: families, backgrounds, ideals, work, things to eat. At ten PM the restaurant started to slow down and by 10:30 it was almost empty. Serge and Steph had not noticed, so immersed in their conversation they had not realized that almost four hours had gone by.

Steph excused herself to use the restroom, and Serge again took advantage of the chance to "check her out" – he could not take his eyes off her. Serge sat back and marveled at the simplicity of the moment, he did not perceived the time until Stephanie had returned and found him looking away to the ceiling.

"Have you lost something out there?" She asked as she sat.
"Huh, what?... no... sorry I guess I was taken by the moment.

A short time later the owner came by, said hello to Serge and complimented Stephanie
"A beautiful signorina."
They smiled and both complimented the food.
"The goat cheese pizza in olive oil base with veggies was delicious, we'll sure come back."

"Serge, you are always welcome." Said the owner

Serge thanked the owner, then raised his mug to drink the last of his beer. He was planning to see Stephanie's cleavage through the edge of his glass but was obstructed by a circular shade at the bottom of the mug, he then frowned. Steph asked him what it was.

"It's a penny ... a lucky penny!" The amber color of the beer had hidden it from sight. The owner was extremely sorry and offered to pay for Serge's dinner, who was more entertained than annoyed.

"Hey, it's a lucky penny. How often do you find a penny in your beer? This is a keeper"

The owner appreciated Serge's attitude and told him he owed Serge for next time. "... and you know we would always want to have you back!"

Steph and Serge smiled and said goodbye. Serge hid the penny in the license pocket of his wallet. "For memory's sake. This penny is special, you know?"

"You are silly, you know? You are a dangerous man but a silly nevertheless." She got close and kissed him on his check.
"See? I got a kiss. This penny is definitely a keeper!" Serge put his wallet away and patted it in his pants pocket a few times, making sure it was in a safe place.

They walked to Serge's car, an old, black four-door Dodge Dart. The car was clean and in good shape but had more than a few miles on it. Serge drove Steph to her place and walked her to the door. They chatted there for another forty minutes, prolonging the night as much as they could.

"I hope you don't think I'm rude, and I know it is late, but I don't want to go. I simply don't want this date to come to an end."

"I've had a wonderful time, too." said Stephanie. "It has been really nice."

"I almost forgot!" said Serge, "I have to give you something!" He ran to his car, retrieved a small box and ran back, climbing the steps two at the time until he reached her again. "Here" he said, excited and panting slightly.

Steph took the box and said, "You shouldn't have. I didn't bring anything for you."

"It's something small." Serge said, "I hope you find it meaningful. Just don't open it yet. Wait until I'm gone, ok?"

"Why?"

"I guess I just want to increase the chances of seeing you again. Maybe this way you'll be at least curious … Would I ever see you again?" He added with a slight tone of resignation. He had had previous experiences where, he assumed due to his personality he was never contacted again, or he simply lost track of the person. This time felt different and he wanted to be sure not to lose what he was feeling.

"Would you ever see me again?" She looked at him with curiosity. " That, I believe, will depend on you. Would you like to see me again?"

"Yes. Yes, I would."

"Then just lighten up, Serge. I had a great time, and it seems to me we have a lot in common." She smiled, again put her hand on his arm, reassuring him that it was ok. "I don't want to rush into anything. I have my studies and I don't want to get distracted from them. Who knows? Let's take one step at a time, shall we?"

He took a deep breath, taking stock of his feelings and himself. I am making a fool of myself, he thought.

"You are right. Sorry. I also had a great time and would like to see you again."

"Then you will."

Serge embraced her with both arms, and she did the same. They held each other briefly but fully. He gave her a small kiss on her cheek and thanked her, took a step back and smiled shyly.

"Call me." said Stephanie.

"I will."

"Thank you. I had an incredible night."

"Me, too. It was very special, good night."

"Good night."

She opened her door and walked in. He stood motionless, taking it all in: the evening, the way they met, the first words, her eyes, the way her hair fell to her shoulders and how it moved when she leaned to the side, her hands … He reached for his wallet and as he pulled it out, he noticed the small, circular bulge behind his driver's license. He traced it with his finger and smiled.

"Lucky penny …" he thought. Then, as if he were standing beside a wishing fountain, he closed his eyes and said, "Help me find my way." He thanked God, nature, the heavens, time, the stars and moon. He was in love.

"Wow!" he exclaimed. "Wow. I feel alive."

The interview

Serge arrived at the Main Plaza Building in downtown Seattle, thirty minutes early. He liked to have spare time on his hands before something important, to prepare mentally for what was ahead. He was excited and optimistic, although he was not sure what was all the fuss about this job. It was a classified advertisement, wasn't it? Yet it was being handled as if it were an executive recruiting situation. It felt good though, for a change. And he was willing to do anything; he had tried before and things worked out; he knew he could do it again.

Looking up at the tall tower of the Main Plaza Building, Serge bent his neck all the way to the heavens. He felt like he was in the movies: business people moving along; flag poles with corporate, state, and U.S. flags; people rushing to meetings; couriers, taxicabs, fountains, vendors. It was an exciting, busy environment.

He saw the main entrance to the building, a huge brass door in the center with revolving doors to either side. He went for the middle one and as he approached, he noticed an attractive, mature woman with the air of an executive, approaching the door from inside. He got to the door first and opened it for her, holding it as she came out. She ignored the gesture, made no acknowledgment; Serge just nodded. "You you are welcome" Serge thought. "Oh well ..." He entered.

Across a short vestibule, at a second set of doors, the same thing happened. An older black woman approached, not so elegant as the first. Serge again held the door, but this time the lady smiled back. She was about to thank Serge when a young man rushed past them and stormed through the entrance. The lady had to take a step back to avoid colliding with him.

"Hey! Careful, man!" Serge said to the young man as he entered, but there was no reply or apology, just a brief, cynical smile and a gesture that said, I'll do anything to get there first." Serge asked the older woman if she were alright.

"Yes, sure." She said. "Thank you, young man. It's good to know there are still gentlemen in this world."

Serge smiled. "You are welcome, always eager to be of help a lady in distress." She gave him a wink and a smile, and exited the building.

Serge could still see the rude young man as he reached the elevators. Still rushing, he stumbled into a black lady of indeterminate age, knocking to the floor some of the file folders she held. He turned around, looked at his watch, and said, "I got an important appointment and I'm late already." He hunched his shoulders apologetically as the elevator doors closed, and was gone. Serge was amazed by what he had witnessed, and hurried to the lady to help her pick up the scattered papers.

"Are you alright?" he asked her.

"I'm ok, son. I just ran into a rude and mean young man."

"Well, it seemed to me he was in a hurry, although that doesn't justify what he did. He should have stayed to help you."

"Not even an apology!" exclaimed the lady.

"Well, better for me. This way, I can help you and be your hero." They both laughed.

Serge marveled at the grace and elegance of the woman. Although dressed like a secretary in a simple, comfortable outfit, her poise and classiness made Serge wonder. She resembled in some strange way someone familiar to Serge, but he could not place the face. Her features were gentle, wise, and she had a big smile. Serge thought about those great women who are heads of families: providers and guides for so many kids without parents.

"Are you going to be late too? Go ahead, I'll manage."

"Not at all. I have some extra time and even if I did not, I would never leave you here on your own like this! What really startles me is that no one else in the lobby came to help you. We all live in our small bubbles."

"What's your name, son?" the lady asked him. Serge had finished picking up the spilled papers; he squared them on his knees and gave them to her neatly folded.

"Serge", he replied "Serge Onamor"

"Say what? You got to spell that for me, and say it slowly."

"Serge," he repeated, and spelled his name for her.

"I'm Roberta Chartres. Nice to meet you, Serge."

"Nice to meet you," Serge replied with a small bow. He shook the hand she extended to him.

"Roberta is such a strong name. You must be a tough cookie to break."

"I am. I'm actually eighty-seven years old; not bad for a grandma, huh?"

"Eighty-seven! No way! You look sixty tops; no way you are even above seventy!"

"Oh ... oh!" She smiled with excitement. "I guess I already like you more. Such a gentleman! I bet your mother is very proud of you."

47

"Well, not sure about that, it's been years since the last time I saw her."

"That is not good, son. Mothers are always there for their kids. You should call her and she will surely forgive you, whatever you did. She'll let you go back, trust me."

Serge smiled. "I'll keep that in mind, though I insist that you should tell that to her. I know it would not be that easy."

Elevator doors opened. Roberta gave him a final squeeze on the hand, kissed his cheek. "For good luck, son. You never know!"

"Thank you. You already made my day!"

"Listen. Before you leave the building, stop by at the seventh floor and ask for me. I might have a surprise for you, ok?"

"I'll try to remember."

"No, you don't," was her reply. "You don't try. I'll be waiting for you; this is an appointment, young man, and no gentleman leaves a woman waiting. Is that understood?"

"Yes, Mom, I'll be there." He gave her a "Bambi eyes" look and squinted his face as kids do when scolded by their mothers.

"Good! Now go on, and thank you. I guess I'll see you later."

"As soon as they let me go," Serge replied. "And you are more than welcome. Bye!"

Roberta walked across the rest of the lobby and disappeared in the crowd of people. Serge stepped into the elevator, the doors closed, and he pushed the button for the fifty-second floor.

When the elevator doors opened at his destination, Serge could see what appeared to be the reception area of a big company. The space was ample, full of light. The ceiling was made of parallel wood beams and lowered edges with indirect light. At the end of the room there was a large granite counter with two receptionists behind it. A dark mahogany corporate logo on the center of the back wall was washed with indirect light from the ceiling suspended lights. The office had been decorated with classic taste, elegant but not extravagant, a good balance. Serge could appreciate the details and craftsmanship of some of the work; marble floors, rich carved wood archways framing doors with classic motifs. On the walls there were lighted niches with antique marble and bronze pieces of artwork. The corridors that lead to the offices were carpeted in rich patterns of color and texture. The indirect lighting of the ceiling on the rounded soffit gave the space a sense of natural light in balance with the character, privacy and scale.

Serge got to the reception desk four minutes late. He introduced himself to the one of the receptionist with a smile. "Good morning. I have an appointment to see Mr. Stafford at 10:30, please."

"You're late. Your name?"

She's probably tired, he thought. "Serge, Onamor." She looked at him quizzically and Serge spelled his name. "It is actually easier than it sounds."

"Please take a seat. I'll inform Mr. Stafford that you are here."

Serge thanked the receptionist but remained standing. He wandered about the waiting area. In one of the corners, a maintenance crew was taking care of a huge plant arrangement. The decoration of the space was achieved with textures, paintings, and light. He approached the paintings and inspected them with a critical architect's eye. He went to the window and saw the view. He examined the large company logo. A placard that had been erected for visitors described the company's business and its performance: they developed GIS and GPS software for statistical, geographical, environmental and planning information; they also had a charitable foundation that operated several programs throughout the world. The company had significant contracts with several city governments. Serge continued his pacing. He stopped near one of the lamps on the wall; it was an interesting design …

The maintenance man, noticing his curiosity, said: "Ahh, those lamps. Let me tell you, they're pretty but they're high maintenance. They're the worst!"

"Why?"
"Cleaning them is always a hassle. Either you get burnt or you leave dust in very narrow corners. Replacing the bulb, which is extremely expensive since it comes from Germany, has to be done in four steps. You almost disassemble the whole fixture!"

"Not very functional," Serge said. "Though it looks great, I must say."

"That might be so, but let me tell you something. Some of these 'designers' should go around asking questions to people like me before making their fancy designs. I tell you, these are the worst of them all. They should make these guys clean them and replace their bulbs once in a while, so they know how hard it is. I hope you're not one of them, right?"

"No, but I am an architect, and sometimes we all get carried away by our ideas and forget what the building is designed and made for. It is hard to resist that temptation. And I have seen it happen many times, in many buildings, that after the opening ceremony the energy bills and maintenance costs skyrocket. You can send your client to bankruptcy, no joke."

"Well, I'm tired of telling them here, I've told them a thousand times, but they don't pay attention to this old guy. Who am I to know, right?"

Serge smiled and shared something this man already knew. "My father used to say, 'youth is a sickness that is cured with time.'"

"Your dad was right. Young generations, always in a hurry, always busy, no time for nothing." They exchanged a brief smile. "
Well, I'm done here. Have a good day, mister." He walked away, pushing his maintenance cart, and disappeared down the next corridor.

More than fifteen minutes went by before someone came to see him.

"Mr. 'Onamor'?" called a young man who looked like an intern.

"Yes?" Serge replied.

"Please follow me."

They walked down one of the corridors that lead from the waiting area, the corridor was well-lighted and full of pictures explaining the company's software. Some of the areas and meeting rooms they passed were decorated with modern art. Serge liked the place.

"Please wait here, Mr. Stafford will join you in this meeting room. Make yourself comfortable. Would you like a coffee or water, tea perhaps?"

"No, thank you. I'm alright for now."

Serge breathed a little bit easier. The receptionist's comment about his being four minutes late had concerned him and he thought that perhaps the appointment would be canceled. It was a good thing, that he had been called to the meeting room.

The young man left the room, closing the door behind him. The meeting room had a large oval table in white marble; a couple of elegant stone basement supported the marble slate. Modern office chairs surrounded the table. Above and suspended in the ceiling was a projector, facing to the wall where an automatic screen descended. Two thirds of the meeting room had a spectacular view of the Puget Sound, the whole city opened for 270 degree unobstructed views. The walls displayed framed awards of the different products that the company had. Serge placed his documents on the table and approached the window. A couple of minutes later, a very attractive woman with an outstanding executive look walked in. She saw him staring out the window. "Good morning," she said in a very sensual voice.

Serge turned around to reply but caught his breath when he saw how attractive she was. He hesitated but recovered rapidly; he hoped she had not noticed. He knew somehow that she had, but he moved on. "Good mor ... good morning, I mean."

She smiled at him. "Quite a view uh? We can see Mount Rainer on a clear day and it looks spectacular. You should see the view from the President's office, which is more impressive."

"Yes, it is quite a postcard." said Serge, quickly turning to the window, to avoid being caught staring at her.

"I'm Alexa, and you are?"

"I'm Serge Onamor, nice to meet you"

"Are you here for the meeting?" She placed a red folder on the table and took her coat off, placing it on one of the chairs rest.

"Not a meeting... uh more for an interview, Mr. Stafford will be here soon, at least that is what they told me."

"Do you usually believe what people say?" She approached him, raising her hand to her face and tracing her finger close to her mouth, trying to make Serge look directly at her eyes and lips. Serge watched her approach; she was teasing him, testing him. He remained calm.

"Yes, most of the time, until they prove me wrong."

"Ah! An optimist. Are you honest, Mr. Onamor?"

He did not know where she was going with this line of questioning. What was all this about? He decided simply to answer in a natural way; it was in the end just a conversation. "Yes, I am. Now, if you are asking if I ever have lied in my life, yes, I have on many occasions. I know who I am."

"Mmm... a straight shooter? I like a man that is direct. Then you will be able to tell me something, if I ask you."

Serge nodded; he was trying to figure things out.

"Ok, then, do you find me attractive?"

Serge frowned. "excuse me?"

"It's just a simple question, you just have to answer. Do I need to repeat myself?

"No need." Serge stood his ground. "Yes, you are a very attractive woman," he said in a carefully neutral tone. "What is this all about?"

"Well ..." She moved closer. "Nothing and yet everything. You see, I'm very picky in regard to men. You know? If they are honest or not, if they are only pretending to be who they say they are. For me, first impressions are important. I have to like what I see first, and I like you."

She took another step toward Serge, getting really close. Serge held for a moment, then took one step to the side and one step back.

"Am I making you uncomfortable? Afraid, perhaps?"

"Intimidated, I must admit." Serge replied

She closed the final gap between them and gave Serge a soft kiss on the cheek, then exhaled a whisper of breath in his ear, making him shiver. His eyes closed involuntarily as he felt her soft hair on his face, took in her scent, felt her soft touch. Her mouth moved to his lips and pressed, kissing him gently. In the same motion, she took Serge's hand and pressed it against her breast. Serge felt a rush of blood through his body, felt the slightly parted lips, inviting him. He responded instinctively and gently opened his mouth, but in the next instant he disengaged, taking a step back and raising his hands, palms forward, in front of his shoulders.

"Wait!" He said, breathing deeply. "I'm sorry. I cannot do this."

She stared at him, her expression a combination surprise, a sense of respect, and a measure of disappointment. "Well," she said finally, "that is a first. What's the matter Serge, By now I can call you Serge can't I? You too afraid? Are we moving too fast for you? Married, gay, dating?" She smiled mischievously so as to provoke an explanation.

Serge took a deep breath, a thousand thoughts in his head. It had been a while since he had felt a kiss like that, or such an attraction for a woman. Finding his footing, he said: "You are a very attractive woman, Miss? ..."

"Lightman, Alexa Lightman, and is Miss as you well state," she said with pride.

Serge was confused. The company owner was Mr. Robert Lightman, so either this was a young, bored trophy wife, a young sister with a mission, or his daughter.

"Ms. Lightman ..." he continued.

"Oh, please. You can call me Alexa – we've already had our first kiss."

Serge blushed at what that could mean or imply. Had he taken advantage of her? No, worse than that, she had taken him completely by surprise and left him without a proper footing in the middle of an important interview.

"Ok then, Alexa," he said, "You are a very attractive woman. I'm sure you have heard that many times before." He continued with more confidence: "God only knows how I feel right now and what I felt when you kissed me. Believe me. Although being bold might mean to take life by the horns and sometimes act impulsively, it also means to act authentically, according to what we believe, who we are, where we are. Please accept my apology. I should not have kissed you. That is not the way I am, or what I came here for. Please accept my apology and excuse me for kissing you. I lost my head for a moment."

Alexa displayed a complex of emotions: she looked surprised, intrigued, embarrassed, apologetic, even confused. It seemed to Serge her reaction was that of someone who either could not accept being rejected, or who was pleasantly surprised by an honest display of integrity. Serge noticed her discomfort, tried to say something to take back the possible hurt or arrogance, if he had been interpreted like that.

At his chivalrous effort, she said, "It's ok, Serge, I understand. I actually appreciate your honesty. We all have our reasons, and your response has been quite refreshing."

Serge was again surprised at this new development. Now she seemed vulnerable, and in a sense touched. At that moment a man walked in to the meeting room, another executive-type.

"I hope I'm not interrupting anything," he said with a straightforward, businesslike tone.

"Hi, Albert. Good timing," Alexa said, her manner once again assured. "We were just talking about the view."

"It's something else!" Serge played along.

Alexa picked up the red folder she had placed on the table, and gave it to Albert. "This is the work I've done and I would appreciate if you can give me five minutes to present this to the Board. I briefed you on it but there are things that I need to explain to them; I'm the only one that knows them well. You can introduce the presentation and after the third slide, I'll take over, ok?"

"You got it, Alexa. Anything for the big girl." She put on an annoyed expression. That meant that she was probably the daughter of the big man, thought Serge. She took her jacket from the chair, nodded slightly at Serge, and walked out.

"She's quite a piece of art, isn't she?" Albert said, looking inquiringly at Serge.

"What do you mean?" Serge replied.

"Well, she is the boss's daughter and a very bright ambitious woman. You have to be careful, she could eat you away.... I would not mind be eaten by her ... if you know what I mean." Albert leered disrespectfully.

Serge, barely recovered from his encounter with Alexa, and who had been subject to an emotional rollercoaster since he entered this building, thought this was too much. First Alexa making those moves, and now this jerk talking like this about a woman; he just did not like that.

"I'll appreciate it if you can keep your opinions to yourself and refer to Ms. Lightman with respect, especially since she has just stepped outside the room."

Albert replied indignantly, "Don't lecture me boy... Who the fuck do you think you are? Do you know who are you talking to, pal?! I'm your god damn recruiting interview manager." He had raised his voice.

"No, I did not know that, and at this time I don't care. I am not your pal, you don't raise your voice to me and judging by the way things are, I might not even be interested in working in a place where these things happen."

Serge picked up his documents from the table and was about to walk out when the door opened again. Albert, who was about to say something to Serge, went silent. The door was partially open and a huge man could be seen through the gap, talking with someone else outside. "Yes, please move everything to the larger meeting room. We'll be holding the meeting there." He then popped his face inside and said, "Albert, we are moving to the east meeting room. See you there." The door closed.

Albert saw that Serge was annoyed and not interested in moving to another room; he was leaving. But before he could speak, the receptionist entered.

"Mr. Lightman will see you now in the boardroom."

Serge was about to say that he was no longer interested when Albert interrupted. "We'll be there in a moment. Serge, please hold a minute."

The receptionist departed and Albert continued: "Please stay, things are not what they appear. Just trust me when I say that you should meet Mr. Lightman, there is always an explanation, we all have our reasons."

Serge had heard those words before. He hesitated. Albert approached, and with a friendly gesture touched Serge's arm. "Think about it for a minute. I'll be outside. If you still want to walk out, you leave. But if you have any questions about all this, please give yourself the chance to meet Mr. Lightman." Albert left the room.

Serge remained, silent and still. He was confused; he played with the edge of the folder that was holding his documents, he looked out the window without enjoying the view, he was confused. He could not make any sense of what had happened. The door opened, it was the receptionist again. "Mr. Onamor, we are moving to the boardroom. Please follow me."

"Excuse me, but I came to see Mr. Stanford, and I don't think I should be included in that meeting."

"Yes, Mr. Stanford is in the meeting. He's there waiting for you too; he asked me to come for you. Now, if you could please, follow me."

Serge followed the receptionist, feeling he had missed something. She took him through a semicircular main corridor, decorated with contemporary art illuminated by receded lamps from openings in the ceiling. The receptionist came to a mahogany double door, and directed Serge within. From the doorway, Serge looked around the room. It was furnished with a conference table that would have accommodated thirty people, was well lighted and with the same decor as the corridor, but complemented with a panoramic view of the waterfront. Serge wondered about the efficiency of meetings with such a view. He saw Albert and Alexa chatting about something with the big man he had glimpsed earlier; two other men stood inconspicuously at the far side of the room.

The three near him turned as he walked in, and welcomed him with smiles. Serge assumed that the third man was Mr. Stanford, who now approached him and extended his hand.

"Welcome, Serge. I'm Ben, Ben Stanford; we talked on the phone. I believe you arrived a little late."

"I know, and I am sorry." Serge said sincerely. Perhaps Ben was waiting for an explanation. Serge did not give any.

"That's it? You don't have an excuse?" asked Ben.

"With all due respect Mr. Stanford, I have learned from the past that it is better to give a sincere apology, than an unnecessary explanation."

"I hope you don't keep all your opinions to yourself, just in case you're interested in joining our organization". He looked quizzical, sounding different than Serge remembered from the phone conversation.

Ben gestured with his hand that Serge should join them at the table, though all remained standing. Alexa took a moment to discuss something with Ben in low tones. Albert spoke quietly to Serge. "About what I said back there … I'd appreciate if you could keep it between you and me." He slipped a hundred-dollar bill into the handkerchief pocket of Serge's jacket, without Alexa or Ben noticing.

With one swift movement, Serge took the money from his jacket grabbed Albert's hand, forced the bill into it, and with a quiet voice told him "I might be looking for a job, and the money could come in very handy for me, but I'd rather earn it. Besides, your opinions are your own; I just asked you to act with respect." Serge was not sure if he wanted to stay any longer. The whole experience had been surreal in nature. Who would want to work in a place like this? And besides, the classified ad had just asked for a household manager.

While Serge pondered, Albert returned to Ben, stood at his left side; Alexa was on his right. Ben signaled to Serge with a nod, as if to say that they were ready. Serge followed the group with his eyes, waited for them to sit, aware that he should be alert. Albert and Alexa sat to either side of Ben. The two other men remained standing, waiting to be introduced or dismissed from the meeting. A secretary entered the room, prepared to take notes. Serge seated himself, again not sure if this was where he wanted to be.

The meeting started with Albert presenting material from the red folder Alexa had given him before. He did the introduction as they had agreed, but never stopped for Alexa's turn. Albert continued, taking credit for each part of the project as if it were his. Alexa's expression became furious; she interrupted the presentation. Albert hesitated and told her that they did not have time for her remarks. Ben agreed: "It's irrelevant at this point."

"No, it is not." said Alexa, "I've worked on this project enough not to let someone else take the credit."

Albert cut her off: "Here we go again."

The confrontation made Serge even more uncomfortable, though at this point he was no longer surprised. Ben said, "Leave your personal matters outside, understood?"

"That doesn't have anything to do with it. It's my project and I can prove it to you."

"I won't go there. I know Albert, and he is incapable of taking credit for something that isn't his."

The secretary continued taking notes. Albert shouted at her in a very rude manner to stop it and get out of the room. Serge could not take it any longer. "What am I doing in this zoo?" he whispered to himself, then added out loud: "Excuse me, Mr. Stafford. Excuse me for interrupting, but I think that I don't have anything to do here." Facing Albert, he continued. "I believe you owe Ms. Lightman and this lady an apology." Glancing to Alexa and the secretary

"What the f..." replied Albert.

"I don't appreciate your attitude or rudeness, even less so in front of a woman. I also would like to point out that Alexa just handed you that red folder a few minutes ago, when she was asking you for time to make her presentation. I don't know if that is her work or not – that is another issue – but the material you are using was handed to you by her."

"Who do you think you are, and who the hell asked for your opinion? If you want to work here you better wait until someone asks you to talk."

"As far as I can tell, I don't want to work here. So if you will excuse me, have a good morning." Serge stood up, ready to leave.

Ben asked Albert to sit down and for Serge to stay a few more minutes.

"Mr. Stafford, I do need the work, but you know, at this point in time I am not interested in whatever you are offering. With all due respect, I won't tell you how to run your business if that is what you are doing here, but I'm not interested in perpetuating it in the same way." He stood up, picked up his material from the table. "Now, if you will excuse me ..."

Serge pushed his chair back, stood and walked through the door. The last thing they heard from him was the deep breath he took as the door closed behind him.

Serge was confused and disappointed. This had been an interview to remember. So many things had happened, most of them weird in nature. It was ok when something odd happened, but all this was just too much, too soon. He went straight to the elevator lobby, past the receptionist who smiled politely but curiously. He pressed the button of the elevator to go down, considered whether to turn his face back; someone might be calling him back, trying to stop him from leaving. He wished that perhaps someone would, but also resisted the idea; it was better this way.

The elevator doors opened and he walked in, never looking back. The doors closed and he felt a certain release. He pushed the lobby button down. He wanted to get out; this was not what he had envisioned, and now he would have to go back to square one, job hunting for anything.

The elevator descended, then stopped at level eight, where a courier entered. The elevator stopped again at level seven. As the doors opened, Serge saw Roberta Chartres standing at a reception desk, looking directly at the elevator. Only then did he remember his promise to her, and he quickly stepped out. She greeted him with warmth.

"I knew you were coming."

"I was planning to, but to be honest, I had forgotten completely until I saw you. It has been a strange morning. Honestly, I was on my way out; I completely forgot. I'm sorry."

"Not at all, young man. You're here, and that's what counts." Her smile was natural and very supportive; Serge felt sincerity in her words and appreciated a little sanity on this strange morning. He thought that he might as well make the most of it by making a good friend or learning something.

Roberta said: "What's the matter? You look as if you've seen a ghost!"

"Looks that bad, huh? I feel like that, maybe worse. It has been a strange morning, I guess."

"Bad interview, huh?"

"Well, most of it strange ... 'bizarre' is the right word. I've never experienced anything like it. In any case, it is behind me. I'm glad that the elevator stopped at your floor, otherwise I'd be gone. Your optimism and warmth might help me recharge my batteries, to be hopeful." And he laughed.

She looked directly into his eyes and placed her hand on his arm, walked off with him as if he was leading the way. They left the elevator lobby behind. "You're in a good place. So, trust me – you'll be surprised."

The decoration on this floor was less exquisite but equally elegant. There were fewer offices and the views to the outside were always available. They came to a very detailed mahogany door, elegantly carved, with a handsome brass handle; apparently there was no lock on it. To the side was a small logo made of the same wood, with what seemed to be rusted cooper and silver in its outlines. The logo had a iconic shape with, apparently, a more personal symbolic meaning than simply a relationship to the company's name or its type of business. It was also, Serge noticed with surprise, the same design as the logo displayed in the main lobby of the company on the fifty-second floor.

Roberta turned the brass handle, passed through the doorway into an office. "Please come in." She said to Serge then Roberta gestured to a secretary seated by the door, who said: "Everything is ready, and he is expecting you."

Roberta again took Serge by the arm, and led him farther inside. The space was decorated with memorabilia, pictures of family, and a few personal items. The view outside, unobstructed by curtains or other elements, was less spectacular than that from the fifty-second floor, but it was a picturesque view of the city and the surrounding historic neighborhood. Serge could see through other buildings the Olympic Sculpture Park, as well as the Space Needle, the bay and waterfront. The air temperature here was milder, perhaps even cold for some people, but Serge felt comfortable. Background music could be heard from an undisclosed source. One of the walls had a huge screen displaying financial information, news, and live feeds from several locations. Facing the screen was a "living room" setting with leather sofas and an ottoman. Against another wall was a conference table made from a large slab of gray- and white-stained marble with black highlights. The base had two pieces, one wooden and resembling the root system of a giant tree, the other an elegant, svelte column of rust-finished steel, fashioned to a smooth appearance. The chairs were a modern design, black leather with a synthetic core material; one on one side of the table, four on the other side. Although the table was covered with documents, it was an orderly display and it seemed that everything was there only temporarily.

"Wow!" Serge said. "Is this is your office?"

"Why do you ask?"

"It is incredible. I mean, it is not over-decorated to make any superfluous statements, it expresses personality and taste, yet it is welcoming, warm, and honest. Whoever works here is not being pretentious and it seems very personal; that is why I thought it was yours. Now on the other hand, I don't see many plants, except the bonsais in the corner, while you seem like a plant lover with a green thumb. If this is your office, do you have an opening for an office manager?" Serge laughed politely.

"No, it's not mine." said Roberta. "It's my son's. I would have put in a lot of plants, and cut down a little on the area, making it smaller. But he never paid any attention to me."

From the back of the office behind them came a man's voice, strong and friendly: "Oh, come on, Mama. You say the same thing about my office every time you're here. And by the way – you know it's true you always get everything you ask of me."

Serge and Roberta turned toward the approaching figure. "Good morning," he said, extending his hand to Serge. "My name is Robert. Robert Lightman."

Mr. Lightman was a wide shoulder 6'3" tall white athletic man. He was probably in his late sixties but appeared much younger. He had a gentle expression and a contagious smile. The long sleeves of his white shirt were rolled to mid arm and two dark blue suspenders framed his large torso. His matching jacket was hanging by an old fashion wood carved coat hanger, a bright orange tie was hanging by one of the side pockets.

Serge received the man's firm, strong shake. "Serge Onamor," he responded.

"Please, sit down over here," said Mr. Lightman, showing the way to one of the leather sofas. "I enjoy this setting better than my desk. It's more personal and comfortable than that work area." He pointed with a certain disdain in the direction of his desk. "Mama, you can sit with Serge ... you don't mind if I call you Serge, right?"

"Not at all, Mr. Lightman," Serge replied.

"Oh please, you can call me Bob. Although Mama here doesn't like it, I've found that it helps people relax around me."

"You know very well how much your parents hated it, when anybody called you 'Bob'. Your name is Alexander Robert Lightman."

"Your parents?" Serge asked. He remembered Roberta calling Lightman her 'son'.

"Well, yes, my biological parents. You see, my Mom gave me birth, and my Dad gave me my name and the foundations of fortune, at least part of it. But my 'Mama' here, she was the one that raised me as her own son: she taught me how to keep my feet on the ground, educated me, and has been with me since I was three. Now I'm sixty-seven. My parents died when I was nineteen, and it took me a while to take control over my family's estate, and in all those years Mama never changed a bit."

"I'm much older now, and tired, but I can still pull your ears if you don't behave," said Roberta with pride.

Lightman said to Serge: "See what I mean? And with a genuine smile he gestured towards the sofa and invited serge to sit down.

"Well, please sit down, make yourself comfortable."

The receptionist appeared, carrying a tray upon which were a pitcher of ice water with slices of lemon and three glasses that she set down on a side table.

"Thank you, Margaret, that'll be all. No interruptions until my daughter comes in, ok?"

"Yes, Mr. Lightman."

Lightman sat comfortably on his sofa, crossing his left leg on top of the right knee. "Serge, I've been waiting to meet you. Mama came here more than an hour ago and told me that you were the one. She was pretty excited and spoke marvels about you. She has a keen sense for people, and can spot a fake from a mile away: a great judge of character, I must tell you. Through the years, I have come to recognize that she has never been wrong, and I've learned to listen to her. Sometimes I wish I had done it earlier!" He sighed, remembering some moment on his life.

"Well, you've come a long way son. And you're still learning," Roberta added.

They smiled authentically at one another, and Serge saw a deep bond and understanding between them.

Lightman spoke to Serge: "First of all, I guess I owe you an apology."

"I don't understand."

"You see, we've been conducting a job search ... well, it's not really a company position ... that's why the search has been a little different and also a bit unorthodox. In any case, I have a need and although we've been searching – and by 'we' I mean mama and me – we have not been lucky enough to find the right candidate. It's been more than a year and a half."

"Almost two years, Robert."

"Yes, almost two years, and we've had no luck until the day you called."

"Me? I have not called you before."

"Well, technically not me, but my company. Let me explain: I run a successful and rewarding business, and we combine it with a small non-profit foundation. I inherited the business from my old man, but made it bigger and have consolidated the company as one of the major players in the industry. At the same time, the foundation receives a lot of donations and support, national and international, to help our campaigns throughout the year. In few words: I don't have too much time to waste.

"For the last few years, my daughter Alexa has been helping me. She joined me here after going through a messy divorce. I loved the idea of having my girl helping me; I don't have any other children and the time she has been here has been the best since my wife Angie, now deceased, was with us. I don't want that to change, but my daughter is being divided between her home and work, between her personal life – which is null – and her children. This is where you come in."

He leaned forward in his seat and looked directly into Serge 's eyes. "When you called us, we called you back …"

"Mr. Stafford?" inquired Serge.

"Yes, Ben. He called you and thanks to him, we decided to act. He had a good feeling about you."

"You mean to tell me that the interview that I was going to have on the fifty-second floor was related to you?"

"Yes."

Well … May I speak freely?"

"Please do," said Lightman.

"Let me tell you the bad news. The interview never happened and from what I was able to see of how things are done here, it really sucks."

Lightman laughed spontaneously; He seemed entertained by Serge's comment. "That bad, huh?"

"Well, bizarre, as I told Ms. Chartres."

"Call me Roberta, son. It makes me feel younger."

"Thank you, ma'am. Well, I told Roberta that the experience was bizarre in nature. Even as I entered this building, all these strange things began to happen."

"I know," Mr. Lightman interrupted him. "Let me tell you, we did a little background check on you, we verified the references you sent in your application and even were able to find some of your personal friends. I know, I know, it was only a few days ago but I have my sources. Your friends, they all speak highly of you; I might say, you have very good recommendations. One of your former teachers said, 'With Serge, what you see is what you'll get. It's that simple.'

"So we decided to see what you look like and verify if that statement is true."

"Wow," said Serge. He leaned back into the sofa cushions. "All that in a few days..." Then he added "You probably talked with Professor Matter ... that is why I gave you the reference in the first place."

Lightman stood up, paced a few steps back and forth, then turned to face Roberta and Serge. "Now the reason I must apologize ... is because the moment you entered this building was the moment we started your interview."

"I'm sorry? ..."

"Yes, well, the first part was actually not completely prepared, but it worked nevertheless. You see, we were giving each interested party a series of tests that would show us, without their knowing, their real personality, not a pose or a rehearsed attitude. When you met Mama in the lobby downstairs, she had gone to greet the other young man; we didn't expect you so early. He was in the previous meeting, ahead of you. He failed the first test. He ran into the building – you even opened the door for him – and he never stopped for the lady who was coming through the doors, or the one ahead of him. He stumbled into Mama and spilled her files, never returned or apologized. He gave priority to his appointment rather than acting correctly, which he should have not only because he caused the accident, but also because it was simply the right thing to do. Then you did help Mama and talked with her. You took the time to help and even arrived late to your appointment. Then, curiously, you apologized for being late but rendered no explanation. That was good."

"Why spoil a honest apology with an unnecessary explanation?" phrased Serge, looking at Mama, who wore a proud smile of "I told you so" on her face.

"Mama was impressed with you and didn't need any other test, but we proceeded as planned. We continued to test this other young man, and he failed the next two trials. He's on his way home now. Some of the other candidates have been through the first two tests, and they're waiting for Albert or Ben to show up, but they've done poorly, and will also be heading home soon.

"You were friendly toward the people you interacted with, regardless of their position; you treated everyone equally and with respect. Mama loved you for that and her opinion matters a lot to me. Then, you were not temped by bribery or even slander, and we liked that a lot. Principles ..."

70

"Do you have a price, Serge?"

"A price? What do you mean?"

"Do you think you could be bought?"

"I want to think I cannot be bought... but you never know. They say that everyone has their price, I truly don't know what is it. I do know my weaknesses, but not my price," Serge replied with sincerity.

"Mr. Lightman, why all that trouble for this position? I truly believed that this position was just the administrator of an estate, that sort of thing. This interview makes me feel that this is way too important for that."

"Yes, it is, and it's way more important than working at my firm, because you'd be working with my family."

Albert and Ben Stafford entered the office, followed by Alexa. The newcomers crossed the room to join the others where they sat.

Lightman said, "I believe you know Albert and Ben. And this is Alexa, my daughter."

"Hi, Dad. Hi, Mama," she replied, sending them both a kiss with her hand.
Albert sat down next to Serge. "Please don't think I'm a slime ball. It was fun to play the bad guy, but honestly, I would have trouble acting like that all the time."

"Congratulations, Serge. You passed our tests with flying colors," said Ben. "That was quite a show you gave us there. I'm glad to know I was right; after our phone conversation, I was feeling optimistic."

"Well, you made me wonder what it was you were up to. You were completely different than on the phone," answered Serge, amused, glad to know that Ben was for real.

Alexa spoke in a combination of discontent and sincerity: "I must admit, I am impressed. Rarely does someone prove me wrong, and you just did." She still did not trust Serge. Looking straight in his eyes, she said, "Let's hope you're who you seem to be."

Alexa, wanting to be independent, wanting to prove that she did not need what her father was doing for her, decided to press forward and test all candidates to a higher limit. If she could prove that all men were the same, that their principles were flexible, their agendas adjustable and their loyalties bought and sold, then probably her father would back away from this search. She was committed to proving her point to retain her independence.

At that, Lightman noticed Serge's discomfort and tried to ease the tension. "Alexa, let's try to make our guest feel comfortable." He walked back to the seating area of his office and leaned on one of his sofas.
"Ok, then. Serge, I want to know if you would be interested in joining us. There will be a lot of responsibility and hard work. I don't doubt you have the guts to deliver, but I want to know if you're interested."

I am here, Mr. Lightman, though I would have left if it hadn't been for Roberta. What is the work all about?"

"I need someone to help my daughter and me. The work involves her estate, her home, kids, life and work … it's a position that is hard to describe. We said 'household manager', because you – well, whomever we hire – will be responsible for her home, and mine, in a way. It's also is a matter of being the coordinator of schedules, kind of an executive assistant, but this person needs to have a family oriented spirit, because he or she is going to interact with my grandkids and closely, real closely with my daughter. So I need a right hand man, someone who can be trusted as if he were part of the family."

"Has anyone done this job before?" asked Serge, curious to learn whose shoes he was going to be filling.

"Not exactly," said Lightman, "This is something I've been thinking about profoundly. I told Mama my concerns, and Alexa, though she refuses to accept this."

"I told you before: I can handle this on my own; we can handle it," said Alexa, still making her case.

"Well, we've been through this before, haven't we? Besides, you agreed to give it a try if we met someone worth the trouble, and I believe Serge here has proven that he is."

Lightman went on: "So no, Serge, no one has done this job before. In a way, if you wanted to put it in words, if everything were ideal, it would be a brother, a son-in-law role, but without the marriage, of course!"

"Father!"

"Sorry, Alexa, but I had to say it. You see, Serge, some years ago Alexa was married but her husband never got involved with family, even with his own kids, only with his work. He never came through as a family man. After the divorce, I gave up on having a normal family for my daughter, understanding that it was her choice and her life. But I still worry."

"That had nothing to do with it Dad". Added Alexa "He was a complete a fraud, he was only interested in a position at your company and the money."

"Well, let's forget that for now."

73

Lightman shifted his position closer to Roberta. "Mama and I know that we need someone reliable close by. She convinced me that you are the one that can do it, and I trust her judgment. I want to know if you're interested."

"Yes, I am."

"Just like that? I haven't covered what we'll be paying you, the terms and details, working hours ..."
"Mr. Lightman, may I speak freely? With all due respect, if you have gone through all this trouble, if we are talking about your family and not your company, I assume that you must be talking about a good, fair compensation. Although," he began, looking at Albert, "although I need the money, I like earning it with hard work, and I know that if I don't do it, you would end up terminating my services. If you like what you see, then you will pay fairly."

"Good enough. I'll have Ben work the details with you, then you think it over this week. I would like to have an answer, a formal answer, by next Monday. Will that be enough time?"

Yes, sir, it will be. I'll give you my answer on Monday. I will call Mr. Stafford with my reply." Serge looked around the group. "If I may add: nice performances, you all. You took me for a ride up there."

"We certainly did. You should have seen your eyes!" said Ben.

Lightman said, "Ok then, it's settled. We'll be in touch. It was good to meet you, and I hope you decide to join us... and please you can call me Bob" He shook Serge's hand and left the room. Albert and Ben said their farewells and left, joking that they should do this more often and that it was fun to 'act' at work.

Serge saw his opportunity and looked Alexa in the eyes. "Miss Lightman, about what happened upstairs ..."

74

"Nothing happened. It's ok, Mr. Onamor." She turned to Roberta. "I have to go, Mama." She nodded in Serge's direction, gave Roberta a kiss on the forehead, and left.

"What was all that about?" asked Roberta, puzzled. "I've never seen Alexa act that way before."

"Well, I guess it was the results of all the trials. I think she was expecting me to fail, especially the one for which she alone was in charge."

"Which one?" asked Roberta.

"You know, the one in the first meeting room ... " Serge suddenly realized that episode had not been part of the plan. He was confused again; rather flattered, but confused. He decided not to say anything more about it, but Roberta pressed him.

"Alexa's test? Ah, I believe I remember," Roberta said mischievously, though she knew there had been no such a test. "Would you care to elaborate?"

"Well, you know, the meeting room, the advance?" He smiled shyly. "She is incredibly attractive and smart ..."

Mama looked at him. "Oh! That test, I almost forgot, Alexa's test, that's right." She tried to hide her surprise, wondering what Alexa had done to Serge and if that was the explanation for her nervous behavior.
On his way out, they stopped again at Roberta's office, where they sipped coffee and chatted a while. He thanked her for her support and told her that he was looking forward to seeing her again. She gave him a hug and said good-bye with a wink. "I told you I had a surprise for you."

Moments later Serge found Ben Stafford in his office, where they discussed the job offer in details. He told Ben he needed to review the whole matter with his son, and promised to be in touch on Monday. Serge left with the sense of something gained, feeling better now that he knew the experience had been something prepared and not merely random acts.

Serge went home with a lot on his mind.

Home

Serge arrived home before Max, and retired to his studio to read and think. It had been a very interesting day, and he was excited about the offer. It was a job that would allow him not to be alone. Max was leaving in a few weeks. He had grown up to be a very special young man; he had his life ahead of him. But Serge felt his own life was in a different place. Losing Steph had been a real tragedy, and although he had tried for the last five years to date again and start a new relationship, it always failed. He would either have different expectations of the women he dated, or he would continuingly compare them with Steph. Max had given up some time ago, trying to find a match for his father, as had Al, who remained Serge's best friend. It was clear that the standard by which Serge measured women was very high, or that he had idealized Steph since his loss. Serge had many friends and went out with them often, but he never made any attempt to pursue a romantic relationship.

Serge's studio was a remodeled attic space. Here he listened to music, read, took in the view and sometime even slept. The studio was decorated with some of Steph's favorite pieces and plants, many too tall and in need of repotting and proper pruning. Her thesis and awards he kept in a special case, with two locked drawers where he kept all their letters, special gifts they had exchanged, and other mementos. He opened the case from time to time, when he needed to make a decision, when he felt alone, when he needed inspiration.

"Help me find my way, Steph," he repeated now, his hands caressing a small stone they had picked up on a special trip and which he regularly held while running. The stone was smooth and shiny, with green and white lines, black flecks. Serge wondered how much of her was still there in the stone or had he already washed it away with sweat, and oil from his fingers. He turned the stone, tossed it repeatedly from hand to hand; it was a therapy to calm his thinking, and he needed clarity to find out what to do.

The thought took Serge back to the moment he and Steph had picked it up, on a long excursion in the desert many years ago. One of their first planned dates was a visit to the Sabino Canyon Reserve. They had decided that they wanted to do something different than going for a drink or sitting in a crowded place or participating in some field trip related to their school work. Each knew the other loved the outdoors, and Serge had asked if she had ever been to Sabino Canyon. Steph was curious about the place, having only heard about it on campus. Serge picked her up very early one chilly autumn morning, and it was still before dawn when they arrived at the trailhead. They needed a head start if they wanted to see the sunrise from the canyon, and also to get the best of the morning without the desert sun.

Serge parked his car in a deserted lot, near an information center. They put on their backpacks headed up the trail, and before long reached a viewpoint towards the east where they could sit. They talked about the hike and the surroundings until the sun started to show up. Dawn washed them in orange light, and Serge put his hand up to show Stephanie how the color united all objects in a same hue. As the sun appeared on the horizon, birds began to fly, bugs altered their noises, and a nice warmth displaced the chill, made them feel comfortable in their hiking shorts.

Once the sun cleared the horizon, they moved forward towards a higher location. There was a particular spot, Serge told Steph, where there was an absolute silence, a place that he called 'sanctuary'. About nine o'clock, they came to 'the boulder point', where an enormous rock had fallen from the higher cliffs, creating a horizontal platform now smoothed by wind and monsoon rain waters. There they took a short break and ate breakfast. All along the trail they talked about their families, in great detail: names, places, experiences, personalities. Serge usually led the way but let Steph go ahead when she wanted. She seemed confident and had a keen eye for details. While Serge enjoyed the scenery, his eyes wandering from side to side, Steph was looking at birds and plants, pointing out the characteristics of the rocks or their strange formations. When she saw anything exciting, she rushed ahead of Serge to inspect it.

Later in the morning they began to feel the desert heat, but they soon arrived at an impressive rock formation, a grotto filled by the runoff from summer rains. The shadows of acacias, mesquites, and old, tall cottonwoods gave an excellent cover from the fall sun. There was no one else around; the two had walked a long ways past the last tourist trail sign. They headed for the water and took a refreshing dip which felt cold and refreshing, but the best sensation came from getting out and laying down on a flat, warm stone in a sunny spot.

"You look like a lizard," Steph commented as she saw Serge crawling on all fours towards the basking rock and splashing some water on it to cool it down.

"It's hot!" Serge replied "I need to freshen it a little. Come over and try it, it feels great."

She sat next to him, and he told her to lay flat on the rock, patting the surface with his hand. "Over here, by my side, like this ..."

Serge lay with his head in the cottonwood shadow, the rest of his body in the sun. "Only your head should be under the shadow, only your eyes, if you can. Hurry! It's amazing."

Steph did as Serge told her and lay by his side, facing the sky, their eyes protected by the moving shadows of the leaves.

"Look up there: you see that?" Serge pointed to the deep blue sky background, floating in it infinite number of cottonwood seeds floated in the air and reflected the sun's glare on them.

"Yes! It's amazing!"

"It's quite beautiful isn't it? I mean, they move like in slow motion. It's like if you were underwater watching plankton move, or in outer space, floating. Seems like time is standing still; the breeze barely moves them and they float so gently down."

"It is really pretty. I like how the sunlight hits them from behind and they shine in the glare."

"Hey, you notice it! Yes, that is why I told you to cover only your eyes with the shadow, so our eyes have the chance to see that glare, and our bodies will feel warm. It looks like an early winter, with no snow... sudden, just an instant ..."

Serge felt her gaze. He looked at her for a moment then nervously looked up again. "It's nice here, and so quiet."

"Serge," asked Steph, "Can I ask you something personal?"

"Yes, sure. Anything."

"Can you feel it?"

Serge turned to see her eyes. He didn't need to ask; he knew what she was talking about. "Yes," he replied, "very strongly. Don't you wish sometimes that you could hold a moment for a while and preserve what you feel?"

"Yes, I have, though sometimes the wishing makes you lose the moment and you stop living it."

"Never thought it that way ... but you are right." "It is happening to me right now, as we speak. I feel so alive but my mind wanders, trying to remember each passing second to recall it later and then, as you say, I'm missing the moment right now."

Silence. It felt good to be quiet and enjoy how those cottonwood seed came gently towards their faces with a glare of snowflakes and stars.

Serge turned toward Steph. They were really close now, and when Serge turned Steph felt it, as they stared directly into each other's eyes. Serge said: "I'm not going to wonder any more, nor think about whether I should or not. Although I want to preserve the moment forever, I also want to feel more, and I'm a little afraid of spoiling it."

Steph looked at him with assurance, knowing where he was going. Serge gently kissed her mouth. They both felt a rush and their hands joined, their bodies pressed together. It was at first a tentative kiss, a tender kiss that quickly grew with the love of that moment. They opened their mouths and then they were breathing each other's breath, so close as if one. In their embrace they rolled to the side, so Steph was on top of him.

"Ouch!" said Serge in surprise, twisting his back.

"Did I hurt you, poor boy?" Steph mockingly.

Serge reached under his back and retrieved a small, green stone. "Yeah, you did. So does this!"

He was about to throw it away but Steph stopped him. "Wait! Don't throw it, let me see it."

"Why? Want to ask for advice on how to break a man's back?"

"No, you silly! I want to keep it." She held the small stone in her hand and after tracing the contour of it with fingertips; she smiled and looked back at Serge. "This will always remind me of this place, this moment, our first kiss … and also the look in your wide eyes when you felt it in your back." She smiled broadly and put the stone in her backpack.

"Now where is all that fine speech about living the moment and forgetting about making memories and such?" Serge told her sarcastically.

"Well …This is my lucky penny!" Smiling, Stephanie looked directly into his eyes. "This is definitely a keeper." She held Serge again. "And so are you."

They kissed again, and with that kiss sealed their friendship with the understanding, trust, freedom, and passion that only love can give. There was no one around to witness their bond, only the canyon and its plant and animal inhabitants. Their relationship came to them as naturally as if it had always existed; they realized that they were meant for each other.

Max had arrived home in a very good mood. He had finished his summer school coursework with very good results. Now he had the time he needed to make final arrangement for college. He did not see his father around, and headed for the place he was sure to be. He climbed the attic steps and saw his father with the stone. Serge turned at the sound his footsteps.

"Hey, champ, what's up?"

"Got great news! I finished today with all my work."

"I thought it was going to take you longer."

"Me too, but there were a few things not required anymore, and I had already earned extra credits, so Professor Valenka signed-off on everything. He wants me to start college; he's been very supportive."

"Yes, he is a good man."

Tegor Valenka had been a friend of Steph in college at the University of Arizona. He was an exchange student from the Balkans with a keen eye for research and since college Stephanie and him had done several projects and studies together. Steph and Tegor had accepted simultaneously two positions at the UW College of Anthropology and become colleagues continuing teaching and research. He now had Steph's chair position at the department and was mentoring Max in a similar free-spirit philosophy as his Mom's, a quality that had distinguished the department as an avant-garde institution since both started there .

"I appreciate he is willing to take so much time with you"

"Hey, old man, what's on your mind?"

"Not much …" Serge replied thoughtfully, though eager to let something out. Max knew his Dad and insisted. "Every time you take that stone and toss it in your hands I know you'll be making a decision. One day you're going to run out of stone … What's up?"

Serge nodded at his son's remark, studying the stone on his palm. "I might, someday." replied Serge. "That would be a great loss. This stone was ours; it has been in my pocket everywhere I go, since your Mom left us."

*   *   *

"Ready for dinner?" asked Serge to Max as he came back from the memory.

"No thanks, Dad. I have plans with the guys. We're going to hit this just-opened pub and celebrate like crazy. Actually, would you like to come with us? That way you can tell me what's on your mind

"No way. It is your party. We will have plenty of time to be together before you go to college. And by the way, is everything ready?"

"Yes, I'm almost done with everything and don't change the topic, why don't you join us?I must say, though, having an old guy around always brings us certain luck with the girls, so you are more than welcome. Besides, the guys know you and enjoy talking with you. The idea is just to have a good time."

"Well, maybe just for the first hour. I've got to think about the new work, the one I told you on the phone."

"The strange interview? smiled Max, making his Dad feel uncomfortable. "Hey perhaps all the guys can convince you what a waste of talent that job is for you, you'll be the family Butler, right?"

"Butler... yeah, right. The position is 'household manager'. For me, at this time, it seems like a strange job but I think it is a little more important than that the title makes it sound. Besides, the way the economy is, and how my connections are, anything is better than being without activity."

"Yeah, Dad, but still ..."

"I know it does not sound appealing son, I think it's more like the administrator of a property, an estate –an important estate. The main reason I'm doing it is because of the trust and the responsibilities involved. I'm being asked to care for and keep an eye on a man's most valuable treasure, his family."

"It's strange ... Have you talked with anyone else about this?"

"No, there is no one to talk to. You know how it is."

"You should hang around more with my uncles and aunts, and granddad and grandma are quite alright, you know?

"I know, son. I knew them before you, remember? But there were things that happened before you were born, then others that you do know about. I don't feel like I belong. I am grateful that you have them as family and that they have an excellent relationship with you, and that for me is enough."

"I know that; we've gone through this before. I just don't want you to be alone anymore. You are very talented and should be working on your own stuff."

"You sound like your Mom. I know what you're saying. I have not stopped doing my stuff. It's just that I don't commercialize it or sell it right now. My work and ambitions were always different things, and as you can see around us, we have never been bad off or without a normal life."

"You need a partner, Dad."

Serge smiled. "Don't worry about me, son. I am alright. These recent years have been for my own growth, and this job might give me the chance to grow some more. I got a feeling about it. Now in regards to a partner … Your Mom is still pretty deep inside me, but I appreciate your sincerity. You don't want me to turn into a grumpy, old, lonely, bitter man. No way! I'm way ahead of you on that someday, someone might come along."

"What about that girl you met at the seashore? Michelle?"

"Yes. Well, she was in a different phase of her life, and probably too young for me. She had a long way to go before knowing what she wanted. Besides, I was not at my best. I might have been too needy; I acted like a wuss. Opened up too fast, might have scared her away."

"Well, the sea is full of other fish, Dad."

"That's what they say."

"I just want you to know that I'm ok with it. I know how you loved Mom, and that means a lot to me, but I want to become the same man you were, even better. You're too lonely and sad, or nostalgic, and I kind of miss the fun and goofy guy that you were."

"Goofy?!" exclaimed Serge with a genuine playfulness. "So that is what I was? Goofy?!"

"Yeah, a real cool and goofy Dad, better than any friend."

Serge hugged Max, rubbed his head and messed up his hair. "Thanks, son, that means a lot to me. Hey, maybe you guys can introduce me to one of your friends. I might be older but who said that everything happens before age forty?"

 "You are way cool, Dad... though not that cool"
Max smiled at the implication.
"Let's go then. I'll keep an eye on you, and you'd better behave."

"Yes, sir, I mean 'Dad'." Serge said with a submissive expression. He realized how much his son had grown, that he could be so serious about him dating but understood that at this point, in this moment, he was being overprotective and that their roles had, in a strange way, reversed.

The Job

Serge became Alexa's Lightman's 'household manager'. He had accepted the position without any further negotiations. He considered the offer generous and understood that the work would not require him to apply any special skills. His talk with Max and his meetings with pillows at night made him see that it was worth a try, even though the job was not related to his profession.

The Lightman estate was located thirty-five miles from downtown Seattle, in a low density residential area. Alexa had moved back to this home after her divorce. Her father convinced that it was a better home for her and her two kids than for him, even though she asked him to stay he moved out to another property that he found more manageable for his circumstance. Alexa never thought that she would ever come back to the same home she lived so many years ago, but it felt like home and the familiarity and warmth of these roots made her feel safe and gave her the confidence she needed at that time.

The Lightman residence measured about five thousand square feet in floor space, though it was not as big as Serge might have imagined, considering the size of their company. Each property in the neighborhood was sited on a minimum of twenty acres of heavily grown forest and ponds. The house had seven bedrooms, nine bathrooms, a library, and an incredible kitchen. Two family rooms were the main gathering places for the family: the more private one on the upper floor, and the more commonly used one close to the kitchen. The house had been decorated with exquisite taste, although in some places the decoration did not reflect the family that lived there, but was more a reflection of the interior designer's preferences. Any corner of the house might have been featured in a design and architecture magazine. An exception to this was the family room by the kitchen, which was warm, bright, full of plants and flowers, and very informal; it was one of Serge's favorite spots in the home. The children's rooms reflected the same informality and uniqueness.

Serge was responsible for administration of the household and for maintenance. His work officially included some family responsibilities, and other things that he had decided to do on his own time, like helping the kids get from one place to another or supporting school activities. He was required to maintain the property, keep an eye on Alexa's agenda, manage the mail, run errands – all those things that always need to be done but are barely noticed.

The other household staff was Lorna and Mon. Lorna the cook was a big, overweight woman from Louisiana. She looked like a traditional German aunt; she insisted on doing things her own way and would not take no for an answer. Serge appreciated her honesty and knew that if he wanted to do something with her, he had to go along with her or make her feel like any decisions were hers. After the first week, they got along pretty well, and by now they enjoyed each other's company. Mon was Lorna's husband, a quiet, tall man who did most of the yard work and the driving when needed. He had a gentle posture and friendly face. Although one might assume that Lorna was in charge, Mon could keep Lorna quiet with just a smile and a nod.

Alexa had two children: Sarah, who was fifteen, and Jimmy, who was seven. She had been divorced for the past six years. Her ex, Richard Sanders, was one of the bright stars in the Lightman Corporation, but had never been a good husband or father. At the beginning, the children were a real challenge for Serge. It was first the feeling of being a stranger, then it was probably a reflection of their mother's restlessness about the whole situation. Serge came to understand that Alexa had a great relationship with her father, but his hiring at the house was one of many impositions that her father made on her. Her marriage had been another. Serge understood her discomfort, but in time, he earned her trust and friendship through his quiet and gentle manner. During the first weeks, Serge continued to wonder if he would like being a "domestic" employee, but he soon grew accustomed to the children and the home. There was an objective, a challenge, to win Alexa's trust and fulfill his promise to prove Roberta right by endorsing him for the job. By sticking up for himself and resolving misunderstandings, Serge became one of the family, at least for the kids. And he liked the idea of being part of an environment that gave him back what he had lost in his own life. This was a new family, not his own, but a family nevertheless. Roberta was a big help, often visiting and always telling Serge how things were, how Alexa and her dad were, and why.

Serge had now been with the Lightmans for nine months. He played with the children and participated in their activities as if he were part of the family. He helped with homework and cleaning, cared for them when sick, and enforced discipline; with him, the kids grew to act with respect and confidence. Serge earned their trust with time and care. It had been more difficult to earn the trust of Alexa, who was still dubious about the need for Serge to be there. But with time she had grown accustomed to his presence and was grateful that he was there to help them the way he did. She spent too many afternoons at work and rarely saw her children, so she was glad they were not alone. Serge brought a feeling of order to their lives.

Max was now completing his freshman year at college in Arizona. He was far away but regularly phoned and emailed his Dad and Steph's family. Although Max had insisted that Serge join him for the Christmas holidays, Serge declined, preferring his solitude and giving Max the chance to be with family from his mother's side. Serge had always thought that that was the best place for him to be; he saved other times in the year for the two of them to take a white water boat trip or other excursion together, without the pressure of a formal holiday.

Serge had kept his condo in Seattle, but had moved what he needed to the Lightman's place, where he lived from day to day in a small apartment above the four-car garage; He had an independent entrance from a side stair and he overlooked the main front yard of the home. There were two small windows which were from the small kitchen and bathroom that faced the back garden which was bigger and had the house amenities and best view. This had become a comfortable spot for him, arranged to his taste and needs.

Over time, Serge had been able to save from the Lightman household budget a significant amount of money, enough to remodel a long abandoned guest-house on the estate. After consulting with Alexa, he convinced her that rehabilitating the guest house could prove to be useful for the family. The guest house had become a warehouse for old furniture and company files, which Serge transferred to the attic adjacent to his apartment. The guest-house project gave him a chance to work with his hands and on several weekends he and Alexa's children had spent whole afternoons working on it together. When finished it gave the family, specially the children, a place to be, play and hang out informally from the decorated and well kept house. The guest-house had become the children's favorite place to hang around with friends. While Serge enjoyed the traditional architecture and craftsmanship of the building, the children enjoyed its informal and free spirited atmosphere. Sarah and Jimmy could have sleepovers and even parties that didn't disrupt the house order. On some evenings, Serge and the children gathered by the fireplace to talk and go over their day.

Serge had earned Jimmy's trust and friendship more easily than Sarah's. Perhaps it was the fact that Serge had a raised a son of his own, that he spent more time with Jimmy. They played videogames, told stories, and worked together on the guest-house. Jimmy came to see Serge as a father figure, although he had monthly visits from his father Richard, they never grew close. Serge taught Jimmy to ride a bicycle, they played catch and, when no one else was watching, he was allowed to drive Serge's car up and down the driveway.

Sarah got along with Serge but they had not become close. She distrusted him just as would any fifteen year-old girl, but that all changed one Saturday night. Sarah did not like it when Serge picked her up at after school, and when her friends would ask her about him, she referred to Serge as a distant uncle, a cousin of her Mom. Jimmy liked being picked up by Serge because it meant arriving home earlier and more time to play, but Sarah saw it as a loss of privacy.

One weekend, Alexa was away on a one day business trip but had given Sarah permission to go on a sleepover with her best friend, Lisa. When Serge picked up the children after school on Friday, he saw something that he did not like, and decided to keep an eye on Sarah for the weekend. Serge was waiting for Sarah in the high school parking lot, and saw a group of older teenagers, two boys and three girls, smoking cigarettes and glancing across the yard at Sarah and Lisa. Serge knew by their body language that they had a plan and intentions that were not good.

On Saturday evening, around nine in the evening, Serge took Sarah to Lisa's home then parked nearby, where he could watch and not be seen. Almost thirty minutes have passed when Serge was about to leave when the garage door opened and the two girls appeared, driving Lisa's mother's minivan. Serge followed from a discrete distance. They girls stopped at a 7-11 where they purchased drinks and picked-up the same three mean-spirited girls he had seen at school with the older boys. Serge did not like what he saw, but there was nothing he could do but wait. It was almost ten thirty when, the two older boys appeared driving a small sports car and parked next to the minivan. There was a brief conversation among the teens, then the vehicles drove off, the minivan behind the sports car; Serge followed them to a house where a party was in progress.

It was eleven o'clock when Serge drove by and parked a block away. He was worried that he had lost eye contact with Sarah. He thought of the promise he had made to Alexa and Mr. Lightman that he would take care of the children. He walked back toward the party and came upon the sports car, now unoccupied; he looked inside and found beer cans and cigarette butts. He approached the minivan and saw that there were people still inside. He saw a faint red light and assumed they were smoking – he hoped that was all but feared that something more was involved. Suddenly the passenger door opened and the overhead light came on. He saw Sarah laughing and smoking; Lisa was being kissed by one of the boys. Serge decided not to act yet. He was not going to embarrass Sarah if he didn't have to, he would watch and keep an eye on her. He wondered if he could watch Lisa, too, and hoped that the two girls stayed together for the rest of the night. Hidden in the shadow of a tree, Serge kept still and watched as the group exited the minivan entered the house where the party was taking place. He cautiously approached and got to the service alleyway beside the house; he needed a way to keep an eye on the girls.

The best he could find was a side window into the living room, where he could watch without being seen. From inside came the sound of alternative music. He saw a lot of kids, with not an adult in sight: a typical teenage party. In the corner on the living room he saw Sarah and Lisa dancing with the two older boys, then felt even more uneasy as the boys started groping at them, despite the girls' protests. He saw two of the older girls go to the kitchen, where through the doorway he could see a counter with bottles and cups. Serge crept toward the kitchen window, but accidentally kicked a garbage can. He heard a voice, then steps coming his way: he was in trouble. The screen door into the kitchen swung open, hitting a cat that screamed underfoot. A young voice yelled at the feline: "Get the fuck off, you dirty cat!"

With relief, Serge saw that no one was coming out. At the kitchen window he watched as the older girls put something into two cups, then mixed the liquid with a knife; the girls laughed and raised the cups in a toast, but did not drink.

They returned to the living room and gave the cups to Lisa and Sarah who thanked them and drank eagerly; they looked thirsty and tired of dancing. Serge continued to watch and soon saw Sarah and Lisa begin to relax and act silly. They had been given something to relax them and would probably be taken advantage of at any moment.

Some minutes after midnight, Sarah and Lisa left the house with the two boys and stumbled to the minivan, the boys fondled them as Lisa searched for her keys. Both girls protested and pushed the kids away but were in no condition to give a better fight. The four got inside and closed the door. Now Serge was really worried; if they tried to leave it would take him some time to get to his car and follow, but fortunately young kid's hormones helped him decide: the boys could not wait to get lucky, whatever they planned to do it was going to be right there. After a minute, Serge knew they were not going to move and that he had better do something or it would be too late.

He neared the minivan, heard the sound of voices and movement. Through the windshield he saw the boys taking off the girls' clothes, the girls protesting, crying and pushing them away but without any strength.

"Stop… no…" was the faint struggle that Serge could hear. Now angry, he went for the door, which the boys had neglected to lock. In one motion, he opened the door and climbed in. The boys were on top of the girls; their shirts had been torn open; they clutched at their bras. The boys looked surprised and annoyed, but in their drunkenness were not coordinating their movements very well. "What the fuck!" exclaimed one in surprise.

"Shut the damn door!" said the other.

"Get your hands away from them," Serge shouted. He grabbed them both by the hair, pulled them out and onto the lawn. Their pants were down and they stumbled about, looking uncertain and fearful. One tried to step up and take a swing at Serge; Serge pushed him away and he collapsed on his butt, completely disoriented. The boys pulled up their pants, looked around. Some of the other party-goers had noticed the event and were approaching; the boys got up and left, running toward their car.

The three older girls had watched the whole episode from the porch and were there now, laughing. Serge stared at them in anger and they froze. When he looked back inside of the minivan both girls were crying, Sarah's looked at Serge embarrassed with a faint smile of gratitude but her eyes kept closing on her. He looked for the minivan's keys and found them still in the door lock. He sat the girls upright, covered them the best he could with his jacket, and fastened their seat belts. He closed the side door and went around to the driver's seat. He screamed at the girls on the porch: "What did you put on their drinks?"

"Go to hell!" one exclaimed and ran inside.

One of the others took a few steps forward. "Sleeping pills … Ruffies… I'm sorry … Are they alright?"

"They will be, I hope. Thank you."

Serge drove away, meditating on what to do with Sarah and Lisa. He decided against telling Alexa about the party; he thought Sarah should tell her. Showing up at Lisa's parents' home with the minivan was not the best option either: he was a stranger, driving their vehicle, with two drunken, sleepy girls; that would only make things worse.

Serge remembered being that age and that sometimes you just needed to be heard, get one chance … The girls had been extremely naïve, but they would probably learn something. He decided to take them home to sober up and rest. He could pick up his own car tomorrow; the girls needed to be taken care of. He called Lorna by cell phone and asked her if Jimmy was ok, if she could prepare some sort of Louisiana hangover remedy. Lorna was surprised by the late call, then annoyed with him for getting drunk, but Serge explained that it was not for him, that he was on his way home and needed her help with Sarah and Lisa. He said it was important that Alexa did not find out. They decided to get them to the guest house to avoid waking up Jimmy this late in the evening, he did not need to know... or tell.

When Serge arrived at the Lightman's guest-house, he found Lorna waiting with an anxious look. She had thought the girls would be much worse and was happy to see them each in one piece. Serge took Sarah and Lisa to the bathroom; they needed to throw up whatever they could. Lorna gave them warm salt water and forced them to drink, and a few minutes later they both began to convulse and vomit. Afterward, they had a tomato based spicy juice for hangovers.
"Go on girls, drink up... this is my old man's special" They drank with reluctance but without resistance, their faces were not pretty and they could barely stand, but already they felt and looked better.

Lorna cleaned them out and helped them get into their pajamas. Then Lorna and Serge put them in the guest's house beds and left them to sleep until morning. Serge cleaned the bathroom, and then told Lorna what had happened, how close the girls had been to being raped.

Lorna gave Serge a big hug and thanked him. "What you did was really good, ya know?"

"I'm glad I was there, that is all."

"Well, many girls go through that experience nowadays, but if we can keep them safe one more day, just one more day ..." she said with sadness.

"Yes, and if they can have a little more experience, we can gain two days."

Mon arrived at the guest-house and told Serge he was ready to pick up his car, they took Alexa's car to pick his car and drove back home. They have thought about returning Lisa's minivan home, but decided against it due to the late hour and to avoid the long explanations. There was no way to know if the girls had permission for the sleepover, the party or the drive. Perhaps a reprimand for taking the car without permission or going out to a late party would teach the girls a lesson too, but without all the ordeal's details. It was already one in the morning when they returned home, they found Lorna in the guest house kitchen taking care of the evening's events cleaning.

"You don't have to do that, Lorna," Serge told her.

"No problem, Serge, I got it, besides I needed something to do anyway seems to me we'll have plenty more tomorrow."

They both smiled. Lorna told him to wake her up if he needed anything, gave him a kiss on the cheek and departed with Mon to the service quarters in the main house. The door closed behind them.

Serge cleaned himself up, and went to sleep on the living room sofa. Lorna had already made it up as a bed. He smiled, sat down, looked outside through the window, looked at the almost extinguished fire in the hearth. He remembered the days of his marriage and the days when Max was still growing. Not so long ago, Max had been Sarah's age and faced with similar choices. Fortunately, Stephanie and he had done a good job raising their son ... Would daughters be different? "Yes," he mumbled, resting his head on the pillow. Thinking about a daughter brought back Stephanie's memory, the family, their plans... It took him a while to fall asleep.

Serge was up early the next morning, went to his apartment and changed his wrinkled clothes and took a fast run through the quiet forest and neighborhood streets. He was home by seven, took a quick shower and dressed in his university sweats. He was getting things ready to cook a hangover breakfast for Sarah and Lisa when at eight o'clock there was a loud knocking at the front door. It was Alexa, and she was mad. Serge opened the door and was pushed back as Alexa came through.

"Where are the girls?! I demand to see them! Who do you think you are? They have their own bed room – you sick bastard!" She slapped him on the face.

Serge tried to calm her down, he tried to explain.

"I got a call late last night from Louise, Lisa's mom, they were not home, the girls have taken the van without permission, and no one knew where they were. Louise called all of Lisa's friends until one told her about a party and how Sara's uncle had drugged them and drove away on the van. I took the first plane back, was relieved to see Louise's van here, but as I walked to her bedroom they were not there. I want you out of my house, you son of a bitch! I'm calling the police and you're going to rot in hell!"

"It's not what you think, Miss Lightman. Let me explain."

"There's nothing to explain, you are alone in a separate hose with two young intoxicated girls in a room, you're barely dressed yourself. As soon as Lorna told me they were drunk and with you, I didn't need to know anything else. I want you out right now!"

"Please, Miss Lightman, don't raise your voice, there is an explanation."

Alexa slapped Serge's face, pushed him back and marched to the stairs, crying and angry, thinking the worst about Serge.

"Alexa!"

Serge turned to the door, Roberta appeared in the doorway, Alexa stopped and turned. "Mama ..."

"Wait just one second. I know what you're feeling, but it's not what you think. Come here and be quiet, girl." Her tone was serene but firm.

Upstairs in the bedroom, Sarah and Lisa were awakened by the noise; they gently opened the door just enough to peek outside; they could hear everything.

Mama, walking to the stairs, passed Serge and as she did, she put her hand on his shoulder and smiled at him. With a wink, she said quietly, "Don't worry. I got this one."

"Come here, dear," she took Alexa in her arms.

Lorna entered the house, wringing her hands in her apron and an apologetic look in her eyes. "Sorry, Serge, she never let me finish when she asked me."

Serge smiled in sympathy, but he was hurting inside. He stood to the side of the door and listened while Roberta told Alexa the whole story. She had been called by Lorna, knowing how impulsive Alexa could be; she decided to be in person to calm her down.

From the bedroom upstairs the girls listened to the story, growing fearful. They did not know if they should announce themselves or pretend they were still sleeping.

Roberta finished the story. Alexa turned to Serge and said, "I'm sorry. I made a mistake. I should not have judged you so harshly. It's hard for me to trust ... men ... sometimes. I'm sorry."

"Miss Lightman," Serge replied, "I believe I know how this might seem, that is why I asked Lorna for help, to keep Jimmy asleep, to help me with the girls to avoid any possible misinterpretations."

"Why didn't you just call me!"

"I thought it would have made things worse."

"Worse than this?"

No, not this, but between you and Sarah. I can see how much you want to be close to her, but it's hard for you with so much work. I know you have had to do a lot on your own with your two kids, and this confirms to me how deeply you love your daughter. I didn't want to tell you because I thought that if Sarah was given a chance, she would tell you herself. If I had told you, there would have been a confrontation and more distance between you. Let her rest, let her think about what happened … She'll tell you."

"I just don't want her to go through what I did. I want to take care of her," said Alexa, crying and desperate.

"Serge's right, honey. Last night you would have been angry and tired and would have grounded Sarah for a month, not have spoken to her for three more, and you'd never have worked this out."

"Miss Lightman, that is true. Please let me talk with Sarah and then let her come to you. She is very much like you, and I am sure you want to talk to your Dad as much as she wants to talk to you. Give her the chance; trust her and let her grow, this day on her own, and then the two of you together."

"I'm sorry. Let me see her, at least."

"This is your home, Miss Lightman."

Roberta took Alexa by the hand, and they walked upstairs. The girls jumped back into the bed and pretended to be asleep. The two women peeked through the door, saw the still forms in the bed, and walked back down.

Alexa said to Serge, "I'm sorry. I hope you can forgive me."

"No problem. I understand." He smiled to reassure her of his sincerity and added, "I'll send them over as soon as they have had breakfast."

"Thank you."

They left and Serge walked with Alexa and Mama to the door. Mama held his arm and thanked him again with a wink: "Good job," she whispered in his ear, and gave him a warm kiss on his cheek. The two women departed.

Lorna, who had been sitting quietly across the room told Serge what had happened earlier. Alexa had returned from the trip in a rush, surprised by her arrival she had let it slip that they were "drunk and sleeping in the guest-house. Alexa had filled in the gaps with her own fears and distrust.

"It's ok, Lorna, no big deal. Besides, I am the one that should apologize: I got you into this, remember?" He smiled. "Forget it. We know that these things happen. The important thing is that the girls are all right. I just hope that they learn, and grow up a bit.

"Oh, Serge, thank you.", you ok with preparing the breakfast here? "I'll probably be burning everything up, but I also have a cure for hangovers..."

Sarah and Lisa were up again, watching through the window as Alexa and Mama, then Lorna, walked back to the main house. Serge heard motion and quiet voices from upstairs, walked upstairs and saw them looking out the window through the opening of the door that was left open by Alexa. He closed the door gently and walked down with a smile to the kitchen, he then started preparing breakfast.

The girls had begun a hushed conversation. "Wow, we are in deep trouble."

"Do you remember all that about last night?"

"Some," replied Sarah, "and some is like a dream. I'm glad Serge was there, or we'd still be in your Mom's car, in the middle of nowhere and who knows in what condition."

"I guess we owe him one. Yesterday, I would've been really upset if I knew he was following us. I'm glad he did, but I'll still tell him "Don't you trust me'?"

"After listening to the whole story I can tell your uncle is a cool guy. I hope he doesn't give us a long talk. … gosh my parents are going to kill me… I need to talk to my Mom!"

Twenty minutes later Serge walked upstairs with two orange juices and knocked on the bedroom door. "Good morning!"

Sarah opened door enough to peer out and pretended not to remember anything. "What am I doing here?"

"Long story … Breakfast is ready. You should eat something."

"Not hungry."

"Smells good!" said Lisa from behind the door.

"C'mon, Sarah, it'll make you feel good. I'll explain what happened yesterday, and how you ended up here, ok?"

"Ok."

Serge prepared scrambled eggs with fresh "pico de gallo" sauce and small fried slices of sausage and refried beans. He showed them how to use warm flour tortillas to scoop beans from the plate in one motion while holding the fork to get the eggs. Breakfast was warm and spicy, with lots of juice. Serge explained why he had followed Sarah and Lisa, what he had seen at school and at the party. He talked to them about who their real friends were, and how they should keep their eyes open.

"Well, it's only sex. " said Lisa, suggesting that nothing else would have happened.

"Perhaps you are right, but you would not have made the choice, not of the place or time. I believe that, yes, you girls will grow and mature and be sexually active in due time, but I think that your first experience, if this is your first experience and it's really none of my business. In any case it should not be in the back seat of a car, in a dark alley with strangers, under the influence of drugs or alcohol. Hey I don't want to lecture you, but your life could have been in danger, or you could've ended pregnant, catch AIDS or some other nasty stuff... and that is besides what all people who were there will be saying to you then.

Serge paused to let the words sink in

"You girls are smart; I know it, and your Mom does, too," he added, looking directly at Sarah.

"No, she does not. She treats me like a little girl. I'm not ten, you know?"

"You certainly are not, but neither you are twenty-five, which I think is mature enough to know the difference between choices and consequences. Listen, your Mom was your age, she went through her own experiences, and the least she could do is guide you. You know it, she knows it. You both are so close to talking freely together, yet so far apart. Give in for once, break the darn silence and talk. Just do it! She loves you dearly, and I know if you give her the chance it will happen. She is a cool mom, believe me."

"Think so?"

"I know so. You say you are a young woman, right?"

"Yes ..." she said tentatively, not knowing what she was getting into.

"So you know your Mom is an adult, right? She should start acting like one, right?"

Yes, but she's always busy, never here, and when she is, she's always telling me I'm doing something wrong."

"Well, you know moms: that is what they do best. But they also listen, and if given the chance they will open up and respond. Give her the chance, talk to her. She is desperately trying to do it; she needs you as you need her. The only problem is pride and stubbornness. Why don't you give your arm a little twist, give a little and ... well, maybe you can start acting like a young woman. Do you think you can handle it?"

Sarah and Lisa sat quietly at the kitchen table, staring at their empty plates. They brushed their hair from their foreheads, exchanged glances, and finally smiled.

"Ok, I'll do it," said Sarah.

"Great! You'll never regret it, believe me."

"You are a cool uncle, Serge," said Lisa. "No one has ever talked to me like that and I wish they had."

"Well, I hope you can use my words for Sarah as if they were intended for you, too. I don't know how well you get along with your Mom, but after last night, you might want to talk to her and ask for advice." Serge took a deep breath and looked at them, his expression serious but sincere.

"Listen. You might not think its true, but every adult went through being your age. Even me, and I'm over forty ... I know, I know, don't smile, it's a lot of years, I know. Even now I still feel I am young, but I remember that it was not until I was twenty-four or twenty-five that I started to feel like the man I am now. Still today I smile at the mistakes I made at 25! The same goes for your parents: they were young, went through the same experiences – different contexts but similar situations. They feel young; they identify with you and care. They can listen, if they see you want to talk, or if you would simply ask."

"I guess we haven't thanked you for what happened yesterday," said Lisa.

"Yes, Serge, thanks, said Sarah. "I'm glad you were there, and please forgive me for how I acted. You asked me to keep my eyes open and I rolled my eyes. I thought you knew nothing ... Thank you."

The girls helped Serge clean up the kitchen and then, gathering their resolve, went over to the main house. Later in the day, Serge was glad to see them with Alexa, talking by the swimming pool. Alexa looked relaxed, and Serge noticed a charm and peace he had not seen before.

*   *   *

It was now almost a year and half since Serge became the Lightman's household manager, and he was glad he had. His everyday routine was far from normal or standard. Some days it was house administration and bill-paying; landscaping days were fun because he loved to get his hands dirty helping Mon, having a professional gardener guide his moves. Serge contributed some landscape ideas and helped make a small rock fountain near the swimming pool. Other days were filled with activities with Jimmy. Serge taught Jimmy to play videogames on-line with Max. and between the three of them, Serge was able to keep up with the latest generational interests.

Both Sarah and Jimmy appreciated Serge's availability, as well as his open mind. Serge always wondered if he was not "adopting" them as his family; first Sarah was like the daughter he never had; then there were things done "as family" he never did with Steph because she died young, leaving Serge alone to raise Max on his own. He always wondered about what might have been, if Steph had not died, and the gift of being able to share in Jimmy's and Sarah's. The children had grown to respect Serge, respect he earned with a steady hand, an open attitude and his gentle ways.

Serge found himself doing more than taking care of the estate. Lightman Industries operated several Non Profit Organizations in Latin American countries, and Serge's sensibilities, experience, and bilingual skills helped them understand and prioritize what needed to be done. He was working on various proposals for the following year's projects in southern Mexico and Central America, and planning a trip there for a delegation of Lightman Foundation officials. Serge had been invited to accompany the group and he was looking forward to the new challenge. Alexa's father, Bob Lightman, had grown accustomed to Serge, and he appreciated that his daughter was not alone, she was being helped by a mature couple and a responsible man in her big house and that his grandchildren were being raised in a steady environment

With time Serge had been invited to apply his professional background by participating in various design processes and creative decisions at Lightman Industries. The departments involved with this work would typically ask him to stay with them, but Bob Lightman ensured that Serge was free to move around the company. This suited Serge very well. He was motivated by a changing environment and by diverse projects; he was never bored. The best thing was that the estate work kept him grounded and in touch with a family, which was what Serge needed most.

All through the first year that Max was in college, he and Serge kept in touch and occasionally visited one another. The two remained close, but with Max's studies, he found it hard to find the time to be with his dad. Field trips and volunteer work took him to Latin America, sometimes for months. His studies were coming along very well but his time was short.
But three weeks before Christmas, Max had a school break and Serge traveled to Arizona for several days together. Max introduced Serge to Julie, his college girlfriend and gave him the full update on his life. They spent an active time together, going for runs early in the morning, canoeing or other outdoor activities the rest of the day.

Max insisted on taking his dad for Christmas with Steph's family. As always, Serge told him he could not go. Max knew the story behind his decision; that it was better for Max to go alone and not risk the chance of a Christmas that was not as jolly as it was supposed to be. Serge was ok with staying on his own, and he told Max that they could always celebrate other days together, that this was a good chance to introduce Julie to family without the baggage of the past and that she would enjoy his larger family.

Serge explained his work to Max, and asked him for some data that he could use for his upcoming trip to Mexico, Belize, and Guatemala.

He would be visiting one of Lightman's NPOs and knew that there were several nearby native communities as well as various archeological sites, that might be of good for his professional interest and where the Lightman Foundation could do some good. Serge knew that both Steph and Max had studied some of these places. Max gave Serge a nice complement to his mom's notes, and with that they said goodbye for the holidays.

Serge returned to work in the middle of December. He had found that he could not go away for more than a week, for if he did, everything would fall behind or work in a different way, and not the best or more efficient. Alexa was glad to see him back and the children were delighted with his stories and presents. There was a sense of anticipation in the house about the trip to Central America, because it was the first time that Sarah and Jimmy would be joining Alexa for a Lightman Foundation activity, and they were curious and excited.

One of the interesting aspects of the trip was the chance to see firsthand what the local, Foundation-sponsored organizations were doing. There were several new programs of "micro loans" and small entrepreneurial investment plans, programs that were making enormously more progress than the usual give-away of money or food. Educational institutions from the US and Latin America participated in the programs and involved students by providing internships and exchange programs. The results they had seen in the last few months had been great. Serge was glad that he had participated in the planning and decision making for two of those programs in Belize. His interest resided in what he had learned years before in one of Stephanie's archeological studies in the area. His understanding and experience was the result of Stephanie's involvement in volunteer work in those rural areas and a previous social services work experience as a graduate student.

Christmas came, and there was a lavish Lightman Industries party made at the Robert Lightman's residence. Most of the employees had been invited for this traditional celebration. Serge arrived with Mama, Alexa, Sarah, and Jimmy. He drove directly to the main entrance and let out his passengers.

While holding the door for Mama, she told him: "I'll be expecting you inside, ok? You're part of the family, Serge. Don't take too long, you hear me?"
He nodded and smiled. "As my kid used to say when he was ten, 'just smile and nod'." They both laughed.

The night was cold and clear, and because the Lightman property was very big and surrounded by acres of forest, there was no light reflection from the city and one could make out most of the stars. Serge liked nights like this, when he would wander in his thoughts and many times get lost. For an hour he stood leaning on his car, arms crossed on chest, breathing deeply as he looked up to the sky.

Out of the corner of his eye, Serge saw Richard Sanders, Alexa's ex, arrive at the party escorted by a young woman in high stiletto heels and a "glued to her skin" kind of dress. He was still working for Lightman and was part of the team. Serge thought that Alexa's marriage perhaps had been one of those stories in which a man seeks a shot to become part of the firm by courting the boss's daughter and then moved on in the corporate ladder. Serge did not spent too much time in that though, he had only met the man a few times, never enough to become friends but enough to get a glimpse of his character, especially during summer and right before Christmas.

The Yard Project

A couple of weeks before the end of summer Serge was overseeing a landscape restoration and pruning project at Alexa's house. He and the children helped the hired crews with the yard work, they had planned a ceremony involving the planting of three trees, one for each member of the family. Serge had explained to the kids that it was really simple to add special value to a common event by having a ceremony and adding some symbolic meaning to it. They were all being working in the garden; most of them were covered in dirt and sweat. It had been a great dry summer and the progress of the yard work was going great. Serge was helping Jimmy and Sarah with their tree, Alexa came to help them, they were filling the voids on the soil to align and level the tree's verticality.

That weekend Alexa's ex-husband came to the house to deliver some paperwork to Alexa and visit his kids. Richard's attitude reflected some jealousy for not being part of the whole thing; after all they looked like a family. It seemed that he did not approve what his kids were doing by mingling with workers. The kids were having a great time. Jimmy called Serge every minute to verify his tree and ask for his help. As Serge was finishing with Sarah, he moved toward Jimmy but Richard cut him cold and told him that he will take care of it..

"This is not rocket science... what is the big deal in planting a tree anyway?"

Serge took it as it came, he understood that it was just part of a father feeling delegated to a secondary role. A way of communicating that he was the father and not anyone else. Alexa was surprised to this new development, she has never seen Richard challenged by anyone before or threatened in his role. But this was definitely not his element. She kind of enjoyed the experience and felt some satisfaction on it.

"This tree planting ceremony you're doing is a waste of time."

"It was Serge's idea," said Jimmy excitedly.

Richard looked over his shoulder and in a soft voice mention to himself "Well, not a very bright idea, but what can you expect from a guy that settles for a mediocre job as butler of the house?"

Sarah joined them.
"Well, for me it's a great idea, being that it's such a small thing and we're all together. I've never been so dirty in my life, and I don't mind it one bit."

"You look all messed up, like a picker in a grape field," said her dad.

"Oh, dad, come on! I couldn't care less, I feel great. Imagine how this place is going to be in a few years, the trees all tall and we'll be remembering this day. It's fun! Besides, I've never seen my mom smile so much simply by being with us, without thinking of work. She looks beautiful."

Sarah watched her dad as he turned to look at Alexa. She did look beautiful. She was by the side of the garden with some men of the landscaping crew. Serge had left the kids with their dad and joined Alexa to review the work progress. Alexa looked excited by the idea of a rock fountain in the pond. She had her own light, a serene smile; her hair shined and moved with the breeze. Sarah saw the look on her dad's face and was glad. She had not approved of her parents' divorce and afterwards had tried to get them back together, but once his father moved in with his young girlfriend she had stopped. Now, since the conversation with her mom after the night at the party, they had become closer, like friends. She knew now and understood that her mom also deserved to be happy, and saw her now as a woman, not only as a mother. Sarah liked the idea of making her father jealous, just for the chance to see him in doubt. She felt like she was in a friendly conspiracy against the boys.

"Yes, dad this is a lot of fun. You should try to lighten up, get dirty."

Richard looked annoyed. He wanted to fit in the picture but was not able to make it his own. "You think that by planting trees and moving some dirt, you can have fun? I make many business decisions each day, and my decision-making affects millions of dollars. That makes a difference in life and makes you feel you've achieved something important, really important. Don't try to tell me to lighten up. Life is not about fun, it's about achievement."

Richard walked away, not in his best mood. He approached Alexa.

"I need to talk to you."

"Hey, Richard, nice of you to drop by. I'm busy right now – can you wait?"

Richard persisted: "This is important."

"You mean to tell me that working on my home is not?" Alexa looked defensive.

"You know what I mean. Gees!"
He breathed deeply and fidgeting his hands in the back of his neck.

"I need to arrange a few things with you before that NPO trip. I need more details on the City deal, and that's an important account for me –just want to be sure you give me the information so I can take care of it. Besides, with all the planning and paperwork for your trip, you're swamped at the office. I don't want to be delayed."

"Oh, so that's why you're here, I thought you might have come because you like to help us, or just to visit the kids. About the City deal: that account is mine and I can handle it. In fact, I've had enough help on that project and it's finished; I have a presentation scheduled in two weeks. In regard to planning the NPO work in

Yucatan … you do know it's in the South of Mexico and Belize, don't you? The Yucatan peninsula? Well, that has also been taken care of. I had a lot of help."

"Well, no one at the office knows anything about it. They told me you brought all the work here." He spoke in a challenging and disbelieving voice.

"Yes –yes, I did bring everything here. Actually, Serge helped me with both projects, and he'll be participating in them from now on. You do know him, don't you? Alexa turned politely towards Serge and introduced him.

"Serge, this is Richard Sanders. Richard, this is Serge."

Serge extended his hand. Richard said in disbelief, … You're in charge of those projects?"
"Nice to meet you, too," Serge replied, smiling.

"… Nice to meet you." Richard ignored Serge's hand. He nodded and turned to Alexa. "You've got to be kidding me. You're telling me you needed his help planning those projects, and now he'll be participating in them with you?"

"I don't see any problem with that, Richard. In fact, the projects have evolved pretty nicely since Serge started collaborating on them. He's got fresh ideas and, quite frankly, knows how to present them well."

Richard looked Serge in the eyes. "And you are? … the 'household manager', right?" He turned to Alexa and added: "He's just the butler, for crying out loud!"

Serge did not like the deprecating tone.

"If you are capable of doing this, what are you doing here and not working at corporate?

Before Serge could reply, Alexa said,
"Richard, you need to change, you know? Just because you see dirt under a man's nails doesn't mean he's ignorant."

"Well, excuse me if I don't agree, but I don't see the value of his work, the butler of the house."

Serge's expression changed drastically, and Alexa saw that he was about to retaliate with a more direct confrontation. She intervened gracefully.
"Well, you might not, Mr. Chairman, but he sure does make a big difference, both with my work, and in the life of my family …"

She was going to add "and my own life" but this was too personal. She regained her composure.
"In any case, you would not believe what Serge put together for both the projects and what we were able to finish in record time. So, no: I won't give you my account files, and you can tell my dad that I have everything under control … No, wait, don't do that. You know what? I'll tell him myself. I have the time to call him. Now, if you'll excuse us, we're busy here. If you can behave respectfully to the rest of the people here, you're more than welcome to help, if you want."

Richard looked confused. He stared at Serge, then at Alexa and then toward the yard. He nodded reluctantly and took his leave. "All right, it's your call, your projects. I don't care."

They nodded back at him as he turned and left for the main entrance where his car was parked.

Serge reflected how much more he had come to know about Alexa and her kids, by being more than just a butler or household manager, but by being a good friend. He treasured the hunger that Alexa, Sarah, and Jimmy had for a family; in many ways it was the same hunger he felt.

"Thank you" he said to Alexa as they saw Richard leave. He appreciated what she had told Richard about his performance beyond his job description. Alexa smiled back at him. "You are welcome, now let's get to work"

The rest of the day went as planned, and in the end, crew and family had a dinner of grilled hot dogs and hamburgers. Stories were told, and friendships made. On that day, Serge confirmed that Alexa had started to trust him, and he knew he had Sarah to thank.

Christmas

Serge leaned on the side of the car, looking away from the house, arms crossed his stare looking up at the sky. The light from the house was distant and did not interfere with the heaven's display. The Orion constellation was visible on the southern sky, visible and captivating as always. From inside the Lightman residence came the noise of many guests. He decided not to go inside; he felt as in the past, that he did not belong in a celebration or being part of a big family.

Once after Stephanie's death, he thought that the sole thought of spending the holidays without her would be too painful. If he could not give his son the best x-mas as they have done with his in-laws in the past , he would not deprive him of one. After Stephanie's death it became apparent that her family would not welcome him in the same manner as with their daughter. Serge decided to send Max with her family for the holidays, allow him the experience of big gatherings and family time. Then Serge and Max will catch up with a personal trip together a few weeks later. That became their tradition and their time and that was what counted for them as holidays.

He strongly felt the silence and emptiness of a family lost and gone, of a love cut short by a fulminating illness. At times, and regardless of the Lightmans' hospitality, he felt like he was just a driver or a butler or a household manager in their home. He liked working at corporate, and the new projects and responsibilities were giving him a professional satisfaction he had long since lost. There is something about work that motivates a man and makes him feel good about himself, especially when he knows he is capable of bigger things.

Out of the house came Sarah, angry and rolling her eyes, and in a low, controlled tone cursing her luck. She became self-conscious when she saw Serge leaning on the car looking back at her. She walked towards him.
"Sorry about that ... Hey, do you mind some company?" she asked.

"Sure – no problem. Though it's not as warm and nice as indoors. Anything wrong?"

"My dad, as always. He sure can get on my nerves, and I hate it when he does that. Can you believe he brings one of his young girlfriends, again, and parades her around in front of my mom? She could be my older sister! He acts as if nothing is happening, and mom acts her part and welcomes her in the house, she shouldn't allow it."

"Hey, Sarah, easy! Want to talk about it?"

"Whatever."

Serge raised his eyebrow and looked back at her.

"Sorry, Serge. I know you don't like me saying that."

"Well, it still feels rude, you cut people right into it, you know?" He smiled.

"Sorry. This is hard on me."

"Listen: your mom and dad decided that it did not work for them. It was their choice and only they know why they did it. You should not be so hard on them."

Serge stood by her in a very casual way, he did not wanted Sarah to feel she was going to be lectured. "Let's see," he continued. "Your dad, he is a good man, he works hard and is very intelligent. From what I've heard, your granddad trusts him very much and that must be for a reason. He is a good father; regardless of what you feel right now. He has been there for you most of the time, and you must admit that you are a tough cookie, yourself. Perhaps you even got it from him."

Sarah smiled briefly; she knew he was right. "I don't know. I hate feeling like this."

"I know, but you should not give up the power you have over these feelings. Think about it. Your father does not want to be alone, no man wants it."

"You're alone, and seem very happy."

"Perhaps, on the outside. I once was married, you know?"

"Divorced?"

"No, she died." He was not ready to talk about this, but he continued. "She died some time ago, leaving my son and me to ourselves. Her name was Stephanie. We were a good team, you know? I don't know why she died, but I had to go on and hold onto my son and do the best I can with him. He has become a pretty good young man."

"Well, you were there for him, not like my dad."

"That is not true. Your dad has been here, too, but we all are different. He has been there for you, in his own way. The only problem I see between you and your dad is his relationship with your mom. You are resentful about the divorce and you shouldn't be. Only they know what they went through, and the reasons behind it. Your mom is an amazing woman, she is strong and I see her treating him well enough, so you should do the same and not worry about that. I'm sure your mom worries about the relationship between you and him, and if she knew you two were alright she would be more relaxed."

"Do you really think so?"

"Yes, I not only think so, but I know so. As parents we worry about too many things; a constant thread of kid's worries... some even very silly"

Alexa had come looking for Sarah and saw them outside talking. Their casual talk had turned into a warm conversation, without letting them know, she listened from a side doorway as they talked. Sarah asked more questions about Serge and his family, a few remaining questions about the party he had rescued her from, and questions about her parents. Sarah's maturity pleasantly surprised her, she wondered why she had not been able to communicate with Sarah as Serge had done; she became jealous, but in a positive way.

"You should go back inside. Look for your dad and give him a huge hug. Just go and do it."

"No way. Never!" she interrupted. "That is very hard to do, getting close to him, you know? It's not so simple."

"What is there to it? It's just your dad. The same man who carried you when you were a baby is the same man who is inside. You go inside, walk up to him, and without saying anything give him a good, sincere hug. Rest your head on his chest and whisper, 'Thank you, dad'."

"It doesn't matter."

"Oh? Trust me, it does. You should give it a try. I'll bet you anything it works, you call it."

"Really? Would you let me see what you write in one of your books?"

"Mmm. For a young woman, you sure know which buttons to press. Yeah, ok: if you do as I say, I'll let you read out of one of my books. You choose what and where in it."

"Oh, you are in trouble, mister," she replied excited.

"How about if you don't do it?" asked Serge. "What is there for me?"

"It's a sure, safe bet for me, because I know I can do it. I hug him and that's it, right?"

"Well, is not "that simple" Serge gestured with his hands in the air. "You go inside, find your dad and give him a good, sincere hug. Then ask him for two minutes of his time, and once you are away with him, tell him you love him no matter what. Then apologize for being rude to his girlfriend but explain why you did it. Tell him you want to be close to him, that you want to know him".

"Hey, that's not fair – you're adding to the deal. I don't know ..." Sarah crossed her arms in front of her.

"I guess you are right, is more than what I said but..." He left a small pause take the moment of a deeper thought. "You do that and I know you'll be surprised" Sarah looked at his with curiosity and he looked directly in her eyes waiting for a response and continued "You do that and you'll see the look in his eyes... Try it" he exclaimed as if it was an amusing challenge a dare. "Disarm him in a moment, see his reaction... and change your life and his. Trust me. There is more to winning this bet than just getting into one of my books.

He paused, he left the words sink in, saw Sarah's head turn, frowning with her eyes looking at something that was not there, looking back at the house, thinking, calculating...
"Besides, what do you have to lose? You just said the words; "it's simple". If it does not work, things will be the same tomorrow, right? Nothing is lost, there is no great relationship, anyway. Think about what could happen; If he turns you down, which I'm sure he will not because he is extremely intelligent, things will be the same. Then you'll have free access to one of my books and secrets... Hey, we'll

even organize a party at the guest-house with all of your friends"
Sarah saw him with a broad smile.
"But…" He raised his right index finger and looked at her quizzically.
"If he does not turn you down, you are up for a big surprise"

"Oh, Serge! You're going to be in trouble. I'll be inviting at least
twenty of my friends, twenty loud, rude, and self-absorbed teenage
girls."

"Hey now that you mention this … perhaps I should rethink this,"
said Serge with a concerned look.

"Oh no, mister, we are closing this deal." She reached out, held his
hand and shook it in the most professional manner, as she had seen
her grandfather do many times.

"Well, get to it," Serge said with a smile. "And just for the heck of it,
let's call it double or nothing. Go give your mom a hug, too, and tell
her how beautiful she looks. Just like that. Remember how she acted
after the party, and how things changed? Well, this is a nice moment
to do it. You'll see it in her face, too."

"You're on. What do I get for hugging mom?"

"I said double or nothing, but to be honest, you'll be feeling like a
million bucks. Do it just for the heck of it, ok?"

Sarah stood up next to Serge, started walking inside, then stopped
and turned around. Her eyes were filled with two sets of emotions,
one of excitement, one of wonder. She ran back to Serge and gave
him a big hug. "Thank you, Serge. Merry Christmas." She ran to the
house, looking for her dad.

Alexa slipped back indoors. She had been listening to the
conversation, she felt touched. She thought about "things to say,
things to do".

She closed her eyes for a moment with a deep sight, life was changing for the good and she knew part of the change had come since Serge arrived. She felt as if the same words told to her daughter were intended to her, "A few words, spoken at the right time, could make all the difference..". She smiled to herself, life sure acted in a peculiar way.

Alexa avoided Sarah as she came in, by hiding in the guest powder room, then returned to the door. She saw Serge, still outside, looking to the sky. She turned inside towards the party. On her way she was intercepted by Mama, who gave her a loving hug, just like the ones she remembered as a young girl; hugs like Alexa had stopped giving some years ago. She had forgotten how sweet and warm they felt. She had not felt like this since she had started working so hard.

"Has it been that long?" she thought.

"Mama, you look beautiful this evening. I love you." Mama was surprised at the tender display of affection. It had been a while since she had seen Alexa with her guard down. They continued walking towards the party, arms held together close to each other. Alexa told Mama she had to find her dad, she was rehearsing in her mind the words given to her daughter a few moments ago by a stranger who had entered their lives in a casual instant.

She found Bob Lightman surrounded by business types and family, and pulled him away, excusing himself. Lightman was surprised and amused by this display of affection, and he looked at her as he had not done in a long time. "Dad, you look very handsome ... Can I take two minutes of your time?"

* * *

After Sarah and Serge shared their heartfelt hug, and she went looking for her dad, Serge stayed outside. He took some more time to look up at the starry sky, to free his mind, to think about Max. Finally, walked to the house as far as the reception foyer, for he wanted to find Sarah in her father's arms. He wanted to be sure she was sticking to her end of the bet.

From across the room, Alexa saw Serge smiling broadly; she was curious and followed his stare. She saw Sarah by the fireplace, looking eye to eye at her father. They were smiling and embraced in a big hug.

She wanted to thank Serge but now saw him moving, walking towards the stairs and no longer looking at Sarah. She turned in the same direction and found Jimmy, looking bored at the base of big stairs. She started walking towards him but Mama intercepted Alexa as she, too, turned her attention on Jimmy. Mama whispered: "Let him do it. I have a feeling he knows what he's doing. You know? I've seen him do wonders with others." She gave Alexa a sweet wink.

"Yes, I've noticed."

From the front door foyer Serge could see all of the decorated living room. A small figure sat by the stairs with a grim look in his eyes. It was Jimmy, looking bored and out of place. Serge recalled earlier years, spending Christmas with a family that was not his, amid an insincere politeness that masked resentment for a crime that was not his. Serge walked in from the foyer, trying not to call attention to himself. He blended well, his suit was elegant, his presence was secure and confident; he could have belonged in a place like this. But in his heart, he did not belong, as in the past, as in his childhood, he felt it all over again.

Serge sat by Jimmy on the bottom stair, and asked him how he was doing. Jimmy just nodded and said, "Ok." Serge gave him a gentle pat on the back. Jimmy looked up to him and gave him a hug.

"What's up, buddy?" Serge tried to sound as casual as a seven year old friend would.

"Nothing." replied Jimmy with a lonely tone, still looking down.

"Are you sure? I don't see you smiling."

"Well, I'm bored. Everyone is a grownup; everyone treats me like a little kid."

Serge smiled at Jimmy's mature expression. For someone his age, he was pretty sharp and perky. "Well, you are a kid, and the grownups have not had the time to get to know you. I guess I know you; what do you think?

"Maybe."

" Hey, what is that in your hand? Let me guess …" Serge paused, rubbing his chin.

Jimmy held out a gold-plated pen.

"That is pretty cool," Serge said.

"It's just a pen, a used pen."

"Who gave it to you?" asked Serge, trying to get Jimmy excited.

"My dad. I think he forgot about us, he always does. I saw when he reached in his pocket and took out the first thing he found. He made it look like it was a present for me."

"Well," said Serge, "what matters is that he thought about you."

"Not really," said Jimmy. "He probably did it because my granddad was around. I saw when he gave a present to his girlfriend, and when he saw me, he pretended the pen was a gift, just to get me out of his way."

Serge remembered those days when he was growing up, feeling out of place and surrounded by adults, most of them strangers. He tried to remember what he would have liked. Serge crossed his legs like a kid, rubbed the side of his shoe with his hand, and with two fingers he walked the edge of the shoe sole. "Hey, have you been outside?"

"Huh? No."

"It's dark and full of stars. Looks like someone scattered them in complete disorder."

"So?"

"Well, I'm not sure if I can tell you this …"

They sat there in silence, Serge testing Jimmy's curiosity.

"What?"

"It's kind of a funny story."

"Is it good?"

"Well," Serge continued, "I was reading the other day about how the stars were made, pretty crazy stuff."

"Why?" Jimmy asked curiously.

"Well, it involved Coyote and his friend, Crow. It is an old Navajo story about how the night sky was created. You know, the Navajos are very brave Indian –we now call them Native Americans – and they have some great stories."

"Would you tell me the story? I'm bored."

"Sure, but don't call me crazy, ok? I just read it in a book. But it makes some sense, because when you go out and look at the stars they do seem to relate to the story."

"Now, for this story we do need to go outside being out is one of my favorite things to do, not everyone does, do you? I know a good place to sit and look at the night and tell you the story"

He stood up and offered Jimmy his hand, which he took. Serge pulled him upright in an instant, provoking a spontaneous laugh. They walked out side by side. Arriving at the car, Serge raised Jimmy to the hood, sat him there with his head propped on the windshield. Jimmy grinned; he was not allowed to play with cars except secretly with Serge, even less to sit on them like this. He felt the warmth of the engine and giggled at the sensation.

"See, it is like you are in the first row of the movie theater!" Serge took his own place by Jimmy's side.

"See up there?"

"Yup."

"What can you see?"

"A bunch of stars, everywhere."

"Nice, huh? You know it was not always like this?"

"No?"

"See how many dark spaces there are, in between each of the stars?"

"Yes?"

"Can you see that there is also, like, a road of stars, there? Can you see it?"

"Yes?"

"Well, that is called the Milky Way. Many people thought the stars were like milk in the sky, and that the moon was made out of cheese."

Jimmy laughed. "That is silly!"

"No, really, people back then had funny ways to explain things. Now this Navajo story makes more sense than that, about that road of stars. You tell me if it's funny or not, ok?"

"Ok."

"An elder Navajo …"

"What is an elder?"

"Oh, sorry. Right, well, he is an old man, an old, wise man. Elders are well respected in Native American cultures. They represent the wisdom and knowledge of many years. They pass to their kids the stories of the past and the teachings of their culture."

"Oh, like my grandpa?"

"Yes, actually. That is a very good example. He is teaching your mom how to do the work of running his business, and teaching you other things he knows."

126

"He taught me how to tie my shoes."

"See? Elders can be very useful."

Jimmy giggled. "He also taught me how to hide food when I don't like it."

"What?" replied Serge.

"You see, you always have to have your dog under the table, or else be close to one of the table legs. If you have a dog, which my grandpa has, you just have to take the food from your plate to your lap and the dog will eat it. You just have to be very quiet when the dog licks your fingers and make you laugh."

"And what is the table leg thing he told you?"

"That is just in case of emergencies. First, you have to sit close to a corner, if there is no dog. You slide the food into a little hole or space between the wood pieces and leave it there. It's very easy!"

"Ewww, that is gross. The food spoils and then it smells pretty bad!"

Jimmy laughed, "No, really, it really works. I think the table eats the food, or maybe ants, because there's always space for it and it doesn't smell."

"Wow. That is a good story. I don't know if my story can beat it... he paused and then continued "There was an old, Navajo, a wise grandpa ..."

"A Navajo elder."

"Yes, the Navajo elder told the story to his people about how the night skies were made. You see, many, many years ago, man was afraid of the skies, because they were always very dark."

"Did they leave a light on at night?"

"Well, they did not have lights like us, only fire. And at night, they did not venture beyond the light and warmth of their camp fire pits, because the night sky was dark. The story says that the gods knew that humans were very smart, so they decided to leave the night sky dark so they could keep men and women under control while they were sleeping. During the day, the men and women felt safe and could move around. So every day they have to collect food and prepare for the next day. That way, man and woman will always depend on the gods for favors and care during the day but at night there was nothing to guide them or to tell them where they were, so they will be afraid and under control without any light.

"Well, one of the Navajo men and women's friends was Coyote, and he thought that it was not fair to leave everyone in the dark. So he went and convinced Crow, who was another of the Navajo's friends, to fly Coyote to the heavens so he could sneak by the gods and steal something that could provide light for men and women during the nights. Crow was a little hesitant but Coyote convinced him that whatever he could get would be good for Crow, too. You see, wherever men and women lived, Crow always made a good living. Crow, agreeing that this was true, took Coyote for a high ride, and once reaching the clouds left him there, by the gates of the gods' house. Coyote sneaked inside and saw the gods playing with golden corn; they were counting the seeds that they were going to give the men and women the next day. Coyote accidentally stepped into a bucket of water and almost fell. The bucket sounded like a big thunder-clap and the spilled water fell as rain from the clouds. When the gods noticed Coyote, they tried to get him. Coyote knew that he was discovered and he ran for the corn, then grabbing the bag with his mouth he ran heading for the door. The gods tried to get him but they could not, because coyotes are very elusive and fast, you know."

Serge winked at Jimmy. "When the Coyote reached the entrance he found Crow waiting for him. He jumped and Crow caught him in the air but he was much heavier now…"
"Yes he was carrying a big sack of corn" said Jimmy
"Yes, and Coyote never had the chance to close the sack so the big sack of corn was open and the corn started to spill. To escape the gods, they tried to fly in a straight line, but not all the corn spilled along their path; some spilled on the left and some on the right. As the sack lost corn the Crow was able to fly farther away and they flew around the world filling up the sky with corn. When the Crow and the Coyote felt safe they came back to earth and landed. The Coyote and the Crow were very happy and decided to visit men and women again. When they arrived to saw them staring to the sky, the corn in the sky had turned into stars! Men and women were amazed with all the light. With the corn that remained in the sack, Coyote made a gift to the men and women. This gave them the independence to grow and harvest corn by themselves so they could eat when they were hungry, and not depend on the tricky gods. Coyote's other gift was that with stars out at night, men and women were able to move around at night and travel without getting lost. As a bonus, when the moon was out, they were able to have even more light because, you see, the moon is the god's doorway that Coyote left open on his way out!"

Serge turned to Jimmy and pointed to the sky. "See that clump of stars?"

"That's the Milky Way, like the candy bar!" exclaimed Jimmy.

"Yes, well, the story says that the golden corn, falling in the sky, turned to stars. If that is right, then the Milky Way is the path Crow and Coyote took when they were escaping."

129

"That is so cool!" exclaimed Jimmy.

"What do you think?" Serge put on an expression of self-confidence and posed as if he was an old chief.

Jimmy laughed.
"What!?" exclaimed Serge. "You think this is so funny?"

"You're silly. Tell me more stories about the coyote." Jimmy said excitedly.

"He is a very mischievous dude, isn't he? Let's see ... there is a story about how the rivers and the mountains were made ..."

Serge and Jimmy spent the next hour watching the stars and talking. They made up new stories. Alexa looked out at them from time to time, wondering what they were talking about that kept them so animated. Then, when the time was right, she came looking for Jimmy; it was time for him to join the party.

"I think Squirrel stole the water from Raven's bath and we made ink from it." Jimmy was saying.

"That sounds good, but we still need to figure out where they got paper from." replied Serge.

Alexa walked to the car and touched her son's shoulder. "Well hello, Mr. Storyteller. What do we have here?"

"Mom! Let me tell you a story about how the mountains were made, and Coyote. He's a friendly coyote, so don't be afraid," he advised his Mom, so as to prevent her from overreacting. Jimmy smiled at Serge.

"Time to go in to the party, young man."

"But Ma, we're busy. We're still working on a new story."

"You'll get to it later. Now it's time for dinner." She turned to Serge with appreciation, "Thank you, Serge."

"No worries, my pleasure. We had a great time, right Jimmy?"

"Yup," exclaimed Jimmy.

"You are welcome to join us, Serge. You know that you're part of the family, and our house is your house."

"Thank you. I'll be there in a moment."

He watched Alexa walk to the house holding lovingly Jimmy's hand, the image reminded Serge of his own family. He had a flashback memory of a time long gone, of Stephanie carrying Max after he had fallen from his bicycle. When Max fell, Serge had not acted surprised but excited, as if Max had done something amazing. Max did not cry, though he was bruised and scratched, and once he stood up, Serge squatted down to his level and looked directly in his eyes.

"Well done, son. That was a good landing!"

Max was holding the pain with a big smile and a proud look on his face. He was soon fighting back tears as the pain from his leg and arm caught up with him, but he picked up his bike with the help of his dad and they walked toward home. As they got closer, Stephanie saw the big bruise and the blood stain on his knee and ran for him.

"Oh my God, are you alright? What happened, baby?" She was anxious and worried and looked back and forth between Serge and Max, waiting for an explanation.

"He had a small crash landing. Right, Max?"

"Yes, but I didn't cry mommy. It didn't hurt."

131

"Small crash landing? You're hurt and bleeding. This is bad, and it's all right to cry if you want. Let mommy take care of it. You're going to be alright." She turned to Serge, who was smiling, grateful for her tenderness and sweet ways.

"And what are you smiling about, mister? You are in big trouble."

"I know." He winked at Max who was also smiling with the guilt of being accomplice to his dad. "I'm glad you are here to take care of both of us."

"That's right, that is what moms are for, you tough guys. Come here, Maxie."

She picked up Max and held him close to her with both arms, leaning her head against his as she walked the final steps to their home.

The vision vanished slowly from his eyes in memory and merged into Alexa and Jimmy as they walked away. Serge found a tear coming, clouding his eyes, and he found a shy smile coming to his heart. He breathed deeply, holding on to the memory one more moment. He followed a little later and spent some time inside the house talking with the guests about work and holidays. He spent more time with a group of people from corporate, talking about the coming work trip, the Mayan culture and the Yucatan peninsula. Serge felt comfortable among the people, he blend in well but the persistent feeling of not belonging pulled to the kitchen where he shared his time with Norm, Lorna, the kids and their friends. Serge recalled holiday season with Stephanie's family, pretty much celebrated in their kitchen and family room; a place where there were no rules, no formalities and where everyone's smile felt like a warm embrace.

The Trip

By the third week of January everything was ready for the long-anticipated trip. Alexa was leading an effort by her father's Foundation to follow-up on micro loan programs in the Yucatan peninsula, Guatemala, and Belize. She had decided to bring Serge with her; not only was he the author of part of the strategy for the programs, he also knew the culture and spoke the language. Having someone who understood their history from the inside could help earn the trust of the communities they would visit, and authenticate the Foundation's efforts. Alexa had decided to take Jimmy with her, as it would be a good opportunity to see different countries and children there of his own age. Sarah would be joining them for the second half of the two-week trip. It promised to be a great journey.

The local Foundation office reported no eminent threat, but recommended caution when moving in rural areas and a security detail of four bodyguards had been hired to accompany the travelers. The lead security man was a seasoned, retired Marine with extensive experience from Panama to Iraq. Samuel Dantz was a self-made, disciplined soldier who based his efficiency on organization and good planning. He had been recruited to make well-detailed agendas and to follow them to the letter. Alexa was uncomfortable with this arrangement, but had to accept it since her father had made it a condition for her to lead the trip. As a further precaution, Dantz and Serge would each be carrying a special handheld GPS communicator, which could be used as a way-finding guide and as an emergency locator and transponder.

Final details were arranged. The team got their visas and permits. They collected descriptions of the places they were going to visit, and contact information for government officials. They got required vaccinations, something Jimmy did not appreciate at first but later found rewarding since he never cried, and this gave him something to brag about to his sister who was very afraid of needles. Some of these precautions were to protect the indigenous people from outside viruses, rather than to protect the team from getting sick.

Robert Lightman invited Serge to his office a few days before departure. He looked concerned.

"Serge, I called you here to ask for a special favor. I honestly did not want Alexa to go on this trip. We have other Foundation representatives that could have done this program assessment, but she insisted on going. She got that stubbornness from me. "I know that you co-authored some of the program plans, and I'm glad that you're going along." He stood from his desk and walked around it, to stand close to Serge. "I remember that you had some military experience, correct?"

"Yes, sir. It started as part of my social service, which was complemented with a certain amount of training in military basics. Later, I was able to have some hands-on experience during some of my volunteer work. This was years ago, but it is still fresh in my mind; I think it's like riding a bike."

"That's good. I certainly hope that this kind of experience is not needed. I had another reason in supporting Alexa's recommendation on you being part of the team. Not only do you speak the language and know the culture, but you add an extra layer of protection for my little girl. Please take care of her and the children as if they were your family. And by the way, as I told you before, please, Serge, call me Bob, ok? After being with us for all this time you have earned not only our trust but a special place within the family."

"Thank you sir" Serge hesitated as he saw Mr. Lightman's expression "Don't worry, Bob. I'll be there with them all the time and will bring them back home safely."

"Thank you, Serge. Please take care of yourself, too, and keep in touch. The Foundation has provided me a list of contact names and numbers, just in case; they assure me everything will be alright, but you never know. Stay in touch. I'm not sure if you'll have cell phones coverage, so use the GPS unit to keep me posted; you can send text messages with it and we can see where you are at any given time. I've been assured that these units have a good twelve hour battery life and are very reliable communicator devices."

"Yes, they are very impressive gadgets."

"Well, Mr. Dantz's credentials are also very impressive. We've never worked with him before, but he was recommended by an associate. Seems like he knows his way around in security, and he has years of experience. In any case, though, I trust you more. Please don't leave my daughter or grandchildren alone for any reason. If push comes to shove, they come first, above any program objective, at any risk."

"Thank you Bob, I'm honored by the responsibility. I'll take care of them, and we'll be fine."

Early the next day, Alexa, Jimmy, and Serge drove to the airport for their flight south.. Alexa looked radiant and ready to go; she was a very attractive woman and her confidence made her even more attractive. For his own part, Serge felt hesitation and was glad to see the very excited Jimmy following her, since he broke the tension of the moment. Jimmy carried a small yellow back-pack and a sweet stuffed toy elephant.

Their plane was a twenty-five passenger, Gulfstream jet. It departed as scheduled on the first leg of the journey, a seven and a half hour-long flight directly to Mexico City, where the group stayed for a day. They visited the Lightman Foundation office for last-minute briefings and met the security team that would accompany them for the rest of the trip.

After introductions, Dantz and another of the bodyguards immediately flew ahead to the city of Merida in Yucatan, from where the group would continue their trip by ground transportation to small neighboring towns; he would prepare the logistics of securing reliable cars, studying safe routes, and familiarizing himself with the rest of the busy agenda. Jimmy was bored, and his Mom had meetings all day: introductions, receptions, award ceremonies for exemplary Foundation employees. Serge decided to take him for some sightseeing while she worked. The other half of the security detail stayed with Alexa, so Serge and Jimmy were able to go out on their own.

Serge took him to the Templo Mayor Aztec ruins and to the old barrios in the historic district of downtown, which prompted brief visits to the historical museums in the area. Their favorite was the Anthropology Museum in Chapultepec. Serge felt almost at home at the museum; so many of his memories of Stephanie related to her passion for anthropology. She had turned their study at home into a small-scale research office filled with books, artifacts, pictures, and a bulletin board covered with maps and other study documents. Being at the museum was no different, except that he was staring from the other side of the rope or glass. He already knew about the subject of many of the displays, the history around them, and the meaning of the rich cultural symbols.

On their return Jimmy enjoyed the subway ride but by the time they got back to their hotel, Jimmy was sleeping with his stuffed elephant under his arm. It had a bright red balloon tied to one of its feet; Jimmy's hands still had the pink residues of cotton candy and the sides of his mouth the stains of a red lollipop. Alexa welcomed their arrival with the warmth of a busy Mom who felt both guilt and appreciation. She herself had just arrived from a final reception and was eager to be with Jimmy, so she was a little disappointed that he was asleep, but his appearance reflected a busy and fun day, packed with history learning and a spoon of sweet candy. Serge laid Jimmy in her bed, and the way he did it was certainly not that of someone doing it for the first time. Not only he was careful, but also loving, which made the whole difference.

Once his little shoes were removed and his sweater taken off, Serge turned to Alexa apologetically: "We only need to brush his teeth, but maybe just one night without might not hurt."

"It's ok. It won't be the first time he goes to bed without brushing his teeth, but it is one of the first times he's been carried to bed with such care and tenderness that he hasn't awakened."

There was a brief moment of silence, one that neither Serge nor Alexa wanted to break, one of understanding, of appreciation, of something deep inside. They could not explain but it felt right.

Serge was the first to say something. "We had a great time. We were very busy and my little partner here held up all the way. He is a sweet kid, like his mom; I believe he got that endurance and perseverance from you."

It was definitely a compliment directed to her. Alexa felt it that way and Serge hoped she sensed it.

"I never thought he could go all day nonstop, without a nap, while away from home. Thank you, Serge. I know he loves you very much. You are very kind with all of us." That was the compliment payback, and she also hoped Serge noticed, especially the part about "all of us".

"I wish you had seen him at the museum, he was so engaged and active. We'll have more opportunities like that on the rest of the trip and I'll make sure we're close to you."

With that, Serge knew he had to leave the room, and with a couple of steps he walked to the entrance, looking at his watch. "We have an early start tomorrow, not at the call of dawn, but early enough. I'll be here to help you out with Jimmy. The flight to Merida is just two and a half to three hours, tops. Plenty of time to unwind for the rest of the day, Have a good night, Alexa."

"Thank you, Serge. Have a good night, too."

He smiled at her radiant face and closed the door behind him. He stood there by the door, his hand still at the door knob. Inside, Alexa noticed that his shadow, projected under the door, had not moved for a few seconds after he left. She smiled, as only a woman can smile when she senses these things.

The next day the trip continued without incident. After a soft flight under blue skies, they made a gentle landing in Merida. The first part of the journey had been uneventful, with no major challenges. Big cities were well connected, had all the usual services and overall represented no major change in everyday lifestyle, other than a busier schedule. All that was now about to change.

Dantz met them with two red SUVs, ready to transport everyone to the city of Progresso, an hour's drive to the northwest. This was the first place where micro loans were being implemented and the first results measured. Alexa was scheduled to meet and greet with fifty entrepreneurial women who had used the money to buy goats, sewing machines, fertilizer and seeds, toys, and many other goods that allowed them to create small businesses that generated revenue for them and employment for others in their town. The area was one of the hardest hit in terms of male emigration to the US. Most of the women had been left behind with the children, and they received money transfers on regular basis, But while the economy had flourished in construction it had not in services or commerce. The micro loans were intended to turn back the tide of emigration, giving the residents a reason to stay and allowing families to improve their living conditions at home.

After Progresso, they continued the trip in the same format, the only things changing were the Foundation partners and locations. They left the State of Yucatan and drove through the State of Quintana Roo where they visited two small towns a short distance from the airport, where they will join the corporate jet again for the flight to Belize. At nightfall they left for Belize, where the trip became more challenging but also more scenic. The plane landed in Belize City and after a five hour visit they had a short, fifteen-minute flight to Belmopan, the capital of Belize. This was the group's last air destination before the final stretch of the trip in Guatemala.

The lack of development and less deforestation made it more complicated to reach certain areas in this region. But for the same reasons, the natural habitat and scenery was more impressive: untouched natural resources, pristine rainforest, exotic animals across vast areas. Here, the Foundation's micro loans were harder to implement using hard currency, so some loans consisted of trading goods to satisfy bartering scenarios in hard to reach areas. All in all, the experience for Alexa, Jimmy, and Serge became like a working tourist tour, rewarding and eye opening.

The visit to the city of Belmopan was brief, with few official events. As before, Dantz had taken care of logistics in advance, though now the four bodyguards were always with the group. The now-standard two SUV convoy made for a comfortable ride among the back roads and trails. The traveling party had experienced a rollover of Foundation support staff and volunteers, who came and went every few days.

On this, the sixth day of the trip, they had a ninety-minute drive along sinuous and sometimes narrow roads through thick rainforest jungle, to the city of San Ignacio, southeast of Belmopan. San Ignacio had one of the more successful programs implemented in Belize. The road was gravel and mud, with steep slopes. As the elevation increased the rainforest transitioned to evergreen pines. They were entering the Cayo District, where the major Pine Ridge Forest Reserve had been established as a natural protected area.

Considering that Sarah will be joining them in a couple of days, they made preparations with one more vehicle. The convoy of vehicles consisted now of three seven-seat SUVs, all communicated with portable radios. The vehicle at the front was driven by one of Dantz's men, with Dantz beside him in front, and a volunteer in the back seat; in the third vehicle were the other two bodyguards a guide and an intern. The rest of the space in these vehicles was reserved for equipment, baggage, and supplies. The vehicle in the middle was driven by Serge with the current Foundation representative beside him, a tall blond named Stephan Ariad who was a third generation Dutch immigrant in Belize. Alexa and Jimmy were seated in the back with their personal baggage. Jimmy was watching a Balto movie in a portable DVD player; he was wearing headphones and you could hear him giggle from time to time. No one knew if he was laughing as a reaction to the bumpy road or at the movie.

"I don't know how Jimmy can see this movie a thousand times without getting bored, but I'm sure happy it keeps him busy and distracted," said Alexa.

"I'm amazed that he is not getting dizzy watching the screen with all this movement," said Stephan.

"On that I'm not surprised. These days, kids adapt to everything. I hope the movie lasts 'til we get there. How far are we from San Ignacio, Serge?" asked Alexa.

"I believe a good twenty-five to thirty minutes, at least. Although distances are not that far, the road conditions are not the best and won't allow us to go any faster."

Stephan added, "You need to be very careful. It get especially tricky where the road gets too narrow, if a farmer is moving a herd, or there is a cart with goods, or you meet another vehicle. It can take you a while to clear it."

"I hope that is not the case."

The vehicles moved forward, spaced a good two hundred feet apart, to have plenty of time to clear the dust or mud thrown up ahead; it made for a faster and safer trip. After watching it negotiate a narrowing curve, Serge noticed brake lights and a sudden slowing by the front SUV, which then continued moving. He slowed down, putting his hand out the window and signaling the vehicle behind him to keep its distance. As he reached the curve he noticed a small cart with bicycle wheels, broken and with most of its cargo on the ground. Whether Dantz's vehicle had hit it or not was not important. He saw an old woman and two children by the road, picking up their goods and looking a little lost.

Serge passed by at a very slow speed, and watched the three through the rear view mirror. He decided to stop and as he did, Alexa said, "Oh, poor people. Imagine: what would you do if you were stranded in the middle of the road?"

"I believe we can help them. I hope you don't mind, Alexa." Serge said.

"Not at all. I wouldn't like to be in that position, without any help."

"I strongly advise we continue, if we want to arrive on time," said Stephan.

"No, we are stopping to give a hand," Serge said with resolve.

The two-way radio crackled; it was Dantz. "What's wrong? Why are you stopping?"

Serge took the radio. "We are helping these people get to the next stop or town, maybe even with their goods."

"You shouldn't stop. Move on. We don't have the time and this is an unscheduled stop in the middle of nowhere. Move on."

It was already too late. Serge had opened his door and was walking back toward the cart.

"Are you ok? Do you need any help?" he asked in perfect Spanish and then in English. He was not sure which language these people spoke, since Belize is the only country in Central America that recognizes English as its official language.

Serge could not guess the old woman's age. She looked in good shape and lucid; perhaps she was in her late sixties but it was hard to guess; many people here looked older than they really were. She had short white hair, gypsy green eyes, probably 5' 5" tall, with a trim, tanned body. Her hands were wrinkled but her arms and legs looked toned; she wore no sandals of any kind. Her face was attractive with a gentle presence. She was probably Caucasian, but years of sun and hard work had made her blend with her surroundings as if she were a native. She was wearing a white cotton pareo skirt around her waist and a colorful sleeveless shirt. She wore a very peculiar necklace, a figurine that hung to the center of her chest from a slender rawhide. It was shaped like the profile of an animal; it resembled a Native American Black Bear. She looked at him with appreciation, holding both children with her hands on their shoulders, and she answered in perfect English that she was ok. Serge could not tell if it was the tone of voice or the eyes that made her so enigmatic, but he sensed that he was in front of someone greater than life: transcendent, relevant beyond common denominators, he could not explain it ...

"Thank you very much for stopping. We rarely see vehicles on the road and sometimes we are not careful enough when we come out of the forest and into the road."

Still startled by her presence, Serge replied, "Are you alright? The kids ok?"

"Oh yes, yes we are. They got a little scared. Hearing a car is a rare thing here, seeing more than one is very unusual. We were on a collecting walk when we entered the road, the other car startled us, and the kids dropped the cart from the noise." Her voice was kind and patient, calming, reassuring as might be the voice of a wise Native American elder.

Serge was already helping with the cart, with one knee on the ground and at eye level with the children. They were probably eleven and nine years old. "Hello, kids. What is your name?" he said to the older one.

"I'm Jonas and he is my little brother, Lou," said the older one with a very casual tone and adding, "And she is our Nana."

Serge looked at Nana, guessing she was the grandmother or guardian of the two boys. Jimmy had gotten out of the van and stood by his mother, looking at the barefooted children and their clothes: they were each wearing only a cotton overall, open on the bottom and tied with a small red rope-ribbon.

"I'm Serge. Glad to meet you all. This is Jimmy, and Alexa." Serge turned to Nana and said, "Ma'am, nice to meet you." He extended his hand to her, which she took in her two hands in a warm and soft gesture. She held his hand for a moment, looking straight in his eyes. Serge had always felt uncomfortable with people who extended or exaggerated the strength of their handshake, but this was different. He felt comfortable but also as if he were being stripped of all his barriers, welcomed but also scrutinized. The moment seemed to last for a long period, how long he could not tell. He came back when Nana smiled at him, showing bright white teeth and a glow in her eyes. The feeling left once she let go of him, and the moment she did so, she grasped the bear figurine of her necklace with her left hand and rubbed it gently.

"Hello, Serge. Call me Nana," she whispered close to him, so no one else could hear. Serge was silent for a moment, smiling but a bit startled.

 "Thank you ... I think your cart is busted. Are you going very far from here?"

"Just a few miles ahead on the road. We live in a small village close to San Ignacio. We were on our way there to sell some plants."

Alexa said, "We can take you there if you want. It's the least we can do, and we have plenty of space. The kids might even enjoy the ride." she said.

"That is very kind of you, but you must be in a hurry. You seem to be busy important people, to stop for this."

Nana extended her hands to Alexa and held them as she had Serge's although to him, watching, it seemed to last only a brief instant. "Hello Alexa, Please call me Lande. Only some old people and kids from the village call me Nana. It has been years since someone called me Lande." There seemed to be a further explanation beyond her words, but she did not elaborate.

Serge wondered why she had whispered "Nana" to him and not to Alexa. He joined their conversation. "There is no problem. There are some things that need to be done regardless of anything else. We can take you there. We can haul your cart and your things on top of our vehicle. You'll be there in a moment." Serge looked at Alexa for approval, and she nodded without hesitation.

By this time, Dantz had returned and the third SUV had parked behind. For a little road, it looked like monumental gridlock.

Dantz said, "We should not stay here. It's an unnecessary stop, and I advise ..."

"It's ok, Mr. Dantz," Alexa said, raising her hand to calm him down and to avoid any further discussion.

Dantz backed down but didn't let his guard down. He looked in all directions as if trying to identify an escape route. He acknowledged Nana from a distance with a nod of respect, and Nana smiled back. Stephan introduced himself to Nana but in a very formal way, and kept his distance. Alexa took note that it did not feel genuine for a Foundation representative to act this way with the people they should be working for.

After getting the cart and sack of plants on the cargo rack atop their vehicle, Serge helped Jonas, Lou, and Jimmy into the third row of seats, then held the door for Alexa and Nana to get into the second seat. Stephan was already in the front passenger seat, but once Alexa had climbed in, Nana asked Serge if it would be all right if she rode in the front with him. Serge said that was no problem, made eye contact with Stephan, and he got out.

As Serge took Nana's hand to help her, he felt again that sensation of comfort and scrutiny; Nana was once again rubbing the stone bear on her necklace with her other hand. She climbed in with a broad smile. "Thank you, son." Serge smiled back. "You are welcome, Nana," and he was surprised to say the name so spontaneously.

Alexa heard Serge call her Nana, and saw how Nana looked at Serge, as if she had seen him before or somehow knew him. She saw the smile, the bright of her eyes, then blushed as Nana turned around to see her, knowing she had been caught staring. But Nana simply smiled and said, "Thank you very much, my dear, for stopping."

"You should thank Serge. He was the one that refused to go on."

"I know."

Jimmy was talking with Jonas and Lou, the three of them playing with wooden toys his mother bought him at the public market in Merida. Alexa noticed Stephan's discomfort as he sat next to her. Perhaps he was too close to the children, seated behind him among the baggage; perhaps he did not want to be in a back seat, a beta dog, out of the position of power. Whatever it was, Alexa was well entertained by all these events.

In a dark corner of the dimly lighted vault, one of the crystals flickers spontaneously for a few seconds, as sudden and unpredictable as thunder, without pattern, sparkling with the brightness of a welding rod making ground on steel. Shadows run out of the vault in a maddening rush. The silhouette of a young woman responds with a sudden movement of surprise.

Serge got into the driver's seat and engaged the engine. Once he had radio confirmations from the other vehicles they continued along the road. Over the next thirty minutes Alexa, Serge and Nana talked about her plants and living in a remote area, the challenge it represented, and some of the Foundation's interests.

They continued a pleasant conversation until they approached a barely visible crossroad, Stephen indicated to Serge that they should be getting very close to Santa Elena, one of the larger towns in the area and recipient of some of the most successful micro loans.

"I believe you can leave us right here, son," said Nana.

"I don't see any town."

"Right by that crossroad. We can walk from here," she insisted.

146

"If that is the case, it should not be that far. Although, if you were still on foot, you would have taken at least five hours to make it here."

"It's ok, son. It's so early that we are doing ok. You can stop there, on your right."

"Are you sure?" he asked.

"Yes. We live in San Luis, just across the Privassion River. Just a thirty-minute walk from Santa Elena; probably a fifteen-minute walk from here."

"San Luis is an abandoned loggers' town. No one lives there," said Stephen.

"Well, we do, and it has been my home for the last twenty years."

Serge smiled and saw Alexa's amused expression in response to Stephen's comment through the rear view mirror. "Then I believe we owe a visit to San Luis," said Alexa, and it was decided.

Nana asked Serge if the other vehicles and their occupants could wait here on the main road, while they continued on to San Luis. Serge pulled to the roadside and stopped. He took the radio and gave notice to the other vehicles that they were stopping and everyone should wait for them to return. Dantz and Stephen both protested; they did not like the idea of waiting in the middle of the jungle-forest and wanted to come along, but Alexa insisted that they wait with the rest.

"Ms. Lightman, your father ordered that ..."

"I know what my father said. We'll be all right. No one is expecting us or will surprise us here. We're going to a small village, where too

147

many vehicles, arms, or strangers might spark some suspicion or concern with the people"

"Call on the radio when you reach your destination," Dantz said to Serge.

"I will, and you can check our coordinates with the GPS unit."

"Agreed."

As Serge got back in the vehicle Nana asked him if he could keep the GPS unit off as they moved towards San Luis. "We want to keep our little town out of everyone's knowledge, if you know what I mean" and with a soft smile she winked at him. Serge nodded and turned the knob on the GPS unit which was on his waist off, he smiled back at Nana and turned the engine on.

After five minutes driving on a treacherous trail filled with turns and forks onto other trails, they reached the entrance to the old loggers' settlement, which seemed abandoned. Nana indicated that they should proceed by foot.

"I hope I can remember how to make it back to the main road. I barely noticed how we made it here," said Serge.

"Oh, you'll find your way. You'll see".

They got out of the SUV and stretched their legs. Jimmy shouted at the prospect of seeing a ghost town, "Wow! Can we go there?"

"We will in a second." Alexa answered.

Jonas and Lou ran off to the abandoned town, and Jimmy was excited to follow.

"You can let him go. It's pretty safe in there," said Nana with confidence, placing her soft hand on Alexa's shoulder "Let me show you our little piece of Paradise."

Serge radioed Dantz, "Ok, we reached the village. All clear; we'll be back in ten or twenty minutes."

"Ok, we'll be here. Report back when you start your return and check your GPS unit I'm not reading your position."

Serge did not reply back and turned the volume down, placing the radio on his waist belt, next to the off GPS unit.

They were no more than two hundred feet from the town entrance, and although the road would have allowed them to drive, Serge saw that it was covered by bark from the old logging operation and grown over with small, fragile plants. It looked more like the forest trails he used on his morning runs close to home. There was some familiarity to it.

As Nana, Alexa and Serge neared they could see that most of the town had been almost absorbed by the jungle but seemed well kept and habitable. The first, dilapidated structures were covered with vines. Old ditches where logs once floated were now used to grow vegetables. Water from a river was distributed through a network of old clay pipes that ended in rain gardens and improvised fountains.

Farther in, the houses where people still lived were more like living organisms. Leaves provided shelter, trunks were the structure, old logs were walls where food could be harvested from, spaces between branches allowed light to be filtered in. Rain barrels captured drinking water, and the overflow drained through rock cracks to replenish the aquifer, or into underground caves for summer consumption. The houses, which might be the envy of any environmentalist, looked more like tree houses built on the ground. Many were remnants of old structures where fallen stones or bricks were replaced by sculpted logs and growing vines. The stucco walls showed a wonderful, handmade pattern in a palette of natural colors: yellows, ochre, greens, and reds. The surroundings reflected a balance achieved between the number of people, the place, and the climate, which fluctuated between a tropical rainforest and a high altitude evergreen forest.

"Nana" Serge whispered, as if he had entered a sacred space. "How many people live here?"

"We are a small town. We have about sixteen to twenty families, depending on the season. People do go to Santa Clara or San Ignacio but always come back: they can't live there. When they leave and come back here, they just say that they are visiting family, or at work, or on vacation. So we have between seventy and one hundred people living here, almost half of them kids under the age of sixteen."

"Oh my, this is beautiful!" exclaimed Alexa. "Jimmy, come here. Look at where your friends live. Lande …" She paused in disbelief. "This is a beautiful place. How come no one knows about it?"

"We like keeping it that way. We live in peace, and can be independent from everyone else. That is where we are going." She pointed to a little yellow house on a corner.

The house was made of old logs piled horizontally by the side of a grassy berm, which made it look like a continuation of the mountainside. The walls were partially covered with a hand-applied stucco finish of a washed yellow color. The door was five wide wooden planks fastened with large brass nails, and a handle that looked like an old, worn horse shoe.

The door opened with ease, no lock needed, just a simple wooden pin in the ground to keep it in place. The round room was simply furnished. In the center of the floor was spread a canvas cloth, surrounded with made up cotton cushions. To one side was a table with a couple of chairs. The wall on the left was finished in adobe and stone, with a built-in wood stove that was raised 9 inches from the ground. The stove had a small grill on top, and two center holes: one for storing wood and charcoal, the other to feed the fire. The wall had shelves with wooden kitchen utensils, clay pots, and some steel tools. On the other wall, imbedded in a niche or small alcove was the bed. Perforating the wall beside the bed were eight small four by four inch square holes for ventilation, open to the dominant winds and used to refresh while sleeping. The center wall had a large window and a door that opened onto an interior patio, where many potted plants surrounded one of the natural gravity fountains. The plants looked regularly pruned, perhaps for cooking or medicinal purposes. The inside temperature was very pleasant.

Alexa and Serge entered the home with respect and almost impulsively, both took their shoes off at the door. The floor was a soft, sandy dry soil, comfortable to walk upon. Nana went directly to the kitchen area and from the oven took a small pot from which she poured a prepared tea into three wooden cups. She brought them to the canvas cloth on the floor, and invited Serge and Alexa to sit upon the cushions.

"This is my home. I've lived here for almost twenty years. When I arrived, only three families were here; they lived under poor conditions in the old buildings and survived on the old loggers' cultivated gardens. There was no water available in town. The springs are seasonal, and the river arrives here contaminated from upstream. We got organized using a few old and traditional ideas, and we have been doing fine since, improving things as we go. We started visiting the surrounding towns and making small commerce with them about ten years ago. Getting here is very difficult and few people know we live here. We keep a low profile."

All this time Nana had been gently touching her necklace figure. The shape of the bear was now more discernable. All its edges were very smooth, polished by years of rubbing or from the craft of its artist. Serge was intrigued by the piece and just seeing it gave him a soothing sensation.

"Do you have any services in town?" asked Alexa. "Doctor, schools?"

"Oh no, nothing like that here. Kids are home schooled in the old ways and we complement their education with trips to nearby towns, where they can see the modern world and learn from it. We grow most of our food: we are very self-sufficient. I gather medicinal plants and treat minor sickness; most of us know a few tricks that have been passed down by older generations. Living close to a nature preserve allows us to keep in balance without raising anyone's concerns. When we need a doctor it is because someone got sick outside San Luis, and when that happens we get treatment in those towns, like anyone else. That leaves the sickness there."

"It must be hard to keep everyone out and your presence undetected," Serge said.

"Oh, that is no problem. Many people know we live here, but they think our life is more difficult. We don't have the regular services, and they would rather live in more modern cities. I see life there as more difficult, while ours here is in balance."

Jimmy entered the house running, and showed the big frog in his hand to a surprised Alexa "Easy, Jimmy. No running inside, remember?" Nana just laughed, expressing no concern. He was excited and wanted to show Alexa something else, outdoors. She stood up with an apologetic gesture and walked out with Jimmy, talking about the frog.

Serge looked at Nana. It was the first time that they were alone. He felt a strong need to ask about the unique necklace. "Nana, may I ask you a personal question?"

"There is no such a thing, but yes, please do."

"Your necklace, I can't take my eyes off it. I'm intrigued by it. What is its significance? What is it made of? Where did you get it? What is it?"

"Well, that was more than one single question." She smiled and pulled herself closer to Serge. "I've been wearing this necklace for thirty years. My husband gave it to me. It represents one of four key strengths or powers in our belief system, in our lives. It is made of an indigenous rock, a stalactite from a secluded cave near a sacred *Cenote*."

"I see you rubbing it constantly, and I assume it calms you or helps you in a certain way. Every time you do, it soothes me, tranquilizes me."

"So you can feel it?" she replied with a tone of satisfaction, or confirmation.

"Yes. It is strange, but definitely present. May I touch it?"

"I was just about to ask if you would like to." She lifted the figure and extended her hand, holding it in front of Serge at eye level. Serge did not touch it right away. He looked at it directly, as when a man buys a precious stone for an engagement ring. Something had captured his eye and he wanted to see it first. This seemed to please Nana, who nodded in approval. After a brief time he touched it with his thumb and middle finger, rubbed it gently with the thumb, then took it in his hand. It was warm, obviously warmer than Nana's rubbing might account for. He looked at the figure intently. "It is beautiful ..." He closed his hand around it and felt Goosebumps rise on his skin. He rubbed it as Nana had. It soothed him again, more than before. He felt no concerns, obligations, or restraints; he felt liberated, like a weight had been lifted off his shoulders.

"What do you feel?"

"It's hard to describe ..." He paused, thinking, trying to find the right words. "I felt like I had returned to a very young age. Then it felt like a security blanket, a comfort toy. Then you grow with it, memories and experiences become so vividly fresh. Rubbing it produces a profound sense of peace, holding it enhances all of my senses. I feel like there are no limits, I feel confidence, motivation, well being ... I believe, in one word, it is peace – no, wait – wisdom ... confidence. No, it is not one single word!"

"You are right. It is all that and many other things. I'm intrigued, though not all that surprised by this."

"What do you mean?"

This stone or figure, as you call it, is a receptor of a living energy, and it works in combination with an arm bracelet. Then it's true potential comes to light. This might sound strange for you, but not just anyone can wear this." She pointed to the figure in Serge's hand, closed her hand on his. "Only those that the crystal chooses."

"The crystal?

"Yes, the source of light, of energy." "Let me tell you something, now that we are alone. When I saw you for the first time you brought into my mind something in my life I had left dormant, something I spent eighteen years doing but gave up two years ago now."

"I don't understand."

"Well, after you stopped the car you were driving, when you walked up to us, you were authentic. I could tell that you had something and somewhere important to get to, but nevertheless you stopped to do what you felt needed to be done."

"It seemed the right thing to do."

"My point exactly: you acted with a genuine heart. Can you feel the warmth of the stone in your hand?" She was still holding Serge's hand, which held the stone figure.

"Yes."

"That is exactly what I felt when I saw you, and the warmth grew as time passed. It reacted to you, to your actions. That is why I was compelled to rubbed it, touch it, to draw that energy to me. It has been a while since I felt this way and I'm glad that you awaken this in me."

Serge was still confused and was about to ask another question.

"Wait, son. This figure matches an arm bracelet that I should be wearing, that was lost, stolen from me twenty years ago and that I have been looking for ever since. I'm getting old and weak and I'm afraid I will not be able to find it. It has been twenty years since I've seen my husband. We are linked through this energy. I left the place where he lives to find the arm bracelet, but now I've given almost all my hope away. I tried to make a life here, and it has been good, but still my objective, my purpose, was to find the bracelet and wear it... match it again with the stone."

She paused and looked directly into his eyes with a deepness that Serge felt was stripping him of any personal secrets or thoughts.

"Have you ever felt that you don't know where you are, and even surrounded by life, still question the purpose of your life, as if there must be something larger?"

"Yes, but don't we all feel that way?"

"Not all, my son. Very few people have that kind of feelings. It's like artists or mathematicians, only three to six percent of people have a call for these things."

A call came through the radio. "Serge, this is Dantz. We need to keep moving if we want to make it to San Ignacio with light. I don't intend to drive these narrow roads in pitch black darkness."

Nana and Serge quickly came back from where their minds had taken them. Nana took her hands from Serge's and Serge let go the stone, with a feeling of emptiness that was hard to describe. There was a separation, as when you miss someone you love. With his other hand he got out the radio.
"Agreed. I'll get everyone ready. We will be there in a few minutes."

Alexa came inside. "What's going on?" She was covered with flowers, in her hair and around her neck. She had a small iguana on her shoulder and was acting as silly as a ten year old girl, displaying all her jewelry and new decorations. Through the door behind her followed seven children, Jimmy among them.

"We need to move on."

"Can we stay? Can we stay?" shouted Jimmy from behind his mom.

Alexa said, "We need to get to San Ignacio, remember? That is our destination. You'll make more friends there and we'll surely come back to San Luis to visit. If that is ok with Lande?"

"Of course, my dear. I assure you, this is not the last time we'll see each other."

Alexa was delighted with the idea, and Nana's tone and certainty made Serge feel relieved; he still had a lot of questions.

They left Nana's home and walked into the street. Jimmy asked Serge to race him to the SUV. Serge was still barefooted and had his shoes in his hand, but when Jimmy started running, Serge started off behind him. All the children, and Alexa and Nana, laughed at Serge's display of dexterity as he tried to run barefooted with grace down the rocky road. He tried to keep Jimmy's speed but his jumps, shouts, and twists made it clear that he was hurt by the uneven surfaces of small rocks, branches and fallen leaves. He was felt quite humble by the time he reached the vehicle, Jimmy wore a gleaming smile of victory as Serge stood by the driver's door, cleaning his feet and checking them for bruises or bleeding.

"Was that a hard road for you?" asked Alexa when she reached them.

"Don't ask … I knew I should have worn my shoes.'

"I won, Mom. I beat Serge running!"

"Yes, you did, fair and square." she replied, looking at Serge's expression of pain and discomfort with a broad smile.

"Ouch. I'm going to pay for this," They laughed with him about it.

They got in the vehicle and said their proper goodbyes. Alexa was riding with Serge in front and Jimmy was in back, standing by Serge's ear. Nana came close to Serge's window, placed her hand on his forearm and winked at him.

"We'll be seeing each other pretty soon."

"Thank you for the tea and hospitality. We certainly hope we do." Alexa said.

"Yes, thank you," Serge said. "How do I get out of here?"

Nana smiled. "I know you'll find your way. You'll see."

He took her answer at face value and put the vehicle in gear. "Maybe that is why we'll see each other again soon," he smiled and winked back at her.

Serge radioed Dantz about their return and drove back toward the entrance to the main road. After a few minutes on the road he turned on his GPS unit to see where Dantz was and noticed a marker on the small screen but before zooming in on the location he decided to take Nana's word and find his own way out, he turned the GPS unit off again.

Dantz was on the radio again. "I got you there for a second but lost you before checking position, everything all right?
"Yes, we are on our way, I believe there is a lot of interference with all these trees" With that he placed his radio back on his belt looked up to Alexa who was already smiling and looking at the road ahead. "We'll find our way out, I know" She added.

San Ignacio

The towns of San Ignacio and Santa Elena comprised the second largest urban area in Belize. The cities, while independent, shared similar issues. The two were separated by the Macal River, connected only by the Hawksworth suspension bridge. Together, the cities represented almost one tenth Belize's population.

The Lightman Foundation caravan crossed a bridge over one of the small Macal River tributaries, and entered San Ignacio. They immediately encountered a small pick-up truck with police markings, with an officer standing at the edge of the street; he raised his hand, asking them to stop.

Serge stopped and got out, walked to the front of the caravan where Dantz was already talking with the two policemen, who apparently had been expecting them. Serge extended his hand with a broad smile. "*Hola. Buenas tardes,*" said Serge in perfect Spanish.

The officers smiled back, and shook Serge's hand. In the most fluent English he could muster, the senior of the two replied: "Welcome to San Ignacio. I'm Captain Joel Ramos, your assigned escort." Captain Ramos appeared to derive from a mix of Native and Spanish Guatemalan ancestors; his demeanor seemed strong and reliable, with a hidden confidence behind his sincere smile.

"Thank you," said Serge. "We are glad we made it. Sorry if we are a little late."

"No problem. We don't expect all our visitors to know the roads as we do. Besides, this is a very remote area and the jungle surroundings change by the month, and even some of the locals get lost from time to time. Please follow us: we'll escort you to your hotel."

By the time they arrived in San Ignacio's town center, the sun was at the edge of the mountains and darkness was falling. Alexa's party was welcomed by a chorus of thirty children singing typical songs of Belize and performing soft dances on a central patio, accompanied by a band playing music with vernacular instruments.

Captain Ramos introduced the group to the Mayor of San Ignacio, and from that point Stephan took charge of the whole event. He was in his natural environment, and in his best mood. This is what he was paid to do, as Foundation liaison with the host town: the welcome party, the festivities, the traditional food, the whole busy schedule for the next two days.

Serge moved aside to talk with Captain Ramos, and thank him for his help. He asked a few questions about the area, local customs, food, Ramos' personal recommendations for what to see and do. He apologized again for being late and explained they had stopped at San Luis.

"Oh, you found San Luis?" Ramos was surprised. "The people of San Luis are very friendly, but also very reclusive. A few of them work and live here during the week, then move back there on weekends. You should feel very honored to earn their trust as first time visitors. This is the first time I've heard something like that from San Luis."

Ramos smiled. "While you are here, please let us know what we can do, so you can feel also welcome here in San Ignacio. We are friendly people, too," he added in a polite and fun-sarcastic way, asking for a chance to prove it. They both smiled and rejoined the welcome event.

The event continued with a group of high school girls carrying a special gift. All of the travelers were presented with a alpaca canvas blanket with bright vertical lines of colors and loose strands at the ends. This symbolized a warm welcome from San Ignacio to them and also the fruits of one of many enterprises founded by the micro

160

loan programs. Jimmy used his blanket as a cape, while the rest used theirs to keep warm in the mild evening air.

As a curious architect, Serge reviewed the buildings around him. With few exceptions the town seemed frozen in the 1950's. Many of the buildings were only one or two stories tall, and their wooden structures gave the town a unique, frontier charm. Most of the old colonial structures were made of stone and brick, claimed higher views, and were silent witnesses of a more promising era when San Ignacio was at the edge of exploration and conquest. Modern signs advertising sodas brands, snack food, and big city life were visible on the terraces of small shops and utility poles. Electricity and telephone cables hung from the poles to tall walls with open windows or to the rooftops of houses. Some satellite television antennas were visible among the inclined tile roofs.

Serge noticed that Dantz had absented himself from the festivities. All through the trip he had stayed close to the group and it was strange that now, during an important part of the journey, he was nowhere to be seen. One of the body guards was close by. Out of curiosity Serge checked his GPS unit, which showed Dantz in a stationary position, two blocks away. He left Alexa and Jimmy with Stephan at the host dining table. On a casual move and in order not to raise any concerns he took one of the foundation report envelopes that was at the end of the table as if to put it away. He then went to check on the rest of the security team.

Serge saw one of the security guards by the edge of the plaza, next to one of the SUVs. He was cleaning his weapons, a 9 mm automatic pistol and a Uzi submachine gun, on a cloth spread over the vehicle's hood. Bullets, magazine clips, and tools were out the public, with no regard for the local people's opinions, concerns or fears. Serge moved with the people around him, being careful not to be seen by the bodyguard. He continued down the block toward Dantz's position, then realized that his own GPS unit could be traced by Dantz in the same way. He made a last check of Dantz's unit's position, made a mental map how to get there, took the report out of the envelope and placed the GPS unit inside its pages and placed both items inside the report's envelope and walked back to the guard cleaning his weapons. "It's been a while since I've seen an Uzi." Serge commented.

The guard turned, raised his eyes and met Serge's. "It's a great 9 mm machine gun. Ten shots per second, light, dependable, and compact."

"Well, you have to keep it clean. It could jam very easily, couldn't it?"

"It's worst in dusty environments. There, you really have to disassemble and rebuild it again to clean it up. But if you get it wet, you only need to dry it out."

"Hey listen: could you please do me a favor? I got this envelope with some petitions for Ms. Lightman, but I'm on my way to my room. Could you make sure she gets it right now? I don't want anyone to think that I did not follow up on getting it to her right away."

"Sure, no problem."

The bodyguard was amused by Serge's visit and though he did not appreciate the use of his time for such an errand he agreed to do it. He assembled the clean weapon back and the put away the cleaning kit. He proceeded to the event to deliver the envelope to Alexa.

Serge continued to the last known location of Dantz's GPS unit. As he got to the designated corner he saw three individuals coming out of a house. He slipped into the dark niche of a building entrance and observed from there. The man who seemed to be the leader had a goatee and long black hair worn in a pony tail; Serge could not make out his face, saw only a strong profile, especially at the eyebrows. The other two walked by his side to a pickup truck with oversized tires. One opened the passenger door for the leader; the other jumped up on the flat bed of the truck and held on to the roll bar. The three drove away. Minutes later, Dantz came out of the house with one of the other Foundation guards and started walking in Serge's direction. He backed into farthest corner of the entryway and tried to be inconspicuous by wrapping himself in his cotton canvas blanket and pretending to be a sleeping drunk. They walked by him.

Once they were gone, Serge ran in the other direction, to enter the plaza from the other side, but he could not find the way around: the streets were not orthogonal, they deviated. It took him two more turns to follow the light and noise to the plaza, where he cautiously looked around for Dantz and any of the other guards. He did not see them.

But as he approached the main area, a voice behind him said" Hey, Serge, welcome back. Everything all right?"

Serge recognized the voice as Dantz's. "Hey, Dantz, I was looking for you. One of your guys was cleaning his guns in public, pretty intimidating for small town people. We want to keep not only a low profile but also a friendly profile. You should talk to him. I asked him to do an errand for me, just to get things out of sight."

"That must have worked. He left his post to come here. Do you think you might need this?" He raised the sealed envelope. His tone of voice was suspicious and calculated, and Serge decided to play along.

"Oh yes, that is it. I can take it from here. Thanks" Serge wondered what Dantz was thinking. Might the envelope have revealed that it contained the GPS or more than the report? Serge was never to let it out of his sight, nor was he to leave Alexa alone. Whether Dantz knew it was the GPS unit, or if he knew Serge had followed him, he could not tell. He had a bad feeling, though, so he determined to keep his eyes open. He went directly to Alexa and sat by her, but did not say anything. He gestured as if pretending to open the envelope, felt for the GPS unit inside, then put it back on his belt under the cover of the table and joined the festivities with the rest of the group.

At the end of the evening, and after what seemed as an eternity to Jimmy, they were guided to their living quarters at the local hostel, a Dutch colonial three-story building with vaulted brick arches and stone walls. Alexa and Serge were able to maintain Jimmy's energy and excitement with the prospective visit to "the castle". They were assigned to what seemed to be monastery rooms, with built-in desks inside of niches, single beds, stone floors, and high arched windows that faced the mountains and the plaza below. The rooms shared three bathrooms, one of which was assigned to Alexa and Jimmy, and the other two to the rest of the party.

Stephan briefed the whole group on the next day's activities. San Ignacio and Santa Clara were the recipients of the most successful micro loans the foundation had. There would meet several micro loan recipients, and a key Foundation contact that had helped implement drastic changes in the area by integrating their work to local culture and respecting a matriarchal system. In the afternoon, there was to be a gathering at the town's main theater where the Foundation would be honored with a varied program of performances and speeches on expanding the program. The next day promised to be one of the most ambitious of the journey.

The Theater

Morning offered a spectacular dawn seen through tall conifer trees and luscious green rainforest; the day was bright and pleasant. The Cayo District of San Ignacio, or "Cayo" as the locals called it, offered the rare sight of a tropical rainforest combined with the charm of a Colorado landscape. The town's narrow streets were already busy with the sounds of vehicles, walking people, market vendors, barking dogs. The air was filled with inviting aromas of exotic foods that, combined with the evergreen scent of the forest, imprinted the memories of every tourist, archeologist, and traveler. The friendliness of the town's people welcomed all visitors in a way that was translated as an open invitation to stay.

The hostel offered spectacular views of the town and the river. From the third floor rooms assigned to the Lightman group they could see the main plaza and the market. Sounds, colors, and aromas reached them through the soft filter of a gentle breeze and the distant thunder of the 150-foot Big Rock Falls on the Privassion River. The Falls served as gateway to the Mountain Pine Ridge Forest Reserve.

The group had a hearty breakfast at the hostel cafeteria, then walked to a nearby school, just a block east of the hostel. They were led to the school's central patio, which was arranged with tables and chairs and covered with a light cotton drape to provide a comfortable shadow. They reached the main table where Nana sat at the center with the rest of the guests. She smiled broadly at them, and winked at Alexa, as if to confirm, "I told you so." Yes, they were going to see her again, and soon. Alexa and Stephen took their places at the main table, and Serge and Jimmy found seats in the first row of chairs along with schoolchildren. The security detail spread to the four corners of the patio.

After a warm welcome by the students, Alexa and Stephan were introduced to representatives from the town, to elders from nearby villages, and to spokespersons for the Native community. After formal introductions, an award was given to the person who had made the most difference in the community: that person happened to be Nana. The master of ceremonies gave a short speech, stating that Nana was a recognized and trusted figure in town and was loved by every child. Alexa gave her a check from the Foundation to reward her and to sponsor more of her activities. The Foundation also gave Nana a framed certificate of appreciation, though Alexa knew it would not likely be hung on the wall of Nana's house.

"Congratulations, Lande. I'm glad that you are the recipient of this award. Why didn't you tell us that you knew who we were?"

"Well, I was pleased to see that you were genuinely the persons that you claimed to be. You offered help to a stranger and that was proof enough for me." Nana gave Alexa a warm hug, as if it was the first time they met. Still Alexa wondered what made her so charismatic: her bright white smile, or the spark in her eyes?

From their chairs, Jimmy waved vigorously to Nana and Serge had a chance to smile at her, too. Nana signaled to Serge, asking to see him later. After the award event, while everyone was making small talk, Serge sought out Nana.

"It's a pleasure to see you, Nana."

"It is nice to see you too. Serge. I need to talk to you. It is a matter of crucial importance and the greatest urgency."

"What can I do for you?"

"Not here. I need to talk to you at my home. Would you be able to go there? It's very important."

"Well, we are on our way to the theater for our next event," he hesitated. "I don't want to leave Alexa and Jimmy by themselves, but I'll take them there and then come to your home. They will be there for a couple of hours and there'll be hundreds of people around them."

"Good. I'll see you there in one hour" With that she gave Serge a kiss on his cheek, all the while holding and rubbing the stone figure from her necklace with her left hand.

When Serge got back to Alexa and Jimmy, Alexa asked, "What was that all about?"

"I don't know. She asked me to go to her house. Seems like she has something important to tell me, and it can't wait. I mentioned that you and Jimmy would be left alone and ..."

"You should go, Serge. Don't worry about us. We'll be there when you get back. Besides, her collaboration with the Foundation is essential to us. She makes things happen."

"Are you sure?"

"Yes, definitely. We owe her trust of us to you. It is because you stopped to help her that we are here today. Anything we can do to foster a better relationship is good. Besides, I'm intrigued ... she is ... so ..."

"Can you feel it, too."

"Yes, and I can't describe what it is."

Under the vaulted ceiling of the Cenote, the sparks of light emanating from the second crystal have become more regular. Two trembling old hands approach its edges and caress it with religious respect. With the touch, the hands stop shaking. The first dimming crystal had started to emanate a stronger light, fully lighting the magnificent space. Silhouettes of an old man and a young woman reflect on the surface of calmed water.

For the short ride to the theater building, Alexa and Jimmy joined Stephan in a SUV with Dantz and one bodyguard, while a second vehicle followed with Dantz's other two men. Serge watched them depart then hurried to the third SUV to drive to Nana's home. He had not given any explanations to Dantz nor had he asked for any, and for someone as methodical as Dantz that was unusual. Serge had a strong gut reaction to this so he knew he had to be fast. He just hoped he remembered how to get to San Luis and back in time.

The theater was a four-story colonial structure fronted with a two story high prominent arcade that gave the building its distinctive character. The Theater covered the whole city block with no surrounding or adjacent structures, its size could be perceived as massive from the distance, but considering the small width of the streets, its proximity to its surrounding buildings lowered its height or presence. The topography of the area made the city blocks irregular, which presented a challenge for visitors to orient themselves. The drive to the theater was a short one, no more than five minutes through narrow streets and small pocket plazas.

Once arrived, they were welcomed at the main stairs by some of the same VIPs who had been at the school the day before. Alexa was hesitant to leave Jimmy with Stephan, she had noticed that he was not good with kids but both of them were seated in the front row of the theater and she would be close by, at the podium. Jimmy seemed tired, and she hoped that once the overhead lights were turned off for the projected presentation slides, he would fall asleep, and with luck would stay that way until Serge's arrival.

The theater program included a roundtable discussion during which Alexa would be answering questions and reporting the progress of Foundation work done in the region. This was the time that Serge felt comfortable leaving them alone. He had given Mr. Lightman his word that he would never leave Alexa and Jimmy alone, and he was concerned he was breaking that promise. He was also concerned how strangely Dantz had acted the night before.

Revelation

Serge took the main road out of San Ignacio until he found the crossroad. He was about to use his GPS unit when he remembered that on his way out of San Luis the first time he had found the way, so he decided trust his feelings again and go for it. He rechecked Dantz's GPS position and saw the indicator steady at the theater location. He then turned his unit off to become also untraceable. As Serge went up the winding road he turned instinctively at the forks and intersections. He found the entrance to San Luis.

Serge walked the last few steps to Nana's home with the same sensation he had felt before, one of belonging, of remembrance of the forest trails back home. He felt at ease. He knocked on the door to announce himself, and Nana's reply came from the window. "Please, Serge, please come in. We must hurry."

"Nana, what is going on?"

"Son, I need to ask you a very important favor, something only you can do. I would not be asking you now but I'm running out of time, and I had given up hope for the last two years until I saw you."

"I don't understand."

"Serge, I know you have questions about this" She took her necklace's stone figure from her chest and held it in front of him.

"Yes ..."

"When you held it in your hands, you felt something"

"Yes, but how do you know? I felt warmth, peace ... belonging. I can't explain it."

"Exactly. It's hard to explain but I'll try to do my best. Twenty-five years ago I was a renowned photographer for the National

170

Geographic magazine. I was in my prime, top of my game. One of my trips brought me here: to Belize, Guatemala, southeast Mexico."

"The Yucatan Peninsula?"

"Yes, but most importantly, the Mayan territory. I came with a team of explorers to record the latest coordinated efforts that the governments of these countries were making in exploring Mayan culture and its archeological sites. It took us more than a week just to arrive at the first encampments. There were no roads, nor the vehicles we have now. Everything was carried by mules or horses using difficult walking trails. We opened paths through the jungle, paths that were closed by the jungle in less than a week. When we got there, each photographer was assigned to a specific exploration team. There was so much territory to cover ... Anyway, that is not important. Let me continue.

"Once we arrived at the archeological sites, it was amazing – oh, God – you should have seen those places: magnificent, unpredictable, hidden. The jungle had taken over at many of the sites. Magnificent mahogany trees grew by the steps of pyramids. Temples were overtaken by vegetation, soil had accumulated with leaves and years of abandon until you could barely make out any sign of human presence, yet there were remnants that we discovered. It took years to uncover the main structures, and to this day maybe no more than twenty percent has been explored, and they don't have enough space to store what they have collected and catalogued. Sometimes the findings were merely recorded and then buried again, in the hope that poachers would not steal artifacts. The success in preserving these spaces has varied, depending on the country and the pressure of growth and development.

"This reserve here in Belize is the last real unknown frontier. For some unexplained reason, which I'm glad for, the British government kept this area untouched and out of the reach of civilization. In 1973, Belize became an independent nation but remained part of the

British Commonwealth, and somehow the preserve has been maintained and it now seems it will remain like that forever. When we arrived at our assigned area, it was as amazing as the others, we walked for miles until we found something that startled all the archeologists. We found several structures in almost perfect condition."

"What do you mean?"

"We found remnants of a small ceremonial complex of six small pyramid bases, no more than twenty feet tall, thirty seven by thirty seven feet in size each. The structures were as if the Mayans had just left them a year after a last ceremony. Fine soft white stucco covered each surface of the structure. All the walls were adorned with almost intact magnificent, colorful paintings of plants, animals, seashells, flowers, and human profiles in rich detail. All the edges were soft and sculpted, the steps were complete, the top of the pyramid was flat as a pool table ... intact. Dried flowers were still present and had been piled on a central polished stone. Only the jungle had grown around it and started to cover it.

"Now, you can go to any archeological site and recognize that many archeologists will interpret information and cannot resist the temptation to "rebuild" a structure according to how they envisioned the original structure. In the end, many are just fakes, cheap interpretations for tourist delight and archeologist fame. But these structures were the real thing. It was by no means big, and it was located in the middle of a meadow, a small man-made clearing where the jungle had been kept in control. That is how we found them.

The discovery took over us and it became dark without us realizing that we have not settle camp yet. That night our team got lost; In those days there were no GPS units to pinpoint where you were, it was dark and although there was a full moon it was pitch black under the jungle canopy. So we decided to make camp and wait until the next day to orient ourselves. We were getting ready to start a fire but decided not to do it this time, to experience total darkness, just for fun, the high of the discovery. We shut off our lamps and experienced this deep darkness, you could barely see the moon light above us through the jungle canopy. It was a very mystic experience, I can still remember the sensation I felt... It was already late, we were tired and decided to wrap it up and get some rest. Each one went to their tent; to finish our notes, check equipment get some sleep. For some reason I was not sleepy, I crawled out of my tent and sat outside again in complete darkness. After a few minutes I noticed light coming from the jungle. It was a small flicker of light ... like sunlight reflected in water on a leaf."

Serge remembered having that same impression, close to home, on his running trail.

"The problem was that there is no sun in the middle of the night! I foolishly thought that maybe the moon had been the source of it. I waited patiently to see if I could see it again, and there it was. It was brief, it took a couple of minutes, but it was there. I walked in the dark toward the last point where I had seen the light, then waited again. I did not turn on my lamp because I was afraid of losing with its glare the sensitivity that my eyes had gained in the dark after a moment, there it was, a small flicker a little light. I kept walking towards the source, then I saw more light, but this time it was definitely the moon's light, perceivable through the jungle."

"You found another clearing."

"Yes, I stumbled by fortune into the greatest discovery. I was excited. In the clearing, in the brightest moonlight, I saw this perfect structure. I was not sure what it was and thought that it might be some other team's restoration effort. In any case, I was excited. I called to my team but they never replied ... My team was supposed to share that discovery, document it, authenticate it, and it was my job, I had the equipment, to record the finding, take photographs as proof and bring them back to the expedition's main camp. But I could not find my way back to my own camp. Walking to the site in the dark, I had lost my sense of orientation. After hours of frustrated effort I decided to stay calm, to stay put, to sleep by the structure and wait until dawn for my team to call me, or to find my own way in daylight."

Serge was immersed in her words. He waited patiently without asking anything else, while Nana handed him a cup of tea and had a sip herself. All this time she continued rubbing the animal figure on her necklace. Finally, she continued.

"Dawn came, and with first light, I awakened to the splendor of the site. I was mesmerized. I forgot that I was lost and walked the site, looked at the paintings, climbed, sat, marveled at it. I'm not sure how much time passed. Eventually, I remembered my team and called them, I shouted their names, hoping they would hear me. I looked for a trail or other sign of where I had come from. I realized I was completely lost and became nervous. I guess I panicked, because I started screaming for my team, hoping that they would be looking for me and would hear my voice. I did not remember walking too long from camp to the clearing, it could not have been that long, they should be able to hear me. They never did … I was lost, I was alone in the middle of the jungle, without any food, supplies, tools, nothing but the clothes I had with me, and with nowhere to go. In which direction should I move? If I move will I be more lost or farther away from a search party? I decided to stay put and make noise until they showed up. They never did."

"But, then, how were you able to survive … to be here? And why have you stayed here?"

"Call it providence, call it destiny … I don't know. Why are you here, for example? Same question. We don't know. What I can tell you is that my new life started then and there, and an amazing journey began."

"What happened, Nana?"

"After I lost my voice for screaming, I sat by the structure hopeless and beaten. I was desperate ... I guess my appearance was not very good. I had not slept well. I was anxious and I felt broken, I questioned my choice of following a light without anyone else's knowledge. I beat up myself pretty good. I guess I fell asleep, after crying like a baby, for what might have been hours. I was awakened by a gentle touch on my forehead, fresh water on my lips, and a gentle pair of hands holding my head. When I opened my eyes I saw two young women smiling at me, native women, with dark hair, beautiful complexions, olive skin, white smiles. I sat up, surprised, looking around me, expecting to see my team or base camp.

"But I was in a small village, a native village. In front of me was a middle aged man, probably five years older than me. He was bare-chested, with broad shoulders, a virile, straight posture, and eyes full of wisdom. He wore a wide cloth around his waist, and a pendant like mine but with another animal figure; his was not a bear but a bird, a raven. His other piece of jewelry was an arm bracelet worn on the inside of the arm, from elbow to wrist. It was a silvery golden bracelet with an indent the shape of the same raven. He was looking at me with a broad smile, waiting for me to calm down. I asked him where I was. 'Arupa,' was his answer. 'Who are you?' I asked. 'A friend' "His answer was straight but he offered no further explanation. 'I need to get back,' I said. 'To where?' was his reply. I said, 'Civilization, any town, a phone, my team: they must be looking for me.' The man said, 'You have been with us for eight days now. Whoever was looking for you has left. We have not seen anyone around us. You are safe with us now.' 'Eight days!? That is not possible. I got lost last night, I fell asleep, you found me ...' He said, 'It is not that simple.'

"'I know that I'm now with you, but where is *here*,' I asked him. 'You are very close to where we found you, and we can take you there if you want, but before we do that you need to eat something and rest.'

"There was something in his voice that made me trust him. I felt hesitant but not threatened, and that hesitancy was soon dissipated by his attitude, his posture, even by the touch of the two young women who were helping me with drinking water. Their assurance and non-threatening attitude tranquilized me. I had thought the man was speaking English because I was able to understand him, but the movements of his lips were different from the words I heard. It was like seeing a cheap Chinese movie with unsynchronized lip synching."

"What do you mean?"

"Yes, I heard the sounds of his voice and simply understood the meaning of the words."

Serge was puzzled. He did not know where Nana was going, what all this meant.

"They fed me corn bread, fruits, and dry meats. I drank the freshest water ever and they made scented drinks, something like tea, a sweet tea … you could compare it to today's flavored waters. When I finished eating, I walked their small village. It had only seven buildings, most of them light, wooden structures with palm ceilings and stone bases. Only what appeared to be the main building was totally made of stone and stucco. I'm not including the ceremonial basement I found. None were very big. Most of the villagers lived underground: you know what a Cenote is?"

"Yes, an entrance to an underground cave system, most of the time filled with fresh water. For the Mayans it served as a water well, a sacred pit, a connection to the underworld …"

"Exactly. The difference here is that for the people who found me, their underworld was their main world, a complete network of

176

underground passages to different areas of the jungle, the forest, the rivers, all accessed through undetected small openings or large Cenote entrances on the surface. On that first day, or the ninth day, according to them, I started asking questions about everything. One day turned to two, then to three, and without me noticing time went by and I started living my life there. I spent what for me was another lifetime of learning, growing and being free and content, without ever missing my former life."

"You said you were there for years?"

"Yes. When I returned I found that only five years had passed, but I spent all my life there."

"You returned … why?"

"I had to. The village depended on me to do it … depends on me still, and will depend on you, I hope."

"I don't understand."

"After a while, probably halfway through the time that I was there, I was allowed to enter the center of their existence, their source of life. This was an underground cave, a magnificent vaulted cave with reflective minerals on all of its walls. This space had four stone bases, with a crystal on each. The crystals are the size of a human heart; their shapes vary, they symbolize or relate to the four cardinal points, the four basic elements, the four dimensions, the four orders. From each crystal emanates a light, some kind of energy that lights the space around it and by doing that provides them with the continuation of their way of life. One crystal was missing, and I never learned the truth behind its disappearance. I simply can't imagine how that space was with four crystals; with three it was magnificent enough. And the people seem to do well with the remaining three. I learned that each crystal is linked to the heart and mind of an elder, two elder men and two elder women. The missing crystal was one of

177

the women's. The link to the crystals is made by some kind of nexus between an arm bracelet and a necklace pendant. Like this one ..."

She opened her hand for Serge to see the stone figure again.

"The villagers perform a ceremony when one of these elders retires or gets close to the end of their life. They know this by the quality and intensity of the light on each crystal. Is preferable that they are alive in order to do the ceremony, that way the crystal is always lighted and continuity of life-light is undisturbed... Now, it is indispensible for at least one crystal to be lighted to assure their way of life, their existence depends on it. Before the end of their time, each elder must choose their replacement, their successor. This honor is a great responsibility, and also an enlightening experience; it falls to the wisest, bravest, and most humble of the men or women in the group. The ceremonies are rare, as these people live a long time, I witnessed it twice. The first time, a retiring male elder chose Norw, the man who had welcomed me to their village, to succeed him. For the ceremony to succeed, one crystal must be active, shining: the other elders must be alive. The passing elder first takes off their pendant, and once this happens the corresponding crystal fades to a dim light, the whole space feels the lack of that light. The successor receives the pendant and wears it close to his heart: this makes the crystal flicker. The elder then pulls the bracelet out of their arm. It is a very difficult task, because the bracelet is linked to your nervous system through the arm; there is a needle-like end that perforates your arm and connects to you inside."

Nana showed Serge the deep scar on the inside of her left arm, at the elbow. "The process takes a lot of time but is almost automatic. The other elders help and guide the recipient through it. Once the arm bracelet is placed in the arm it molds and adapts to the shape and size of the recipient's arm, and at the moment it finally links to the body, the crystal fully lights up. The recipient, being younger, has more energy and the emanating light shines brighter, stronger. There is a staggered process for the passing of elders, so there is always young blood as well as old wisdom in the four elders, the crystal holders, the leaders. This incredible ceremony is a celebration in all its meanings. Everyone is present, the departing elder falls into a deep sleep, no one cries, there is no sorrow. The elder is taken to the surface and placed on the exterior basement, the structure I found. The other elders care for the recipient while the process completes. Outside, the passing elder is left to sleep and his body eventually vanishes. I never learned what happens there, for no one stays to witness that."

"The ceremony clearly has a sacred and symbolic meaning."

"Yes. The recipient gradually receives the wisdom of all the generations before him or her, a process that tests the heart of the recipient. By tradition, if this person is not worth of the responsibility, not only does the crystal not shine, but the bracelet does not merge with the body and a new successor must be named by the other elders. But as far as I know, it has never happened."

"If your pendant is the real thing, where is your bracelet?"

"Well, time passed by, and Norw became a great leader with the other two other elders. I developed a close relationship with Norw, which grew with the time and we married after an incredible courting which stole my heart away. This stirred up some trouble because, in the end, I was an outsider and had been there only two years … or whatever the time had been. One family in particular was not satisfied with Norw's decision to marry me, and they created a breach of harmony and peace within the village. Nothing major happened and apparently, with time, balance was restored. But another crystal transition occurred, and the woman departing chose me as her successor; she told me that I had proven a to have a good heart and that I, being an outsider, might help the community grow in different ways. By this time I had given birth to two children, a girl and a boy. They seem now to be five and seven years old … that is why I never understood the time difference … I was there all of my life, Serge."

"This new succession must have made things worse."

"Yes, unfortunately, and it concentrated the community's power in one family, something which was not uncommon, but it had never involved an outsider. My ceremony was the same as Norw's. I was left with Norw and Jelal, the other elder in the central space while everyone else took Elene, my predecessor, out of the *Cenote*. As the bracelet was placed in me, the crystal shone brightly, and I lost consciousness, at least this existence's consciousness, because I entered a dream where I received the wisdom passed to me. I lived all the former elders' lives in my mind. I found out that the fourth crystal had been taken by a recipient from a dissident family that decided to move away. They just left one day with the crystal. The moment the crystal is removed from its base, it stops shining outward to the cave and instead shines within, storing its energy or light. The people assumed this family would place the crystal on a base in a nearby cave, to share its energy with the rest of the community. We have been looking for it ever since, with no luck.

"Since there was only one crystal elder remaining who was a woman, and I was to be that woman, Jelal's family, the same that had objected to me marrying Norw caused trouble again, As I was recovering from the ceremony, one crystal was taken away, mine was left in place as first they needed both bracelet and pendant to remove it. They were generous enough to leave Norw's in place but left all the community exposed to disaster. Remember the transition? The other crystals are needed for it."

"They numbered the days of you all."

"Yes, our future was now counted in the years that Norw will live. This was a tragedy. The family of Jelal, the third crystal elder left. His pendant and bracelet were gone. While I was still recovering from

180

the transition, I was assaulted and my bracelet forcefully taken. I awakened in pain as they took it, but I held the pendant in my hand and lever let go. I screamed for help, I knew Norw would come to my aid, he was never far from me. Norw was too late. They left, took my bracelet with them and left us all."

"Did you all search for them, did you catch them in time? What happened?"

"We could not leave … only I. Jelal and his family left our village and went to the outside world, out of the Cenote system, out of the village and into this world, this realm. The only one capable of following them was me, because I had the pendant. You see, the pendant reacts to its bracelet and links to it. In the ceremony the bracelet is placed in your chest, on top of your heart, where the pendant lies. There they became one. That is why the indent in the bracelet corresponds to the pendant."

"Why did they not take your crystal?"

"They could not. They needed the bracelet and its pendant to remove the crystal from its base. As I screamed, holding the pendant, they ran away and never had the chance. My crystal still lies in that cave, and it must be flickering from time to time, especially if my heart gets closer to an answer or has new hope at the end it would not have any constant light as the link to the bracelet was broken. . Until then, Norw and the community are left without hope."

"So that is why you returned to this world."

"Yes, only because of that; otherwise I would still be there. I had to find the bracelet, the bracelet is essential for renewal."

"You said you had given up hope."

"I'm an old woman, Serge. I searched everywhere, but Jalal vanished. I looked for them for eighteen years, and spent the last two in resignation and sadness. I'm afraid I have not proven to be worthy of the responsibility."

"But them leaving and taking your bracelet was not your fault. You should not give up; there must be a way."

"There is, and that is where you come in. That is why bringing you here this is so important."

"You need my help?"

"Not only your help, Serge … your life."

"What?"

"Yes. The day I met you I felt you had a good heart. You showed generosity and strength, leadership and commitment. You were kind to an old woman and two kids lost in the middle of the jungle, and despite your other responsibilities, you did the right thing."

"But how can I help you?"

"Serge, I'm making you my successor, my replacement."

"Me? How would I replace you? I don't know what the bracelet looks like and have never been at your village."

"I know, but I must take the chance. I feel it is the thing to do, and the old wisdom that was passed to me tells me it is possible. The way the pendant reacts to you, and to my touch now, is very strong. I'm sure the crystal is flickering at the cave, it must be giving hope to the community, to Norw."

"Why you never returned, asked for their help, explained what happened."

"I can't. Unless I have the a bracelet and pendant together I can go back. Having only one is like a one way ticket, you can only go out. Once both, the pendant and bracelet are out the crystal fades, it only flickers in the cave. That is why Norw could not follow, there is only one crystal left, his. Norw could have come out if my crystal was still lighted, but it is not. Only the elders can open the door between the two worlds, the two realms, leave and come, bring or take things or people with them. The energy feeds the community. I left them in darkness, hoping to help, restore balance... they will perish and with that, one of the oldest, if not the oldest, culture will vanish."

"I understand. But me ...?"

"Serge, you have proven your worth in the few days I have known you. I have been outside for twenty years and have never felt this way about another person. I was ashamed and hopeless until I met you. If you find the bracelet you can go back to them, light my crystal, then come back to find the missing third crystal. Most importantly, you could help Norw with his replacement, who I'm sure is now a very old man. Time there passes faster in our minds ... somehow my kids grew to be five and seven in two years. Norw must name a successor soon, but there is no crystal light to back up the community. They can't do this in darkness."

"What do I need to do?"

"Just open your heart and receive my pendant, look for the bracelet, and give an old woman the hope of life. I still feel them, somehow I do."

She held both his hands with hers, drew him closer and as they embraced, she transferred the pendant from her neck to his. Serge immediately felt the warmth of the link between them; it was from heart to heart. There was an energy that moved through him, but he also felt a void.

Nana was crying. Serge was unsure what to do. He continued to hold her. "Nana, are you all right?"

"Yes, son, I'll be all right. Don't worry, I won't die like my predecessor. I'm incomplete but now I have hope. I'm mortal again as I was before and will die when I'm supposed to … This is uncharted territory; we are writing history. This is what is so important. Please, Serge, find the bracelet and save them. I know I'm placing a big burden on you, but it is my only and last hope."

"I'll try as hard as I can, Nana. I hope I can prove the trust you have placed in me. I'm not sure what to do next, but when I finish with this trip and return Alexa and Jimmy home, I'll come back and do this."

"Serge, it will be hard for you to leave Belize…. The pendant's strength depends on proximity to the crystal and to the bracelet. If you go far you'll feel very empty. It has been hard for me here, but I know I'm not that far away, because the emptiness I feel is not unbearable. Be careful: the crystal energy is something that can fill your life as well as drain it to the soul. I'm sorry. I should have told you."

"There is nothing to apologize for, there'll be a way."

The two shadowy figures witness the change in flickering energy from the crystal: now it was stronger, but paced at longer intervals. The young woman runs out of the cave. The old man falls to his knees and weeps.

Escape

Serge left Nana at home, resting on her bed. She looked tired and anxious; she felt she had lost her cause. The pendant had given her comfort and now she did not have even that. In sympathy, Serge had made tea for her, and reaffirmed his commitment. He drove from San Luis holding the pendant on his chest; somehow stroking it gave him peace and strength. The way back felt easier, and without thinking about which road to take, he arrived at San Ignacio in minutes. He decided not to turn on his GPS unit yet. He wanted to be sure that everything was well.

He parked a block away from the theater, grabbed the GPS unit and jogged the rest of the way. He paused at the last intersection, looking for Dantz's team, but saw nothing irregular. The outside of the theater was quiet. One of the Foundation SUVs was parked close to the main entrance. He walked cautiously to the back of the building, where he found the big pickup truck he had seen the night before, parked by the service door. He checked the adjacent buildings' windows and roofs: no one was in sight.

Then, from the corner of his eye, he noticed movement behind the truck. Two men were carrying something big wrapped in black trash bags and secured with duct tape. By the size and shape, Serge guessed it was a body. He was alarmed, he thought about Alexa. Serge recognized one of the henchmen of the man with the pony tail. When one of the men made a movement to clean his hands of dust, and arranged his shirt and jacket, Serge saw he was carrying a gun, the same 9 mm that Dantz's man had been cleaning the night before. The men entered the theater service door, laughing. Something was going on.

Serge ran around the back of the building, looking for a side door, but it was locked from the inside. He tried to force it open it with no luck. He had to move fast: whatever was going to happen would be

185

happening at any moment. He ran to the back again, then with caution moved to the tall pickup truck. He climbed to the back and checked the bag. It was clearly a dead body. He took a knife from his key ring and opened the black plastic wrapping. He saw the fabric of a jacket, a hand, and a diver's wristwatch. He recognized the watch from one of Dantz men, the driver of the second SUV, he had noticed the diver's watch when they met. They even exchanged a few words about diving certification and best places to dive. Serge was alarmed, if this was one of Dantz men and he had been eliminated, who else was on his side?

He reached inside and searched the corpse's pockets, he found what he was looking for, the second SUV keys. He checked for weapons but found none. He had left his own gun in his vehicle, parked van a block away. He regretted that, then thought about it: he was no match for three or six armed men. His best option was to get Alexa and Jimmy out and away.

Serge entered the back of the theater, and heard an amplified woman's voice announcing names, interrupted by applause. He still had time. The two men from the pickup truck stood in the wings, watching the stage. Serge grabbed a service cap and jacket from a nail on a wood column and put them on, found a box of brochures to carry, and in this disguise walked naturally behind the men, not even looking back at them. He did not know if they would recognize him, but Dantz and his team would. He found the side door and checked its lock, which was just a steel pin with a wire. He removed it and slowly opened the door. The SUV was parked forty feet away. He closed the door without locking it, walked to the auditorium door and from the side of the stage area he peered inside to see where everyone was. He was on the same level as the first row of seats where Jimmy was with Stephan, sleeping with his toy elephant on his lap. Alexa sat smiling at center stage, listening to the speaker on the podium, and applauding with the crowd.

To the side of the stage he saw one of Dantz's men. One dead, two were missing: one was probably by the front entrance, and Dantz must be with the ponytail guy, but where? There was only one way to find out. He took out his GPS unit but decided not to turn it on, not yet. He opened the memory card compartment and removed it; he would use the GPS unit to his advantage. Serge turned it on, and on the display saw the indicator for Dantz's unit, coinciding with the theater building: Dantz was nearby. Serge scanned the audience again, methodically he started from the front and combed with his eyes each row until he found him, third row first seat on the right, a short distance from the stage.

The theater was fully seated and some people were standing in the side aisles. Serge could not pick out the pony tail guy. He accessed the settings of his GPS unit, hoping that Dantz was not looking at his own unit. He disabled the feature that allowed the unit to be tracked and then dismantled the access buttons, making it incapable of modification but still displaying the information; the screen froze on the theater location with the two indicator dots merged. He walked up through the outside corridor up to the theater lobby, took the jacket and cap off and enter again, walking down the right side aisle, knelt by Dantz and touched his shoulder in a friendly gesture. He whispered: "Hey, Dantz, I'm back. What is going on?"

Dantz was startled. He turned around and looked up, recognized Serge. "Nothing. Everything is as scheduled. Where were you?"

"I went to the hotel, had an upset stomach, needed some Pepto. Not feeling too good."

"I checked for your signal. You were nowhere to be found; my men even checked the hostel."

Serge knew it was a risky move and probably he was caught in a lie, but he had to play along. "Well, I was there. Not sure if I wanted to be found where I was, not with my pants down. Have you checked your GPS unit?"

Serge took his out, confirmed that the signals were merged, and with a hand gesture asked for Dantz's unit. Dantz held his unit for Serge to see; the two displays were almost the same. Before Dantz could react, Serge grabbed the device and, turning away, switched the units, apologizing as he did to a man standing in the aisle, as if he had stepped on him. He hoped Dantz did not see the switch.

He gave Dantz the disabled unit, saying, "Looks fine. Not sure what happened. Let's check them. They were supposed to be trouble free. Let's check them before leaving here."

Dantz looked annoyed, but Serge did not care. All along he had not liked him. "I'll be back. I want to apologize to Alexa for being gone." Alexa had spotted him and smiled at him.

Serge walked to the side of the stage and entered the wings behind the side curtains. He located a panel of light control switches and counted the steps to it. He moved backstage, saw the two killers on the other side of the stage, avoiding making eye contact. Still no pony tail guy. The auditorium lights had been dimmed and a spotlight illuminated only the speaker. Serge walked across the stage at a crouch, hoping the light did not reveal him. He reached Alexa.

"Hey, Serge, very good to see ..." He did not allowed her to finish, whispering: "Please listen carefully. We need to move out, right now." He slid the SUV keys he had taken from the dead man onto her lap and continued explaining.

"Don't turn now, but on your left there are two guys, brown jacketed and with broad moustaches. Not of the theater crew, bad guys, saw them yesterday with Dantz. Don't ask, I'll explain later. When I give you the signal, which will be me rubbing my forehead, I want you to briefly excuse yourself, then walk to the side of the stage to your right. Once you reach the wings walk up through the service corridor, about thirty feet and you'll find a side door. It is unlocked."

"Jimmy …"

"I'll get him on my way out. You go out the side door, where you'll find one of our vehicles. I hope these are the keys, but if they are not, run as fast as you can and hide at the first open restaurant you find, and I'll meet you there. If the keys work, turn on the engine, open all the windows and drive to the side door. Thirty seconds later I'll be running out with Jimmy. Be sure to unlock the doors. Once we are in, press the pedal full to the floor and head to the street. We'll turn left, and in the next block we will switch places and I'll drive. Now act normal and wait for my signal, then be quick."

Alexa kept smiling, while Serge made apologetic expressions then walked offstage. He checked on Dantz and the killers, everything looked normal. He waited a couple of minutes, then making eye contact with Alexa he rubbed his forehead.

The next minute lasted a lifetime to Serge. Alexa discreetly stood up and walked to the side of the stage. The two killers stood talking and either thought she was someone else or that this was part of the program; Alexa continued through the corridor until she found the side door and walked out.

Alexa was blinded momentarily in the intense sunlight, but once adjusted she located the SUV and hurried toward it. Serge made sure Alexa was out, then turned to Dantz, who had been following her with his eyes, no doubt wondering where she was going. Serge looked at Jimmy, still asleep, right by Stephan. He estimated the number of steps to him, and walked back to the electrical controls. He closed his eyes and counted to twenty, then killed the energy to the whole theater, which went dark.

Serge opened his eyes, partially adjusted to the darkness. He quickly traced his steps, touching the edge of the side curtains to guide himself. He imagined the distance to Jimmy, and entered the auditorium in a crouch. All around him he heard the sounds of surprise and giggles from kids; the master of ceremonies shouted for everyone to remain seated, that power would soon be restored.

Serge found the front row of seats and grabbed a knee. He continued two more seats and felt the softness of Jimmy's elephant. He found the boy's neck and legs and lifted him to his chest, walking immediately to the side door. He hoped Alexa was there, otherwise it was going to be a mad dash, running with a little boy in his arms to who knows where. He stepped out and saw Alexa at the wheel of the SUV with its windows and side door open.

He jumped in and shouted, "Let's go! go, go, go!"

The SUV accelerated to the street, no wheel burning but fast enough, then turned left toward the main road out of town. Inside the theater the power was restored. Dantz could not see Alexa or Jimmy; he shouted to the two killers and issued commands on his radio.

"We got a problem. They're gone. Fast, to the exits and check the roads!"

The killers ran to the back door, and as they exited they saw the SUV moving out. While one radioed for assistance, the other took out a handgun and started shooting.

"They are leaving in a SUV, south side!"

Dantz heard the shots, shouted to anyone who could hear, "Stop shooting, stop shooting! We want them alive!" He ran to the theater entrance, pushing through the startled audience who were now filling the aisles. "Move, move!" he shouted frantically. "Everyone to the vehicles. We are moving out, south road, heading to the main road out!"

The big pickup truck with the two killers roared and headed after Serge and Alexa; the other SUV caught up a few seconds later, Dantz and the two body guards on board. San Ignacio streets were not made for motorized vehicles, much less for big, fast moving vehicles. Alexa tried to steer without knowing where to go but forward.

"Serge, what is going on?!"

"I'm not sure. Steve, one of Dantz men, the driver of the second SUV was killed. Dantz has been acting strange, meeting with other men here. They were going to do something, I assume kidnap you or Jimmy, ask for ransom, take revenge, who knows?"

A couple of bullets ricocheted off the vehicle, making a "thump" sound. They crouched in their seats, Alexa lost sight of the road and hit an adobe guard barrier, braking it in pieces. The SUV jumped and slowed. Serge shouted, "We need to switch places!" Another thump.

"Dantz went missing last night, so I followed him with the GPS unit. I found him with three very suspicious guys; it did not feel right. This morning when I came back from Nana's, I found them surrounding the theater, watching all the exits but the one you took."

"But why? Dantz was highly recommended, clean. Why now?"

"You never know … At the next corner, turn left and stop. I'll drive."

Jimmy had woken up, restless and startled, the face of fear started to show on him. Alexa turned left and braked to a complete stop. Serge jumped out and ran around to the driver's side, while Alexa slid over to the passenger side with Jimmy. She had not taken the SUV out of gear, and it started moving when she released her foot from the brake. Serge struggled to get behind the wheel, and was still not seated properly when the pickup truck rammed them from behind. Serge took the impact on his side; Alexa and Jimmy crashed against the dashboard. The pickup had hit a glancing blow to the SUV, then a wall, and now blocked the street, motionless. The pursuers of the pickup truck were not expecting them to stop on the corner, the driver took an evasive action by reflex but hit the van and a wall, stopping almost completely. The momentum of the impact moved Serge's van forward, diminishing the damage to the vehicle but sending him backwards.

Serge was still holding the steering wheel. He pulled himself erect in the seat, put his foot to the accelerator and pressed to the bottom: the engine roared. They were free but slowed by the damage from the collision. One rear tire was touching metal as it turned; it would surely break in a minute or less. Serge felt the friction building; the sound of metal rubbing, the smell of rubber burning. He pushed the engine and started moving fast. He looked for the rear view mirror but it was gone, he had knocked it off when they were rammed, he found only a cracked windshield. He looked in his side mirror and saw a cloud of white smoke from the damaged tire. He saw the pickup truck still motionless back at the corner, blocking the street. A few seconds later, Dantz's vehicle reached them and had to stop. Shots were fired. Serge crouched but looked through the steering wheel to the street ahead.

Dust was being lifted from the trail they were leaving. Tourists and locals shouted for caution as they drove fast through the streets, hitting fruit stands and bicycles, other cars.

"We need to find the way to the hotel, then out to the main road to Belize City."

Serge handed the GPS unit to Alexa, instructed her to text the emergency code and to activate the emergency locator beacon. A red light confirmed continuous sending of a distress signal to Lightman Industries.

"Let's hope they get this message and send some help," Alexa said. "What about Dantz's unit?"

"I took care of it. They can't use it to find us."

Dantz saw them leaving, he saw the trail of smoke and knew they could not go much farther. He checked his GPS unit, saw one bright dot still at the theater, and the other locator not visible at all. He tried to reboot the device, and discovered the jammed controls.

"Damn! Son of a bitch!" He threw the unit at Serge's vehicle in frustration. "We need to get them. Move this trash from here!"

The big pickup truck was totaled. Dantz used his SUV to move it to the side. The pickup driver jumped in with Dantz; the other man never got out. They speeded up, trying to follow the trail of smoke in front of them.

Serge and Alexa had reached the street of the hotel; they knew which way out of San Ignacio. Serge checked his side mirror while speeding up, no pursuers in sight, but the smoke and the smell of burning rubber were increasing,

"Alexa, grab Jimmy and stay down!" She held Jimmy close in her arms, the GPS unit in one hand. Her knuckles were white with tension but she continued comforting her son.

The road to the hotel was straight, and wider than the others. Serge saw the end of the road and the entrance to the town 100 feet ahead, they passed the hotel at best speed; they were nearly out of town. Serge knew that they could ask Nana for help, that she would hide them. They just had to make it to the jungle and use the GPS unit to find her village. Dantz would never find them without a working unit. Suddenly the left rear tire blew and the SUV wiggled.

"Hold on!" The vehicle swayed increasingly from side to side. Serge tried desperately to counter the movement with the steering wheel and reflexively pressed the brake pedal, which made things worse. The brakes were uneven and he released them, but it was too late. The SUV moved suddenly to the left and was about to roll. It crossed the opposite lane and hit a parked car, bounced back to vertical. It made a violent 180-degree spin, and came to a stop facing the direction they had come from. The cloud of smoke and dust caught up to them. Serge had hit the side of his head and was disoriented. Alexa came out from the floor in front of the seat with Jimmy, who was crying now.

"Serge, Serge! Are you all right? Serge!"

He turned to her and slowly came back to his senses. He tried to open his door but it was jammed. Alexa's door was so close to a parked car that it was useless. Serge climbed out through the window, fell hard to the street. He stood up by reflex, still disoriented, and looked to the sides, through the dust and smoke.

"Hurry, we must go."

Alexa gave Jimmy into Serge's hands then she climbed out without difficulty. "Oh Serge, what are we going to do?"

"Out to the jungle. We'll lose them there. You have the GPS unit?"

"I don't have it!"

Serge looked inside, saw it on the floor. He opened the back door and climbed in, reached and retrieved it.

"Let's go!" They ran down the road, out of town. The jungle-forest was in sight.

Dantz had reached the main road to the hotel. He saw the cloud of smoke at the end of the road, the wrecked SUV.

"Good," he said, "if they are not unconscious they will be on foot."

Waterfall

Serge ran holding Jimmy who was hugging his elephant and crying. "It's ok, Jimmy, we'll be home soon, ok? Don't worry." He tried to keep Alexa's speed, but his bleeding head and the weight of Jimmy made it hard. He was having difficulty breathing and was almost sure he had a broken rib.

"You're hurt bad, Serge, give me Jimmy."

"No, don't stop, or they'll catch up. There." He signaled to a small trail and they ran into the jungle. Once in concealment, they proceeded slowly, moving branches aside and looking for a clearing to orient themselves.

Dantz reached the crash site. The dust had receded but smoke from the engine was still significant. The air was filled with the smell of burning rubber, oil, and dry soil. He and his men got out of their vehicle, weapons drawn, and saw that the crashed SUV was empty. They saw blood inside, and a trail of blood on the road.

Dantz said, "They're heading to the jungle. You get your boss on the radio and ask for help. We're going to need a good search party, ASAP." He gave a radio to the pickup driver, signaled the other two and ran toward the town's exit.

Alexa and Serge had reached a clearing. There was a small opening in the jungle canopy, where sunlight came all the way down. They stopped, and Serge asked Alexa for the GPS unit. He accessed its memory, displayed Nana's house as a blue dot, then checked where they were: perhaps thirty minutes away, walking at this speed. Not enough time, Serge thought, Dantz must be coming very close. He signaled to Alexa, and they continued on the trail. After three hundred feet, he stopped.

"Wait!" He gave Jimmy to Alexa and handed her the GPS unit. "This is where we are, this is Nana's home. You run as fast as you can on this trail until you reach this point." He pointed at dots on the screen. Alexa held Jimmy, his head on her shoulder, her hand on his head.

"What are you talking about? We can make it together."

"No, we can't. I'm going to slow them down, create a diversion."

"You can't leave me now, not in the middle of the jungle. You can make it, too." She was shouting. He placed his finger on her mouth and calmed her.

"You know this is the best bet. Don't lose any more time.

"But Serge," she cried, "I can't make it on my own. And what about you?"

"Oh yes, you can make it. You must. I have seen that you are a very strong woman. It is not that far, you can't get lost. Follow the dot, you'll be there in less than thirty minutes. If you don't go, you and Jimmy will not be safe. I don't know what their plans are. You know this is the only way, now hurry."

He gave her the GPS unit. "I already sent the emergency message but once you reach Nana's home and things have settled again, you activate the beacon. Your dad will send the cavalry and you and Jimmy will be safe. Then you can send a search party for me. It will be easier for me to move by myself, knowing that you both are safe."

He turned to Jimmy. "Hey, buddy, can I borrow your friend to help me out?"

197

Little Jimmy's red eyes looked at Serge from his mom's shoulder. He breathed deeply and in the most natural way handed Serge his elephant. "He can help," Jimmy told him.

"Thank you, Jimmy. I'll take care of Mr. Elephant." He reached for Jimmy's feet and took one shoe off. Alexa did not know what was going on. "Now go! Don't stop for anything." He gave her a kiss on her cheek and turned in the direction she was supposed to go, pushing her. "Go!"

He ran cautiously back down the trail toward the road in the same direction they had come. He was very cautious first, but after two hundred feet he stopped and returned to the clearing, breaking branches and leaving stains of his blood on the leaves. Twenty feet from the clearing, he cut a piece of his shirt and placed it on a thorn. After several more feet, he dropped the elephant then continued, making the trail wider. He reached the clearing and reviewed his work. He could hear shouts in the distance. They were coming fast and closing on him. He turned ninety degrees from the trail and walked inside the thick jungle, very cautious not to leave a trail. He turned and bent a single branch at eye level, walked a few more steps inside the jungle and left another bent twig, daubed with blood. He threw Jimmy's shoe on the ground, then ran for his life.

Dantz and the two henchmen reached the clearing a few minutes later. They saw the trail continued and started running in the same direction, they found the traces of blood, the cloth, and the elephant.

"They are becoming sloppy," said one of the men.

Dantz held Jimmy's stuffed elephant in his hand, thinking suspiciously. "Too sloppy … This is too obvious. You," he directed his men, "run up the trail and see if you find any other traces. A hundred feet tops, don't go very far."

"We are going to lose them."

"No, they have a kid, and they're injured. They won't go far, but I have a hunch ... this is not right." He searched the clearing with his trained eye, and after a few minutes shouted, "Bingo. Nice move, Serge."

He had found the first tweaked branch. His men returned. "The trail narrows ahead. Not that many traces."

Dantz said, "Never mind. We are moving in this direction. Keep your eyes sharp."

They moved into the jungle and after a while found the other blood traces, then Jimmy's shoe "We're on the right track. Let's move!" Dantz ordered.

The three men continued on Serge's path, giving Alexa and Jimmy the chance to find Nana and be safe.

Serge moved forward, but he was not sure he was not going in circles. It was very easy to get disoriented in this thick jungle. From time to time, he stopped to break a branch, though he was sure that if they were behind him, they would be finding traces that he was not aware of leaving. He found a small stream and followed it down, hoping to find a river and then a town. Moving in the stream was smoother than through the thick vegetation, and after fifteen minutes of walking and running he found a river. He continued downstream along its bank. There was almost no vegetation on the riverbanks, so he could move faster. He was tired, breathing was difficult. All this time he had been touching the bear figure on his chest, finding some strength in it. He hoped Alexa had made it. Suddenly he heard voices through the jungle, behind him, and he started running.

Alexa came to a place that the GPS unit indicated was Nana's location, but she was still on a trail She walked a little farther and came to an opening, saw the entrance to San Luis. She smiled and breathed deeply. All the time she had been looking back, hoping Serge was going to catch up with them. It never happened. She entered the desolated part of the town, Jimmy asleep on her shoulder. She was bruised, dirty and wet, anxious and tired, but in control. Nana saw them from her garden and ran out. Alexa stopped and activated the emergency beacon.

"What is wrong, my dear?" Nana said with honest concern. Alexa fell into Nana's arms and started crying.

*   *   *

In Seattle, Bob Lightman's cell phone rang: his office was briefing him regularly. Since they received the first emergency signal. His staff had already arranged for the Foundation's office in Belize to scramble a rescue team, apparently it was already on the way to San Ignacio. Lightman had become very anxious since the first signal. Mama had joined him at his office after the first message, she assured him that his daughter and grandson were all right because the text message that followed the beacon activation:
"I'm fine. Jimmy is with me. Dantz and Co failed kidnapping us. Serge saved us but he is lost, this is his last known location. Will prefer to stay here until sure who we can trust, then will help in the search." The message included a set of coordinates.

*   *   *

Dantz and his men reached the river. He became concerned, because there was only one set of footprints. "There's something wrong. There's only one set of tracks. We might have overlooked something," he said.

"They might be running on the water, parallel to the river as a diversion, with the kid carried by one of them."

"Perhaps. Keep looking." Dantz contacted Pony tail guy on the radio. There was a lot of interference but he got through. A small chopper and five more men would be joining their effort.

Serge knew his pursuers were getting close, the splashes of their steps in water and their shouts were now more audible. He had been running for more than an hour. He took his shoes off and entered the shallow river to disguise his tracks, but found it difficult to walk, much less run, on the rocky bed. He remembered Jimmy beating him when they raced from Nana's place to their vehicle. He smiled at the thought; If Alexa and Jimmy only knew that the little guy had really beat him running on the rocks... He decided to put his shoes back on and continue along the riverbank.

He fastened his shoes and stood up. There was a loud gunshot, and a streak of water rising beside him. He turned and saw Dantz and his two men running toward him. Serge started running, too. A couple more shots followed, but missed him. Serge did not turn back. He ran along the sandy bank, trying to get some speed. The men followed him.

The river became more agitated, shallower and with a faster current. Abruptly, the river divided into two into two branches; one shallow and fast and the other deep and wide. Serge decided to follow the shallower for speed, but realized that he had made a mistake. heard a thunderous sound, rising in volume. He had come to Big Rock Falls, a 150-foot waterfall on the Privassion River that ran through San

Ignacio and Santa Clara. He was at a dead end, trapped, with only one way out. He had to jump into the abyss or give up.

Dantz was within shouting distance. "I believe there's no way out for you. Serge, give it up. Where is the bitch and the kid?"

"Use your GPS unit, that will tell you," Serge taunted. He backed to the edge of the waterfall. While not afraid of heights, the scale and sound of the waterfall were intimidating and diving had never been his sport of choice.

"That's funny. I'll try to remember that when I'm asking their location with my bare hands." The men walked towards him, spread out and guns drawn, aiming at him.
"What's the matter?" Serge shouted. "You lost the tracks? I thought you were a resourceful Marine. Planning an early retirement, perhaps?" He looked over his shoulder again at the cliff edge, took a few steps towards Dantz, then turned and ran. They realized he intended to jump and fired a barrage of bullets. There was no turning back.

Serge reached the edge, landed his left foot on the dry side of a large, sunken green rock, and as he found his footing to jump, a bullet hit his left calf just beneath his knee. He lost momentum and height but his speed was enough to carry him over the falls. He shouted in fear, imagining that he was going to crash into the closest rocks.

Serge descended, spinning and covered with white water. The noise around him was a roar that lasted a lifetime. He felt an endless, slow motion fall into a void, with images of his life passing in front of him. His last thoughts were of Max and Stephanie, and he felt strangely peaceful. His eyes saw only a disoriented commotion of blue sky, the white wall of water, and the dark green river bottom. He impacted the water surface on his back and shoulder, was sucked into the waterfall's vortex. Serge felt an urgent need to breathe. He felt the water surface on his head and was able to pull a brief gasp of air then was sucked back in. He knew it would take a few seconds for him to pop up again, but was not sure how long he could hold his breath or will to survive. He thought that it was going to be ironic to survive a bullet and a waterfall, only to drown, pinned down under the water's backwash's persistent pressure. He extended his body, hoping that his limbs might reach the bottom, a floating branch, anything he could hang on to that would stop his spinning.

Just when he was about to give up, Serge felt his hands touch something like a rope or a soft root. He extended his arms again, opening and closing his hands, hoping he could hang on to it. He was dizzy and disoriented, about to give up, when suddenly he grabbed it again, definitely a piece of rope. He held tight with his right hand, then his left. He felt the pull of the water sucking him up but he was no longer spinning. Using both hands he pulled himself forward, but he felt he was going deeper, his legs still sucked by the current but he was leaving the vortex behind. He felt the edge of a rock, continued pulling. The noise and movement of water and movement diminished; this allowed him some sense of orientation. He was underneath a rock that started to slide up, hopefully to the surface, to some air.

Serge continued pulling until he felt his hands break the surface. He instinctively pushed his head out of the water and heaved a big breath. He felt the sudden rush of oxygen in his head. Dizzy and tired, he opened his eyes to a dark, quiet space. A faint trace of light entered from beneath him, from his entry point, enough to see that the only way out was back through the waterfall. The ripples of water on his shoulders, the cold shivers, and the pain in his leg told him that he was still alive. He pulled himself out of the water, breathing heavily; he rested there on his hands and knees. He let go of the rope and fell face first into soft dry sand. He turned to lay on his back, and his right arm hit the edge of a log. He pulled himself into a sitting position and rested his back against the log. To his side he felt a bundle of dried ropes; he moved it away. Now only his feet remained in the water.

Serge lifted his left leg and felt the pain, felt the warmth of the blood coming out. He pulled up his pant leg to reveal the wound. In the minimal light he was only able to see a black stain, but he traced the wound with his fingers and felt a strong pain. The wound was wide: he felt torn skin and muscle, a loose piece hanging by the wound. He cupped water in his hands and tried to clean the wound as best as he could, squirming and crying in pain as he did. He took the loose piece of flesh and instinctively placed it in the opening, filling the void. He felt along the surface of his calf and found no other wound. He took off his wet shirt and knotted it around his calf, then applied pressure to the wound. He hoped that would stop the bleeding and close the wound. He was exhausted and needed to rest; he closed his eyes and fell asleep.

Dantz and his men stood at the edge of the falls. They looked for Serge's body but did not see it resurface. There was only what appeared to be a faint trace of blood on the water that diluted almost instantaneously. "No one survives such a fall," one of the men said.

Dantz said, "He was shot before falling, and it will be hard for him to swim in this current … if he survived. In any case, this is our only lead. We don't rest until we find him or his body. Call the rest of the men to this location."

In San Luis, in Nana's house, Alexa set the GPS unit on the table and sat down. Nana was at her side, holding her hand. Jimmy was outside, barefooted, playing with Jonas and Lou. Alexa broke down and started to cry. She found shelter on Nana's shoulder and let herself go as she had not since she was a young girl.

The Find

Hours later but with the dim light of the afternoon still illuminating the cave through the waterfall opening, Serge awoke with shivers and a strong pain in his leg. He released the makeshift tourniquet a little until the numbness receded, he felt his wound for any new bleeding: it seemed ok. He felt pain with every beat of his heart but it receded, he then applied pressure again.

By now he could see a little more and could make out the size of the cave. It was about six feet tall and ten feet wide; the opening to the waterfall was five feet long and wide. On the water surface little bubbles from the near waterfall filtered light from the outside, making small traceable ripples on the water. Serge turned his attention to the log and felt a straight edge, then a hollow core: it was a native-style, carved wooden canoe; the jumble of ropes had come out of it. His chest was suddenly very warm, unusually warm; he reached for the bear pendant, which was hot. Somehow, as if instinctively, Serge felt compelled to get closer to the canoe. He painfully tried to get up, placing his weight on his left knee and extending his right. He reached inside the canoe, looking for anything helpful. If the only way out of this cave was through the waterfall, then he could try to improvise an escape using the rope and the buoyancy of the canoe. His hands felt what seemed to be bones of a foot. He let go and sat back down.

The old man looks at the crystal, flickering with an intensity not seen in many years, he begins to feel a deep sense of connection. Suddenly he springs into action, knowing he does not have much time. With the agility of his younger years, pulling strength from his hope, he runs to the deep Cenote's entrance. At the edge of the water he looks up to the blue sky. This part of the Cenote is very deep, the water crystal and transparent at the edges but deep blue at the center. The old man walks upon the water's surface but there are no ripples from his steps. At the center of the Cenote, his arms extend to the sky, his eyes close and he begins to levitate. A trace of light shines from his necklace's pendant, a stone figure of a crow. He rises to the surface, suspended in mid air above the Cenote's center. He continues concentrating, eyes shut, arms extended, legs straight. His forehead furrowed, he reaches, provokes, communicates ...

Serge again felt an urgent need to reach inside the canoe. He thought to hear a voice saying, *"Reach inside, reach it, reach it ..."* In the faint light he traced the skeleton's shape, he felt the leg bones and then a leathery surface, what seemed to be the garment used by this person. He realized he had found two embraced skeletons, still wearing ornamental jewelry. One seemed to be holding the other on its chest. At the other end of the canoe Serge finds a curved leather bag with loose leather strips and embroiled decorations, with a long shoulder strap.

Again he felt the impulse:. *"Reach inside, reach it, reach it ..."* Serge moved closer, making an effort to put his weight on the healthy leg. He tried not to disturb the skeletons as he moved to the end of the canoe and reached inside for the bag. As he opened it, the impulse increased; he touched the soft smooth surface of an object the size of a pear: he felt a connection to it. He felt another object, moved his hand and traced it with his fingers. It was cold and long ... *"Reach inside, reach it, reach it ..."* Suddenly the surface felt warm and then hot, He grabbed it with his hand and took it out. He studied it: a cylindrical-conical shape, seven inches in length. There was an inscription on it, barely visible in the dim light, and an indentation, where something could fit in. He thought he heard a voice repeating, *"Wear it ... wear it, place it on your left arm, wear it ..."* The impulse he felt to place it on his arm was very strong. It seemed like he was being told to do something but at the same time he felt a need to do it .

He did not know if he was dreaming or hallucinating. Nothing felt real anymore. He was suppose to be looking for a way out, but at this moment he was acting as if he was a little kid in a candy store, exploring the mysterious cave without regard for his precarious situation. He held the object with his right hand, and as if trying it to find the best fit, he simulated placing it on his left arm. It seemed that it could fit. *"Do it, wear it … put it on, do it, do it, put it on …"* He lowered the object onto his forearm. The sensation, the warmth increased, and in an instant he felt the object embracing his forearm with its two sides closing upon him. From the upper side of the bracelet a claw shaped edge grew and closed on the inside of his arm. He felt a strong pinch, then excruciating pain. It felt as if a transfusion blood needle had been placed in his arm. The pain increased, now with a sense of numbness. He moved his arm upward, shook it to take it off, tried to grab it with his right hand but it felt too hot to touch. He looked at it, afraid, disoriented, dizzy, his mind racing with strange images and visions from the past or future. He began to hallucinate, everything moved around him. With his right hand he grabbed his left by the wrist, pulling it close to his chest. He instantly felt an electric shock all through his body and lost consciousness. His left forearm wore the conical shaped object. Its indentation matched his pendant which now lay embedded and fused inside this object … an arm bracelet.

Not far from Serge, suspended above a Cenote, the old man finally released his effort. "Yes … at last. Yes!" he exclaimed, starting to cry. He had completed his purpose. Exhausted and completely drained he descended down to the Cenote, away from this world. He knew he had been seen but had to take the risk, to stay there until the connection was made. Inside the Cenote, the light now was intense. There were four bases, two with crystals: one shining steadily, the other shining with an outstanding intensity. The whole cave was illuminated, showing the magnificence of its construction. Light reflected from the crystalline walls and onto the ceiling, from where it was channeled through the center to the rest of the cave system. The young woman entered the chamber, and amazed by the light she shouted excitedly to someone outside. She looked for the old man, then realized what might be happening. Continuing to shout to others, she ran toward the Cenote's entrance.

*   *   *

A green military Huey helicopter flies toward San Ignacio, where at the north edge of town there is an improvised airstrip. A young woman is in the pilot's seat. She and the copilot and a man seated behind them are wearing military uniforms. There are two other passengers dressed in civilian clothes, one of them wearing the logo of the Lightman Foundation on the lapel of his jacket. The copilot suddenly breaks the silence: "What the hell? Look down there, by the Cenote, nine o'clock!"

The pilot adjusts the helicopter's pitch in that direction, and one of the passengers notices in the middle of the jungle a huge clearing, the entrance of a Cenote, and a human figure suspended above it, floating in mid air. "What is that?"

The helicopter levels flight and moves to fly over it the Cenote. The pilot rotates the helicopter to the left, curving in an arch and gaining altitude, but when it returns to the Cenote entrance there is nothing to be seen.

"What are we looking for?"

"What I saw was a man, or a human figure, suspended in mid air, arms extended. But he was suspended in mid air!"

"Yes, I was able to see just a glimpse of him. but it was too fast. I lost sight of the Cenote with the turn and I can't see him anymore."

The helicopter hovered over the Cenote entrance, those on board looking for an explanation: perhaps it was an explorer climbing on an interior wall, a shadow or a mirage on the water surface. Suddenly they noticed a smaller Bell helicopter flying from the north in their direction. It was flying at low altitude along the Privassion River. The Huey pilot tried to make radio contact with the other aircraft but there was no response. The helicopter, painted black and gold but with no distinctive markings, was definitely flying a search pattern.

"That is unusual," said the pilot. "There were no other aircraft scheduled to be flying in this area today. We are aware of certain drug routes in Belize where traffickers venture into deeper areas of the jungle to avoid detection before reaching the permeable boundaries of Guatemala and Mexico, but this is way too far to the east." The copilot logged their location and radioed for instructions: a plane would later be scrambled to the area to search for the mysterious helicopter or for flight permission verification. They returned to their search above the Cenote, but could not find anything. After five more runs they record the unexplainable event in their log, but with no positive confirmation it would soon be forgotten. The Huey gained speed and proceeded to San Ignacio.

*   *   *

The old man rested at the base of the Cenote. He was wearing a broad smile when the young woman arrived. She helped him move out of sight of a passing helicopter. Although he was very weak his mood reflected the same excitement that was apparent in the young woman's face. When their eyes met she nodded and he closed his eyes, saying, "Yes …" Other members of the community arrived; a broad shouldered man with long black hair and a Spartan look stood by the side of the old man. "Father." The old man opened his eyes again and smiled. He placed his left arm on the young man's neck and head, his arm bracelet with the crow's indentation reflected his image. His right hand touched his pendant.

"Aio, there'll be a transfer after all." He smiled broadly again. "She did it. I know she did it."

"Nana?"

"Yes, and someone else."

The next day Serge woke up inside the waterfall's cave. Almost twelve hours had passed since he found the bracelet; it had been sixteen hours since his fall. He had a strong headache and was disoriented. He barely remembered where he was, but the pain in his left leg had receded. With both hands he touched his head, then his leg, then noticed the bracelet on his left arm. It did not hurt anymore. It blended into his muscles as if it had been custom made. Its smooth surface reflected the dim light coming from under the waterfall, and he could feel and see the patterns on it and the indentation, the same bear shape as his pendant.

Serge checked his watch it: it was almost seven a.m. He wondered if he had lost one day or two. He was thirsty and hungry. With one of his hands he cupped water and drank without hesitation. He then took his pendant and slowly placed it inside the bracelet's indentation, hoping to not be shocked with a thousand volts of electricity. It fitted perfectly, and nothing happened except that a

210

total inner peace came to him. He thought about the mere random event by which he had come to find Nana's pendant, and that hopefully, in some remote area, a crystal was again shining strong. He knew that he could now return this gift to Nana and go back to his life, though it was going to be hard to give it up.

He looked inside the canoe again, and found that one of the skeletons had an arm bracelet on the left arm and what seemed to be a pendant at the bottom of the rib cage. He could not discern its shape but it was almost certainly these were what Nana had described to him as the bracelet and pendant that were taken from her village twenty years ago. For some reason these two persons had adventured on a canoe down a river that seemed calm, making the same mistake he did, never realizing that they were close to a big waterfall until they could not go back, and by then it was too late. After the fall they were trapped as he had been, under the waterfall's eddy. The floating canoe must have escaped the vortex, and they were pulled into the cave by hanging on to it. He had found them in an embrace, they had died tired or injured trapped in the cave. Serge did not know what to make of all this. But he had to find a way out or he would share their fate.

Dantz and Co. were still looking for Serge, it was the second day, one after their failed attempt. The bell helicopter was flying down the river, covering more distance now, looking for a sign of life or a body. If alive he will guide them to Alexa.
Dantz was tracing his steps and guessed that he had been fooled by Serge the day before. He had anticipated his expertise will see the obvious as a decoy and the hidden or almost unperceivable as the right track. If this search gave nothing, he will have to go back to the beginning of the chase, move in the opposite direction at the clearing in the jungle, avoid the diversion and continue for any new lead. He knew he could trace Alexa and the kid as they surely left a trace, but the sooner the better. He left his men in charge of the search and contacted the chopper. A few minutes later he was riding

it with the pony tail guy piloting it. They left for San Ignacio, with luck and after one day, there will still be some traces of their tracks, he might follow her instead of Serge. He knew he did not have too much time left, If Serge had switched the GPS unit, help would be on the way. They have already seen a military helicopter heading to San Ignacio the day before, just 4 hours after the chase. They have heard a lot of radio chatter and movement in town and in the air. They might lose the advantage they had and would have to move to a ground search soon or hide away. He knew he must use this day to its fullest or then go underground.

At Nana's home in San Luis, Alexa received a text message on the GPS unit. "Support team arrived at San Ignacio, awaiting instructions. Search party on the way, government contacted to deal with Dantz and Co. Dad will join you the day after tomorrow." She showed Nana the report. Alexa wondered about Serge and his whereabouts. It had been almost a full day without any news, and she hoped he had made it to safety.

Nana had changed. She no longer had her pendant. Her energy had diminished, though not her determination or wisdom. "I know he is all right. We'll hear about him soon, you'll see."

The afternoon caught up with them. In silence they listened to the sounds of the river, the living jungle, leaves moving to easterly winds that smelled like rain. The following days would determine the future for many people. Without either of them knowing how, Alexa's and Nana's lives would never be the same again.

*   *   *

It was night, and Max was studying in his dorm room at the University of Arizona. The room was Spartan, painted white with a central light fixture that was turned off. The walls were decorated with a collage of photographs from ancient lands and archeological sites. A large calendar hung behind the door, bookshelves were filled with articles, folders, and books. There were a few magazines on the entrance counter. The window was open, the blinds pulled all the way up. The humming of a standing fan disguised sounds from the outside world. The desk and chair and a double bed were the only furniture. Max sat in front of his computer with open books on his desk and a set of earphones plugged to his ears. He received a phone call from Mama.

"Max?"

"Yes, who is this?"

"This is Mama, Mama Chartres from Lightman Industries. I need to talk to you, son."

"Hello Ms. Chartres. My father told me all about you. He's got a deep respect and appreciation for you. What can I do for you?"

"It's about your father …"

"What's wrong? Is he ok?"

"He's missing. We lost contact with him in Belize."

"But …" Max could not speak or think of anything to say. He was still processing the word "missing".

"Your father helped Alexa and little Jimmy escape a kidnapping attempt. We don't know the details yet but a search party has been sent to Belize. We know he saved them. But then they got separated, and they haven't heard from him since yesterday afternoon. I want to assure you that we'll do everything we can to find him and bring him back home safe."

"But what do you mean, 'missing'? Is he dead?" Max found a knot in his throat at the possible affirmation from the other end of the line.

"No. At this time we don't know too much, but we are doing everything we can. Mr. Lightman, the Foundation and all of us will take care of everything. You shouldn't worry. I just wanted to let you know where we are. I know you would have wanted to know."

"Yes, of course, thank you ... You said there was a kidnapping attempt?"

"Almost ten hours ago, Alexa contacted us via text message, not too specific. We're trying to find out more. She simply said that she was fine, that an attempt on her failed, thanks to your dad, and that he was missing since noon today, Belize time. She was at a safe house."

"She didn't say if anyone was injured or where she was?"

"No, but apparently her security team was involved in it. That's all."

"Why?"

"We don't know. Money, perhaps. It'll be ok, you'll see. Let me give you my phone number, and you call me if you need anything at all. We'll take care of you, ok?"

"Thank you. Please contact me as soon as you learn anything. I'll make preparations tonight to fly to Belize, and I'll join your search party. I've been there in the past, my mother used to take us there. I know my way around and can help look for him."

"No need at this time, son. I believe it's better if you stay where you are. I know your dad would be more comfortable if he knew where to find you, and was sure that you are all right."

"I need to be there. I can't stay here and not do anything. I'll make preparations and wait for your call. Please call me as soon as you know anything, please. I'll contact you when I know my travel arrangements to Belize."

"If you insist, son. There's no need, but I understand. Let me know your travel plans ... Hold on." She paused, her hand over the phone's mouthpiece.

"Max, we are sending our plane to pick you up. When do you think you'll be ready?"

"In a couple of hours. Just need to contact my department, pack, and I'll be ready."

"Ok. We'll be there tomorrow morning. Mr. Lightman and I are going, too. We'll contact you when the plane gets near Tucson, pick you up at the airport, and you'll fly to Belize with us. I'll see you tomorrow."

"Thank you very much. I look forward meeting you. Please call me if there's any news, will you? I'll have my cell phone with me at all times."

"Of course. Don't worry, I know your dad is well and good, I can feel it."

"I know, too. He knows how to take care of himself. He better be good or I'll kill him." Max smiled, wiping a tear from his eyes. "Thank you for the call, Ms. Chartres."

"Oh, son, you can call me Mama, and you're welcome. Your father must be proud of you. Have a good night, son."

"Thank you, good night to you too."

Max moved the books away, sat on his chair looking at the pictures on the wall and at his desk. The family photo was at the center, everyone smiling. "Don't take him away from me, please ..."

Max made a few calls to friends and advisors. The first call was to his uncle Al, Al Gadgett, his father's best friend. He gave him a rundown of what Mama had told him, and Gadgett confirmed to Max that he would join him for the trip and help with the search. They planned where to meet, to go together to the airport and then to Belize. An hour had passed since Mama's call. Max was comforted that a close friend was coming with him. He got his backpack from the outside closet and started packing.

Found

In the cave, Serge checked the condition of the leather bag: it was sturdy. He removed the bracelet and pendant from the skeletons and placed them in the bag. He felt the smooth surface of the pear shape object and took it out. He held the crystal in his hand, it felt smooth and cold. It was semi-transparent and shapeless, but it was not ugly. The crystal reflected the dim light that was on the cave in all directions but it was not shining. While its shape was organic its material was transparent, quartz like but with an interior pattern that resembled a mesh or grid like connection system. Serge was intrigued by its complexity, he needed more light to study it but that was not his first priority. He placed it back in the bag and looked around for any other objects inside. He found a small pouch with what appeared to be seeds or small stones; a stone carved knife and a long cord made out of some plant material. He looked for any other relics, but found none. He no longer felt much pain in is injured leg, and when he removed his shirt from around the wound noticed only a horseshoe shaped scar. There was no inflammation, just a dull pain when he applied pressure. He moved his foot, extending it and retracting it, moving his toes. He was able again.

Serge washed his injured leg, then cleaned his blood-soaked shirt as best he could; the water stained every time he rinsed it. He soaked his shirt and applied it to his forehead, he drank some water, then sat on the sand with his arms over his knees. It had been a couple of hours since he awoke and now, more rested, he started looking for a way out. His eyes had adjusted to the low light, and he was able to see a little farther. He explored the cave as best he could and at the far end found an apparently dry passage but it seemed too narrow to move through and was extremely dark. He decided against it, as he was too cold and weak to make the attempt, especially without light.

He noticed another underwater passage where the water was calmer, and there were no bubbles coming out from it. He decided to test the passage beneath the calm water; he grabbed a piece of wood and threw it in that direction. It settled in the water and floated calmly. Serge thought about swimming through this opening to get out, but swimming down could use most of his air, risking drowning. He thought about a diving technique that used weights to go to the bottom and simply swim your way out. He ripped one of his sleeves from his shirt and tied wood and sand in it, testing its buoyancy until he found it neutral. This took him quite some time, but showed him that there were no sucking currents that would trap him inside this passage. He checked his watch. It was 11:00 a.m. perhaps of the next day, since he was feeling hungry but he was not sure what day; his analog watch did not have a calendar.

He tied the canoe ropes to his wrist and went in the water. On his first try he floated too much and surfaced back into the cave, he added sand to his pants and tried again. With each subsequent try he went farther down but his buoyancy gave him a bad time, every time taking his strength, testing his endurance, and making him colder. After five tries he rested for a time, then decided to add more weight to himself. He found a stone that he estimated was heavy enough to neutralize his buoyancy. Holding the stone, he jumped in the water and went straight to the bottom. He opened his eyes and saw a way out, there was light at the end of the passage, perhaps sixty yards away from where he was. He released the rock and swam toward the light. He struggled to swim, bouncing against the ceiling of the cave and fighting his buoyancy. It was very hard to swim downward without hitting himself on the head or losing momentum, wasting energy and air in the process. He panicked, he had no more air. He knew he was not going to make it. He grabbed the rope with both hands and pulled himself back into the cave.

Serge surfaced without air, extremely tired, cold, weak. He had to try again. If he waited longer he would only be weaker. He grabbed the leather bag and placed over his head and arm. With the long cord he closed its opening and tied it as close to his body as possible. He then loaded his pants with sand and rocks, got in the water and tested his buoyancy: it was almost neutral. After a brief rest, shivering in the cold water, he found another large stone that he could carry with him. He checked the knot on his wrist, tested the rope, and went submerged. He knew that with each try he could endure a little more under the water, but if he pushed himself too much it would be fatal. He sank to the bottom, opened his eyes and again noticed the light sixty feet away at the end of the passage. The cold made it difficult to hold his breath. He released the stone and this time did not float to the top. He swam calmly toward the exit. He knew he had to make a decision soon, before he passed the point of no return.

Weighted down by the sand and rocks in his pants, he dragged himself along the bottom of the cave. He saw more light ahead. He was not going to make it … Serge stayed calm. He noticed an air pocket above him and with his hand tested its height. He put his mouth into the pocket, and breathed in. The air tasted damp and cold, but it was breathable. He rested a few seconds, then took a deep breath and went down again, and after a seemingly endless succession of moments, reached what appeared to be the end of the tunnel.

Nearly blinded by light and feeling a distant sun's warmth, he looked up and saw the mirror of the surface above him. He took the rope from his hand and let go. He opened his pants and let out the sand and rocks, pushed himself up from the bottom. He felt the pull of his natural buoyancy, and started swimming up. He surfaced, about two hundred feet east of the falls. Although he could hear them he was not able to see them. It was 6:30 p.m.

Serge took a deep breath and felt the sun's warmth on his head and shoulders. He looked around for the closest edge, swam to a sandy bank and pulled himself out of the water. Still laying with his face in the sand, he checked the leather bag, everything was still there. He wanted to take just a brief moment to rest and regroup but felt overwhelmed by exhaustion. He closed his eyes, pulled his legs to his chest and wrapped his arms around them to gain some heat. The pain in his left leg returned and he grimaced, but felt alive. He leaned his head against the trunk of a tree and fell asleep.

*   *   *

Dantz had returned to where Serge's vehicle had crashed. Police and military units were everywhere. It was almost twenty hours since the incident. He moved with caution through town, wearing a canvas hat and dark sunglasses. With Pony Tail Guy and two other men, he drove by the accident site to the edge of town, intent on followed Serge's trail back into the jungle. After two days, tracking someone's movements becomes more difficult, but Dantz was confident he could find a new lead to Alexa. The vehicle slowed down and stopped by the trailhead. All except the driver got out fast and entered the trail fast to avoid calling for any attention. Their car continued along the road and disappeared in the distance.

Once on the trail they moved fast to the first clearing. Dantz could see remnants of tracks. He moved in the direction of the other lead, the obvious one that Serge had created as a diversion to his own tracking. They were able to track for a couple of hundred feet until it became difficult. The jungle had taken over, rain and vegetation erased any traces of human activity. Dantz had to rely on his experience and keen sense of observation. "This is going to take us time," he said, "more than we expected."

"You assured me that you had everything under control," said Pony Tail Guy. "We have five hours to find them or I'm pulling the plug. Two hours after that, your face and your friends' will be on every local and Interpol wanted list. You are becoming a liability I don't need to deal with."

"Let me worry about that. In the end, it's my head that could roll. Just have patience. I'll find a lead."

*　　*　　*

The Lightman corporate jet landed in Belize City after a seven hour flight without incident. Max's "uncle" Gadgett had arrived to Max's dorm to stay with him for the evening and leave the next morning. They had dinner and talked about next steps once they got to Belize, the next morning they took a taxi to the airport where they boarded Lightman's Jet. The flight had been a new experience for both Max and his "uncle" Gadgett, one they wished could have been experienced under better circumstances. Neither the personal service nor the spacious seats helped Max relax his mind. He was anxious to get to Belize to join the search.

The Gulfstream jet was elegant and spacious without being pretentious; it certainly was different than flying on a commercial airliner. Max was grateful to be able to come, considering that only one day had passed and that in other circumstances it would have taken him at least a couple of days more to get there. Still he felt anxious to get there. On the plane the passengers had the chance to get acquainted. Gadgett was introduced as Al, Serge's best friend and Max's godfather. Max saw that Bob Lightman was a very demanding but generous man. He had heard his father speak of him and of Mama, about the interview and the family he was living with. Max had never felt that his father's job suited his training and experience, but he noted that he was happy and that was all that mattered. After he met the others, he understood why his father had accepted the job and why it meant more than simply making a living.

The first thing that Max noticed when the door was open again was the heat and humidity hitting his face. He remembered experiencing the same sensation with his mother, years ago on one of her archeological research projects. Outside the plane, a large group of people welcomed them and guided the group to two military buses. The Belize government had made arrangements for them to be transferred to a nearby Army heliport from where they would be flown directly to San Ignacio. Max was surprised by the efficiency with which things had been organized: he was told that in less than an hour they would be joining the search.

Welcome

Serge awakened rested and dry. He opened his eyes and saw a wooden and straw roof above him with a small opening close to the center. He turned his gaze to the sides and found he was inside a small hut, with wall of adobe and stone to the first three feet of height and then a wooden structure made of straight tree limbs for the rest of the eight feet. He was resting on a soft bed of leaves, with a fresh, bright yellow cotton-like sheet. He felt the heat of the day but he was not overly warm. He raised his back and sat up in place, not knowing where he was. By the side of the makeshift bed was a small three-legged table upon which were his clothes, clean and neatly folded. He looked at himself and found he was only wearing something like short pants made of the same cotton-like fabric as the sheet. The shorts were very comfortable and fit him perfectly.

He looked at his left leg, where his makeshift shirt bandage had been replaced with a rawhide bag and green leaves. It also fit nicely, neither loose nor tight. He did not feel any pain. He saw that he was still wearing the pendant and bracelet, and that his body had been cleaned of all the mud and sweat from the past three days. He heard noise outside: children playing, people talking in a strange language he could not understand. A dog barked in the distance, and he heard birds in mid-flight, not so far away, making the sound of a gentle breeze. It made a peaceful background noise. The intensity of the light inside of the hut indicated that it was midday. He wondered what time it was but could not see his wrist watch anywhere. He thought that maybe a day had passed after coming out of the pond from the cave. He stood up, testing his leg for support. He was able to walk, feeling only a slight numbing sensation, and pain like a sunburn. He walked to the hut's door, his formal hiking shoes were on its side, neatly clean and pointing towards the exit. He moved the fabric covering to the side, and walked outside.

223

To adjust to the brightness of the sunlight, Serge shaded his eyes with his right hand, and then a small hand clasped his left. He looked down and saw a beautiful girl, perhaps eleven years old. She smiled at him and, holding his fingers, she guided him to the middle of a courtyard, where more than twenty children were playing with wooden hoops, spears, leaves, and rocks. He was greeted with smiles and cheers, and Serge smiled back at them. He saw genuine wonder in their eyes, pure innocence, sincere appreciation and curiosity. He knelt down to be at their level and when he did, his left leg hurt, and he tipped to his right and fell on his butt.

The children laughed at him. Two of them brought leaves and flowers and placed them on his shoulders and over his head. Another placed a small tortoise in his right hand; the child's smile was shadowed by his missing front teeth, but was still broad and sincere. Serge smiled, rubbed the boy's head and nodded at him, gently touching the tortoise's nose. The tortoise did not hide in its shell, it looked back at him and closed its eyes. Serge felt a sense of peace. He didn't know where he was but he felt confident and safe. He remembered Nana's story of how she had been welcomed to the ancient community and how she felt there, forgetting the outside world and the worries of the past. He knew, somehow, he was in the same place.

He raised up his eyes and saw adults walking towards him. An old man led the group, with a young man and woman by his side. Serge stood up, the tortoise still in his hand. The children laughed at him, he looked silly with flowers on his head, awkwardly walking barefooted and still struggling with only one good leg.

At a signal from one of the adults all the children moved to the side and stood with deep respect, though still giggling and smiling at the adults as they came to Serge. The elder was wearing a bracelet and pendant, and Serge guessed he was Norw, Nana's husband. The old man extended both hands to Serge, who tried to do the same but the tortoise in his hand made him hesitant, and the children laughed again. Serge felt embarrassed and the adults smiled at him. The old man held Serge's left arm with both hands then, in what seemed to be a symbolic gesture, placed his bracelet right next to Serge's. It was a left arm shake where both hands held the inside of the bracelets as they rested side by side. The old man got close to Serge's face, looked straight into his eyes, and touched his forehead to Serge's.

"Welcome."

Serge could see his lips making another sound but he understood the word. He remembered Nana's story but resisted asking where he was. Instead he answered naturally, "Thank you."

*   *   *

It had been two weeks since the kidnapping attempt. Alexa was talking to her father on the phone when Max entered the hotel conference room in San Ignacio, all sweaty after a search trip. The makeshift search and rescue office was filled with military and police personnel. The walls displayed maps covered with grid patterns, there were computers, and radios to communicate with ground crews and three helicopters. Max approached one of the maps and crossed off one of its grid squares; the map was almost completely covered with crosses and he was running out of places to search. It had been a combined effort between the government of Belize and the Foundation to find Serge. Bob Lightman had left after ten days and had given Alexa five more before returning home. Alexa did not want to leave but she knew she needed to take Jimmy and get back home with Sarah. When she left, the search effort would be left to a four-member team that would support Max as long as he needed. Max stood by Alexa's side and with a negative gesture indicated that

225

there had been no luck today, either. They were running out of time and they knew it.

Alexa and Nana had spent most of the days together. Nana had taken her to San Ignacio the day after her dad arrived in Belize and together they had been monitoring the search effort. They had bonded together more strongly, especially after the second day, when she asked Alexa to call her Nana and not Lande anymore. They now behaved as if they had known each other all of their lives. After the fifth day, Nana told Alexa that she felt responsible for Serge's disappearance. She had told her part of the story of her past and the personal favor she asked Serge to do for her, told her she thought that somehow this had something to do with his disappearance. But Nana still kept secret her knowledge of a lost culture that might still be found. She was not sure anymore if she could get back to that hidden community without the pendant's guidance.

Nana had been surprised how much Max reminded her of his father despite not having such a strong resemblance to him. "Son, you are so much like your father ... Still, you don't look like him."

"I know. I have more from my mother's side, but everyone tells me that I'm a lot like my father, though more in a non-physical way."

She and Max had developed a good friendship and, perceiving his nature, she had asked him to call her Nana, as well, from the day they.

The search for Serge had been fruitless. There were a few leads and tracks but as time passed all leads were turning cold. After ten days the search crews had been reduced by half and soon the search was going to change to a recovery effort, or simply flyovers and waiting for news. Max knew that he could not stay much longer, but after spending all this time in the forest and jungle, he was feeling desperate. His final hope was to find Dantz or his accomplices. Interpol had been advised and photos circulated in the area. If the authorities could find him and learn Serge's last location, learn if he had been killed or injured, that would help Max cope with the uncertainty, but there had been no results on that front, either.

Gadgett, walking into the conference room after completing a helicopter search, saw Max staring at a map on the wall, marker in hand, looking at the grid and wondering where to continue.

"Max," he said, approaching from behind, "I think we should give ourselves a time limit, and rethink our next steps. As time passes, all our leads turn colder. I trust your Dad's resilience, but it's been too long. You can't continue like this, and he wouldn't approve of it."

" I can't give up. I know he's out there, alive. I can feel it. Nana expresses it the same way. I need to know that he is all right, that he will come back … I can't let go. I can't, and I won't."

"I know, but if we don't find him in the next couple of weeks we need to be realistic. Think about your future, and about remembering your dad through your life, not through your suffering."

Max turned to face his dad's friend. Gadgett had always been there for Max, as a godfather, as a friend, as a confidant for a teenage boy who got in trouble for drinking too many beers, or missing a red light, or arriving home too late from a party at "my uncle's home". Max embraced him and cried softly, tears of desperation, a mixture of tears between his mom and now his dad.

"I know he's alive. I know, and I can feel it."

*   *   *

Not that far from his son and friend, but still not close enough, Serge was interacting with the community. For him, it had been more than six weeks since his arrival and he felt a sense of belonging, the same sort of feeling as Nana had described to him. He also felt a deep sense of accomplishment with every task he completed and everything he learned. His most fun moments were spent with the children, teaching them Spanish and English, drawing on sand or paper, playing with balls made of natural rubber, throwing rocks at holes or branches, painting their bodies, or swimming in the Cenote. The children in return would pull him by his hands to a nearby river to fish and teach him how to track animals and persons in the jungle or forest.

In all the time Serge had been with them, he had never used his regular clothes, only the cotton-type garments that they all wore. The only thing he used were his hiking shoes, because he had a hard time walking barefoot along the river on the loose rocks and slippery pebbles. He could barely stand erect for the pain of sharp edges or an uncomfortable stone in his toes. The children laughed at his awkward movements, trying to maintain balance, and if pressured to walk he always fell down, finding himself on the water's edge, sitting on his butt with children jumping around him. He could not be beaten the same way when he wore his hiking shoes; then he was as fast and reliable as any of them. He was known among the people as "barefoot challenged" and his hiking shoes became his trademark among the community. He felt comfortable walking barefooted in the village but hesitated on any outside trip.

Serge had participated in hunting trips, fishing excursions, adolescent initiations, and community gatherings. He had learned basic woodcarving, and gone on long food gathering excursions in the jungle, collecting medicinal plants and exotic fruits, things that made a difference in everyday life. He spent late afternoons with Norw; learning their language, sharing the history he acquired through his transfer, gaining experience. The evenings among all were filled with storytelling and music. Some adults performed with elaborate

228

costumes for the children stories of the past; among them it was a way of bonding and sharing, talking with each other.

It was until Serge had his turn to talk about his life and about Nana that he remembered the outside; Max, Stephanie, his former life... it all felt so distant. When he felt nostalgic he hesitated and paused. Norw knew the dilemma he was facing; he had seen the same reaction from Nana. Being from the "Outside" as it was known by all, was not easy. When this happened Norw will divert the storytelling to him and cover the rest of Serge stories with all what he had learned from the conversations with him. By now, the community had welcome Serge as one of their own. They had accepted that it had been a random fact of life what had made Serge cross Nana's path, how he had found the missing crystal, how he had became an Elder among them. They never questioned if he had the right to wear that title. Their experience had proven many times in the past how life was filled with random events, shadows of instants that changed his life's course and determined new beginnings.

After eight weeks Serge was completely immersed in this new life. He had not spent any time thinking about the outside world, he was learning, observing, evolving and time went by without him noticing. As a crystal bearer he had been invited to be part of the transfer ceremony for the third crystal, the one he had found behind the waterfall with the lost bracelet and pendant. The ceremony would confirm the privilege to bear the crystal, and this time it had been given to a woman, the same young woman who had accompanied Norw in the Cenote. Serge knew that because he was wearing Nana's bracelet and pendant that balance must be restored gender-wise, so the recovered crystal would be placed in a woman's custody.

The ceremony was different than Serge had envisioned. After annunciation and confirmation, a date was set to perform the ceremony. Early one morning, after a simple breakfast of fruit, honey, and bread, the community gathered at the main building where the crystal and jewelry were kept. Earlier, all the objects had been placed underwater at the edge of the Cenote, for cleansing and safekeeping. In a very simple ritual, all the elders walked to the Cenote, followed by Viladi, the young woman and next carrier. Norw and Serge followed behind, Norw carrying the pendant and bracelet and Serge carrying the crystal in a leather pouch. They all came to the cave, but only Norw and Serge entered the vaulted chamber. In awe, Serge saw the splendor of the light inside and how it was carried deep into the cave system. The light flowed up through glass-like walls and into an inverted pit, where it was distributed to other areas of the caves, places he had never been but knew he would in the future.

Norw and Serge placed the crystal in its proper base, opposite the other two. Serge saw the empty base of the missing fourth crystal. He wondered, again, how all this came to be, what was behind the crystal's energy, what was behind the light, the symbolism of the pendant animals, their connections to man and woman. Norw sensed his questioning thoughts and nodded at him. Serge interpreted him to mean that there would be an explanation, perhaps soon. They returned to the antechamber of the cave where Viladi lay upon a stone base, the elders circling around her, alternating women and men. Norw explained to Serge that he would place the Jaguar-shaped pendant on Viladi and that Serge would place the bracelet on her arm a few moments later.

Viladi was in her late twenties and had been one of Norw's closest apprentices. She was an active member of the community who volunteered for any needed work, who's loyalty and wisdom had been proven by her actions, and who had the affection and approval of everyone. She looked up at Serge and Norw when they entered and smiled at them. There was a slight hesitation on her face, maybe even fear, but also a sense of complete honor to be the recipient of this gift. Norw simply nodded.

He walked to her right and Serge to her left, and without further ceremony Norw held the pendant above her face then placed it between her breasts, passing the leather string over her head. Serge waited a few seconds, watching Viladi's eyes as they looked to the chamber ceiling. Then their eyes met. Serge smiled at her. He stood close to her left arm and oriented the narrow end of the bracelet in the direction of her hand. He lowered it onto her forearm, opening the two ends, and saw what had happened to him behind the waterfall, but had then been unable to see: the bracelet closed on her and adapted its shape to her forearm, the wider side now showing a sharp edge that penetrated Viladi's inner arm, making her grimace in pain.

What happened next was something he could not explain. He sensed an explosion inside the cave, not of tremors, noise, or movement but of new energy created. The third crystal in the vaulted chamber behind them began flickering repeatedly, then steadied into a constant bright glow. The three crystals shone with a brighter intensity than he thought possible, the light now reaching the farthest ends of the cave system. Serge was amazed at the energy stored or generated in the crystals, wondered at the origins of it all. Any explanation or stories that had been transferred with Nana's ancestral memories; the images he had seen before passing out in the cave after the bracelet found its place in his arm did not reach back to the origins of all this; they included only the experiences of the former carriers.

Viladi had closed her eyes and was probably going through the same process he had: a complete shutdown of mind and body until the final fusion occurred. He placed her left arm on her chest to complete the bonding process. Serge saw the pendant fused to the bracelet indentation, perfectly fitted as his' had, making contact between the crystal and the carrier. Norw and Serge stayed with her a long time, taking turns wiping her forehead of sweat, monitoring her sleep, guarding the transition. The rest of the elders left the chamber, smiling and conversing among themselves. The future looked bright again for the community.

*   *   *

231

In Seattle, three months had passed since the Belize incident. At the Foundation, things were getting back to normal, though at Alexa's home they were not. Serge's absence was evident and it showed in the moods of the children and staff. Alexa perceived a void created in everyone. After more than a year, Serge had become familiar to them; someone who had begun as an estate administrator had become a mentor, a friend, and in many ways a member of the family. She also felt that during their last months together, she and Serge had developed a deeper relationship, something more meaningful. She was used to his presence, his gentle means, his sense of humor. She missed him not only for saving their lives but also for the support she found in him. She remembered the last time she saw him, as he pushed her along the trail, his head bleeding, his eyes focused and concerned, his comforting touch. She remembered the night in Mexico City when he laid Jimmy on the bed, the quiet silence between them that needed no explanation, the way he looked at her, his chivalrous and embarrassed departure when he, too, felt the attraction.

Since Alexa's return Mama visited more often, spent more time with them. They read Max's e-mail reports in the following weeks of the search, waiting for any good news. They were disappointed when the search was called off, but by then it had been two months since Serge disappeared. The frequency and length of the reports gradually diminished with each passing week. Alexa wished she could do more for him.

Max had returned from Belize after two and a half months. Although he had the support of the Foundation to continue in Belize, Gadgett convinced him that he had to go back to his life, as his father would have hoped. He sent his final report to Alexa from the hotel lobby, and flew back to Arizona where he settled back into his daily routine at school. He drifting into a quiet, lonely existence of resignation that he covered with work and increased responsibilities, a trait that was typical of his mother. Gadgett had seen that many times before and tried to keep close to Max to break this behavior. He knew that, as with Max's mother, it was a matter of time. He remembered Stephanie dealing with stress and how Serge gave her space to come back.

From time to time, Max felt his dad talking to him, telling him he was fine. Max had never been able to easily recall his dreams, but in the past six weeks he had remembered vivid dreams of his father's voice talking to him, and at times had feelings similar to déjà vu, or daydreams, charged with hope. It was perhaps the only thing that he had left of his father, these memories and encouragements to keep on going. He was planning to go to Seattle to get his father's belongings. He shared his desire with Alexa and discussed the idea with her. She assured him that he had all the time he needed, that they had not touched his place since their return and would like him to be first.

*   *   *

In the jungle-forests of Belize, Serge felt as if it had been more than a year since he left the outside world. He had learned the secrets of life there: how to gather food, identify plants, fish, hunt, make fire, speak the language, observe nature and communicate with it, as part of it. Two of his favorite activities were carving wood and making papyrus-like paper. He had manufactured a small book of uneven pages, bound in a leather enclosure and tied with rawhide and cotton-like strands from the Maguey plant. He sketched and wrote what he was living on a daily basis, using carbon sticks to draw and writing with pens of cut feathers and bamboo sticks. He manufactured ink with grass, water, and ground, colored minerals, using tree resin to keep it fluid and stable. He taught some of the children how to draw on paper, practicing in the sand at the banks of

233

the river. In return the children taught him how to carve wood for tools and spears, toys, animal shapes, furniture and hunting traps. With each passing day he mastered the practice of tracking and gathering techniques.

On one of his excursions with children he developed a strong bond with Nana's grandson, a twelve year old named Alter. Serge called him Al, like his best friend from his past life. Al helped Serge find a special branch from a twisting tree, with an unusual bend that allowed them to make a strong spear with a hook at the end. This tool was very handy for capturing animals without hurting them. It made an excellent hunting weapon and also a comfortable walking stick.

Many times during these days Serge wondered where they were in the jungle, for in all his days with the community he had never seen any manifestation of the outside world, not the sound of a distant engine, no strangers or lost wanderers in the jungle, or even the lights or condensation trails of a high altitude airplane. Only his thoughts bore witnesses to the outside world, and most of the time these were about Stephanie and Max. Every time Serge thought about his son and felt restless, he touched his pendant and calmed down.

He also applied a meditation technique he learned from Norw. Serge had inquired of Norw if there was a way to communicate with someone at a distance. Norw told him that there was, that it was limited but possible. Norw said his best example was the way he had reached out for Serge from the Cenote. Norw possessed the experiences and techniques of a life time, even to suspend himself in mid air. He did not share with Serge how he had done this, but did teach him the technique he had used to persuade Serge to wear the bracelet when he found it behind the waterfall. Sensing Serge's proximity to it, and through the manifestation of the light in the crystal, Norw had known he had to reach out and help Serge make the crucial connection. Serge remembered the voice inside his head, the impulses, and was satisfied with the explanation. Serge practiced the technique in quiet, during the day or before sleeping, either sitting or laying on the ground. At first he was easily distracted by his surroundings but now he felt he could reach a deeper sense of peace in meditation and at times, when he needed, he felt he could reach out to his son through his thoughts. He practiced tenaciously, and hoped that when the time came, the natural bond with his son would help reach him, and that Max would realize that it was his father's voice.

With time he became more confident about it, since he was being more successful in connecting with Norw and Viladi in that way. At least once a week, he took the time to think about his son and tell him he was fine. This created an internal conflict for him. On the one hand he was living an exciting journey, one he felt he belonged on and which was hard to let go, and on the other his sense of responsibility and love for his son wanted to pull him away.

Serge learned how to move stealthily in the jungle without being noticed. He had mastered a way of walking and running and being still that allowed him to be at arm's reach of animals without them noticing. He enjoyed doing this when he felt the need to be close to nature, to observe life as if no one were there. He heard from some of the young men that there was a way of moving in water whereby not even ripples were noticeable, a movement so patient and timed that the skin was dry after surfacing. This represented a major challenge and was something he was eager to learn to become more a member of the community. Day by day, Serge learned and integrated into his new life. For the first time he felt a sense of belonging and peace, and without Serge noticing, time moved fast and months went by.

The members of the village always moved freely in the jungle and forest, never encountered anyone from the outside. Serge asked Norw about this, and learned that there was something about the Cenote cave systems and the crystals that acted as a gateway to the same world but in another time. Perhaps this was the reason behind the perception of time, as Nana had explained to him, how her kids grew all the way to seven and twelve years old, after only five years of outside time being married to Norw. Nana had felt her five years in the community to have been a life time, only to find out when she returned that just ten years had passed. The perception of time as lived and experienced was relative, more related to things learned and done than to physical aging.

Serge spent some time thinking on this. Al was Nana's grandson, and he was twelve. His father, Nana's son, was seven when she left, twenty outside years ago. That meant that in order for him to have a son he had to be thirteen, and although this was possible, he looked to be in his late thirties. The same with Norw, who seemed many years older than Nana, in his late eighties, while both were in their late thirties when they met. nana's physical age was probably sixty-five and she had mentioned that she felt herself growing old upon her return to the outside world. While she felt and remembered that she had spent almost half her life in the community, at least twenty years, it simply did not add up to the time she was gone.

It was at the end of the eighth month of Serge's time in the community, late one afternoon, when the normal peace of the community was disrupted. A group of children were swimming at the major Cenote, climbing the edges and jumping and diving, testing who could go higher on the Cenote, or deeper into the water, or who could hold their breath longer underwater. One of them climbed close to the exterior rim of the main Cenote entrance and was spotted by someone from the outside. Such a rare encounter almost never happened, and there was almost always an adult who could mitigate the encounter as if it had been a mirage. But this time the children had gone farther than allowed, into an area designated as a gateway to the outside, an area where only the carriers of pendants were safe to move, and no one was close to help them out.

236

Among the group was Alter, or "Al" as Serge called him. He was Serge's favorite child friend and Nana's grandson. It was Al who had given Serge the small tortoise as a welcoming gesture on his first day in the community, when he came out of his hut. Al was with the others, swimming and diving in the clear waters of the Cenote. One of Al's friends went farther up, reaching the rim of the Cenote. When he reached the rim and shouted for the rest to look at him, a stranger caught him by the arm. Al saw what happened and quickly cautioned the rest to hide in the caves. He ran back to the village and found Aio, who was helping the women fishing. Aio was Norw's son and the probable successor for his pendant. He heard Al's cries for help and ran to him.

"What is going on?"

"They got him."

"Calm down. Who was caught? Who is 'them'?"

"Outside people got Ksed. We were out in the Cenote swimming when they took him away."

Aio calmed him and gave him instructions. "Go back to the village and warn the others. I'll go to get him back, hurry!"

Aio turned toward the cave entrance, heading to the Cenote, hoping that even with the time difference between realms he would be able to find Ksed.

Outside the Cenote, Ksed was held by a group of five white men in military fatigues, one of them with long dark hair. They were worried that their animal traps or illegal poaching activities might be discovered.

"Who are you, and what are you doing here, huh?"

Ksed understood some of the words in English, Serge had taught him a few words of English/Spanish. "I em Ksed"

"Cerseed?" They laughed at his name. "Do you speak English or Spanish?"

"Little ..." Ksed said. "Serge is teaching me."

Unfortunately, the sound of Serge's name inspired more interest from the long-haired man. "You said Serge? Is he living with you? Where did you hear that name?"

Ksed, who had never been exposed to this kind of treatment, was intimidated. He remembered some of the elders' teachings about the outside world and knew he needed to be in control.

"He is good ... friend ..."

"Where is he?"

"Home." Ksed looked down into the Cenote.

The men followed his eyes. "You live down there?"

Ksed knew he had made a mistake, and diverted their attention by pointing his finger beyond the Cenote. "Home." He made gestures implying a river and a mountain.

"I believe we might find the guy who screwed you over, months ago." said the man with the long dark hair to a hooded man at the edge of the Cenote. "You might have a chance for revenge, after all."

Dantz turned around and looked Pony Tail Guy directly in the eyes. His faced was covered with a long beard, and wore a tired expression. He had been living in Belize all this time, hidden and

238

making a living as a poacher, hunter, archeological trafficker, and mercenary.

"Is that so. I had forgotten the damn bastard." he replied.

The men made Ksed walk for two hours until they reached their camp. Ksed was tied by the hands and seated between traps and cages of captured birds, monkeys, and reptiles. Some of the cages were stained with blood, as were the clothes of the men. Dantz walked up to Ksed and with old accumulated rage in his eyes, yanked him by the arm and raised him to eye level. "Where is Serge?"

Ksed looked directly into Dantz's eyes and said nothing.

"Where is he?" Dantz shouted.

The silence of the boy unnerved him. With disdain, he threw Ksed back to the ground.

Dantz said to the others, "We must head back to that Cenote and find a trail to their town."

From the top of a nearby tree, Aio witnessed the interrogation of Ksed. Fortunately, he had been able to make up for lost time with a fast run, and the men had left plenty of tracks that were easy to follow. There were seven men in the camp, five of them armed with handguns and rifles, the other two only with machetes. Aio studied them for a while, looking for the best moment to get closer to Ksed and free him. Ksed lay on his side, head on the ground, hands tied behind his back. The most important thing for Aio was to let Ksed know that he was not alone. He whistled softly, a bird's chirp they used on hunting trips. When Ksed heard the whistle his eyes opened. He waited for confirmation, the whistle repeated. He tried to sit up, and after the second try he was able to look up. Resting his body on a cage, he kept his head still while moving only his eyes towards the probable source of the sound. From the tree, Aio signaled him to be quiet and gave him a reassuring smile, which Ksed acknowledged with a slight nod.

Aio trusted his ability to move in silence through the jungle, he was one of the best in the community. He studied the best way in and out of the camp, then waited for evening to make his move. He descended the tree and moved closer to the camp.

*   *   *

Al and the rest of the children arrived at the village exhausted from running. They found Norw by the entrance to Serge's hut, under a large Ceiba tree, training Serge in a wood carving technique. Serge stood up immediately, trying to understand what Al, who was gasping for breath, was trying to say. He knelt down and held Al by the shoulders.

"Take it easy, Al. What is wrong?"

"Aio asked me to come for you … Ksed was caught."

"Caught?" The same question came from both Norw and Serge.

"Yes. We were swimming at the main Cenote, Ksed went too far up and got caught by outside men. I found Aio. He told me to come to you for help. He left for the Cenote to get Ksed. We ran as fast as we could to get here."

Al explained what happened to Ksed and how Aio had gone out after him. A moment later, two teen age boys arrived, one of them was Ksed who was sweating, muddy, and stained with animal blood.

240

He related the events of the last hour to Norw and Serge; Aio ran into the outside world and followed him to help, When it had turned dark, Aio had released him, but as they were trying to escape he had triggered a booby trap cord attached to glass bottles, which made a terrible sound and awoke everyone in the poachers camp. There were shots fired and Aio was wounded. Aio told Ksed to leave him and run for safety. He did not want to leave him but the men were getting closer and Aio shouted at him to leave. He did, and returned to the village for help.

Aio had been captured and hurt. The last he saw of him, he had been tied-up on a boat and he was bleeding. As Ksed finished his account,

Norw hesitated. Aio was his only son and his successor, the next carrier of his pendant but only carriers could be outside on a permanent basis and Aio's life was in danger. He needed to do something fast, but the other men of the village were out on a hunting trip and there was no one to go after Aio. Serge stood before Norw and in a reassuring voice told him that he was Aio's only chance. He would go out and try to get Aio back, he only needed Ksed and the teen aged boys to show him the last place they saw Aio. Serge entered his hut and grabbed his spear, tied its leather rawhide cord to his wrist and rolled the excess around his right hand. He looked around to see if he needed anything else, nothing came to mind and he walked out. He told the boys to take him to the closest exit on the way to the river to the last place they saw Aio.

Serge gave Norw a hug and ran off toward the caves, with Al, Ksed and the other teen boys behind him. As they departed a little girl came out of Serge's hut with his hiking shoes, calling for Serge to wait until he had them. Norw placed a hand on her shoulder and stopped her, letting Serge go without them. He smiled at the little girl, then turned to face Viladi, who had just joined them. She saw the shoes in the little girl's hands and nodded to Norw in approval of his decision. She turned to watch Serge and the boys run from the village.

Dantz's men attended to Aio's injuries. He had been hit twice, on his left arm and on his waist. The bullets had gone through, leaving one wide exit wound in his arm and a large bracing scratch on his waist. Both injuries were not life threatening but impaired Aio of any free movement. They had let the boy run away, but Aio represented, in their estimation, a much more valuable catch. Aio could be tortured and would eventually take them directly to Serge.

Serge ran with the teenage boys to the caves. They entered the system and went through a couple of tunnels, some directing to the Cenote entrance and some to other areas of the jungle. Serge asked them for reference on regards to estimated movement on where they might be, they agreed that the last they saw of Aio was moving down the river and that they could make up for lost time if they ran through the tunnel system that went under the river and close to the falls. After a couple of minutes running, Serge heard the sound of moving water and saw natural light filtered by water at the end of the tunnel As they got close to the river' Serge told Al to go back and tell Norw he was on his way. He asked the Ksed and the other boys to follow him, and jumped into the water. He saw that he needed to dive to go through an underwater opening, and without hesitation he did, the two boys following him. Al ran back to the village.

The flooded passage resembled the one Serge had taken behind the waterfall, but there was no draft and Serge reached the surface of the moving river without trouble. He emerged and swam to the river's edge. Once the three of them were together they ran downstream along the riverbank for more than five minutes. They approached a bifurcation in the river and Serge recognized the place from his pursuit by Dantz. He recognized the sound and rock formations of the waterfall, this was where he had been shot months ago. Downstream in the distance he could see the river turning, and a small boat that fitted the description of Dantz's.

As they were running he asked the boys for confirmation, directions, and estimated times. He knew that if he followed the gently flowing branch of the river he would not get to Aio on time, he weighted his options and decided to take his chances and jump the waterfall as a short cut. He increased his pace, leaving the boys behind and shouting them to go back to the village.

"What are you doing?" asked Ksed

"I'm jumping. I can't afford to lose any more time."

"But it is a very tall fall..."

"I know."

He waved them off, continue running through the shallows, moving steadily through rocks and water puddles. He saw the same green rock with its soft edges and gracious curves, he remembered stepping on it before, and falling through the waterfall after being hit by the bullet. He reached the point of no return, his speed and determination were already taking him over, and with one final thrust his feet landed on the center of the green rock. No slipping, no movement, just a firm landing: he impelled himself forward, extending his arms and throwing his body over, head first.

Serge felt himself falling as if in slow motion; the moment became silent, his racing heart slowed to a rhythmic beat, the same sound of falling drops of rain in his shoulders as in his morning forest runs. He extended his arms as he has seen the boys do at the Cenote, as he had been taught by them. This was called the Seagull's dive, and it needed a high jump with a strong forward thrust to be successful: keep your body straight and away from the edge where the jump originated. He saw the sky, then the jungle, and then the water getting closer beneath him. In mid fall he let go of his spear, throwing it to the side. The leather strap extended from his hand and once he felt the tug at the knot on his wrist, he extended his arms to the sides of his head and in the direction of the water.

He entered the water vertically, and as soon as his hands felt the water he opened them to slow his descent, he bent his knees gently inward to provoke a sudden turn of his body, slowing his trajectory to the bottom. He opened his eyes and saw the river bottom, behind him the white turbulence and foam of the waterfall. He swam underwater a couple of strokes and emerged close to the river bank. He wiped his face, pulled his spear close and started running again downriver. He had not noticed or even thought about it, but his feet were moving smoothly on the rocky beach. He did not feel any discomfort, his eyesight was focused ahead, his only thought of reaching the moving boat with Aio on board. He ran without feeling tired, he turned with agility to miss passing branches and low hanging leaves. He jumped over obstacles: fallen trees, rocks, wide puddles. His movements resembled those seen only in the most experienced men of the village.

At a "u" bend of the river he saw the boat ahead of him, he thought that by cutting through the jungle he could make up for some time. He was getting closer. Once he reached the river again he saw the boat in the distance. It was moving at a very slow speed. He could see only three men onboard, and some boxes covered with a dark dirty canvas: Serge thought those would be the cages. He did not see Aio, and hoped he was there. He whistled a loud birdcall, hoping for a reply. There was none. He tried again, and this time heard a faint, similar sound from the river. He guessed that Aio had heard him. Serge was within swimming distance but he knew that in order to rescue Aio he needed to move ahead, board the boat from the front and rescue Aio. The boat was approaching another "u" bend and Serge decided to again cut across through the jungle again, to get ahead of it. He ran and jumped through dark soil, branches, and rocks without any trouble, his concentration focused on only one thing, getting Aio back.

He came to the river again and saw that the boat had not yet made the turn. The river narrowed ahead of him, a perfect area to plan something. He stopped and thought for a while, looked around and decided on his next steps. He ran back into the jungle and collected four of the longest tree vines and roots he could find. He tied one end of the ropes to a large boulder at the water's edge and then swam across the river where he tied the other ends to a tree. He swam to midstream and, holding the ropes, he tied a series of roots and branches, making a rude net where he expected the boat to go. He waited until he saw the boat coming, then swam close to his trap. When the boat neared he submerged himself, holding the rope and holding his breath.

The boat closed on the tied, floating branches and turned to avoid them, floated against the rope. The boat engine stalled as the propeller caught the tangle, and stopped. Serge surfaced by the boat's side, spear hook in hand. A man appeared. Serge hooked his shirt and pulled him to the river, shouting in surprise. He elbowed the man's neck, blowing out his air out and leaving him helpless. Serge quickly tied him into the floating branches then dived under the boat to the other side.

Serge emerged, grasped the gunwales and thrust himself aboard, landing in the center of the deck. One man peered over the side, his back to Serge, and another was bent over the engine. Serge kicked the first man in the back, and he fell to the water. The man at the engine turned around, his long black hair flying to the sides, and when he saw Serge he reached for his side holster. Serge swung his spear, striking him in his arm and chest, knocking his gun from his hand. It was Pony Tail Guy.

With the strength of his blow, Serge spun completely around to face his opponent again. Pony Tail Guy was startled by the hit but lunged forward and tackled Serge, knocking them both to the deck. Serge struck his head and was stunned; he lost his grip on the spear. The men struggled around the boat, jostling the cages, and the trapped

245

animals erupted with screams and shrieks and howls. Serge was still a bit disoriented by the blow to his head but was able to get his hands between them and then catch the man's shoulders. Serge pushed him away, but Pony Tail Guy took Serge by the neck, strangulating him. Serge gasped for air. He could not slip his hands between his throat and his assailant's hands. He suddenly remembered something he had learned in a self defense course, and with both hands he struck into the man's armpits, provoking a reflex reaction. Pony Tail Guy recoiled in pain. Serge took a deep breath and with all his strength kicked the man in the chin, sending him backwards into the cages.

Pony Tail Guy lay sprawling against the toppled cages, struggling to release a knife from its sheath at his waist. Aio appeared, arms and legs still bound, and threw himself at Pony Tail Guy. The man's head struck the deck, he lost consciousness and lay inert on the boat deck. Serge hurried to untie Aio's legs and arms.

Aio's expression changed, and Serge sensed that someone was behind him. He crouched, pulling Aio with him off to the side. A loud bang exploded behind them. The man Serge had kicked in the river had climbed out again and tried to hit them with a length of heavy pipe. Serge grabbed the pipe and the two men struggled for it, but with one kick to the groin Aio disarmed their opponent. Serge twisted the man's arm behind his back and forced his face against the boat's deck. Serge and Aio tied him with ropes, then did the same to the still unconscious Pony Tail Guy. Serge then examined Aio's wounds. They were bleeding again from the fight, but his eyes reflected his determined spirit and courage.

"Are you all right?"

"Yes. Thank you for coming, Serge. Is anyone else with you?"

"No, this is it. The rest of the men were hunting and there was no time to wait."

"You did well. Is Ksed ok?"

"Yes, he arrived with Al. They all are waiting for you."

The third man, sputtering and still trying to catch his breath, surrendered to Serge and Aio. They pulled him from the water and tied him with the others amid the cages. Serge jumped in the water and untangled the boat's propeller from the ropes and branches, then released the tangled mess of his trap. He climbed back on the boat with the jungle vines and roots so no other boat would get untangled. He then started the engine, moved to the edge of the river, where Aio opened the cages and freed the animals. Pony Tail Guy cursed loudly through his mouth gag, but Aio signaled with his hand and a small smirk that the man should be quiet.

Serge again tended Aio's wounds, staunching the bleeding with some of the plants from his pouch. They heard another boat from up the river and looking back saw it had the same configuration as theirs, with a canvas covered mound in the middle, of what appeared to be boxes or cages. This was probably the rest of Pony Tail Guy's gang. Serge jumped back to the boat's wheel and moved away from the bank. He took the boat down the river, toward San Ignacio; it was probably an hour away down the river. He increased his speed and disappeared around the next bend.

In the other boat Dantz saw them moving away. He wondered what had caused his other boat to stop, and why they were out of communication. He tried the radio again without success, then ordered the man at the wheel to catch up.

Serge gave Aio basic operations for the boat and had him take the wheel while he broke up the wooden cages and threw them overboard. Pony Tail Guy's eyes were filled with rage, and he struggled to free himself, kicking fiercely as he saw his traps destroyed. Serge paid no attention. Intent upon his task and with the

247

noise he made smashing the cages, Serge failed to notice Dantz's boat approaching. There was a barrage of bullets. Aio first instinct was to turn the boat sharply and push the throttle all the way forward. From behind the cages Serge saw Dantz and two other men shooting at them.

He scrambled to the rear of the boat and saw the other approaching fast. He found a shotgun on the deck, grabbed it and fired back. On the other boat the men ducked and assumed a more defensive stance, but continued firing. Aio maneuvered the boat on a zigzag course. Serge's fired the shotgun's eighth and final shell. He searched for another weapon and could not find one. The cages remaining on deck swayed and slid with the sudden turns, making the boat less stable. The three captives did their best to stay on deck, certain that they would drown if thrown into the river.

Aio managed to put some distance between the two boats, while Serge kept busy throwing more of the cages into the path of their pursuers, hoping to foul their boat's propeller. Hefting a sturdy and heavy metal cage, Serge had an idea. He tied the two ends of a long rope to bumper buoys he found hanging against the side of the boat, and tied the cage in the middle. He threw the cage and buoy in the water, and the cage left a white streak of splashing water as the rope played out. the buoy bouncing on the water's surface.

Serge secured the second buoy to the rail, and the rope trailed behind them. He had Aio slow the boat, and the cage sank beneath the surface. Aio drove the boat slowly across the river until the cage was suspended in the middle. Serge estimated depths and lengths, as Dantz's boat neared again. Gunshots from the other boat began to fall on them again.

On Serge's mark Aio increased the boat's speed. Serge released the knot on the rope and let the second buoy fall into the water. The propeller on Dantz's boat caught the rope, and pulled the metal cage into it. The engine stalled and died, the exhaust choked with smoke.

248

Dantz's desperate curses, screams, and gunshots quickly faded behind as they roared downriver.

San Ignacio appeared along the riverbank a few minutes later. At a public pier Serge and Aio docked the boat and moved their captives to shore. The commotion of shots and fast moving boats had been audible for miles, and a curious crowd of fishermen and townspeople quickly gathered around. A pair of police officers appeared, one speaking into his radio. Serge explained who the bound men were. He pointed out the boat, the cages, the guns. The officers recognized the men as poachers and they would take care of them.

"You look familiar ... I know you," said one of the officers to Serge.

Serge recognized him. "Captain Ramos," he said. "I'm Serge. You were part of the welcoming party for Alexa Lightman. You gave me directions when we arrived in San Ignacio. These guys kidnapped and shot Aio, and they tried to kidnap Ms Lightman a few months ago. We disabled another boat up the river. You can catch the others if you hurry."

"Serge? That was almost a year ago ..." Captain Ramos hesitated.

"A year ago..?" Serge asked him in disbelief then smiled, extending his arm. They shook hands.

"We looked for you for months, we all did. Your son was here ... Where have you been?"

When Serge heard that Max had been there, his whole reality shook. He was jarred back into a world he used to be part of, acutely aware of the ties here that pulled at him. It was the village that seemed far away now, but Aio was a reminder of that dream, that dream that was also a reality.

"My son, Max?"

"Yes, he was here for months. With Ms Lightman, a big search party, reporters, curious people, government officials. Where've you been? You look changed: fit, trim, taller, tan ... not lost at all." Ramos placed a hand on Serge's shoulder. "Lost?"

Ramos reported by radio and called for support. The police would go for Dantz's boat, and keep Pony Tail Guy and his men detained.

A local reporter had followed the crowd to the river, as well as two French filmmakers who were making a documentary about the rainforest and eco tourism. When they saw the almost naked bodies of Aio and Serge they began filming the encounter as if they were natives of a lost tribe.

The reporter had worked on the search for Serge, and when he overheard Ramos and Serge conversing, said, "I recognize you. You're the guy who was lost in that car chase. We looked for you for months. We thought you were dead."

Serge silently pleaded with Ramos for a way out. Aio's injuries needed medical care, the reporters were too intrusive, there were too many questions ... Ramos nodded and pointed out his official vehicle. Serge moved fast, hoping to leave as soon as they could. He retrieved his spear from the boat, took Aio by the arm and made their way to the police pickup truck. In less than half an hour the peaceful docks of San Ignacio had become crowded with curious onlookers, tourists, and police officers. Serge drove away with Aio through the confusion. Serge intended to disappear from San Ignacio, get Aio to Nana, and then reunite with the whole community.

After a few minutes driving, they were back on the road out of town. Serge strained to remember the way to San Luis. Ramos called by radio to report the capture of a second boat of poachers with two suspects on board; neither fit Dantz's description. Serge took the radio and replied: "One still missing … but Gracias from San Ignacio" Serge hoped that Ramos would figure out from the reference that they were heading to the reclusive people's town of San Luis to hide. Dantz was still on the loose, and might be listening to police broadcasts. Serge now concentrated strongly on Nana, hoping to find the way back to San Luis.

Rendezvous

Although it had been a year, or months, Serge drove as if by instinct, like a returning salmon, or migratory bird, or a bee to the hive, he returned to a place he felt was home. When he stopped the police truck at the entrance to San Luis, the children of the town came running, and with their help carried Aio toward the homes. Nana stood in her doorway, and as they approached Serge saw tears in her eyes, and smiled back at her. He turned to Aio who was now crying with happiness, his face wearing a broad smile. "Mama!"

The moment had been emotional, quiet, pure. Serge had given Nana and Aio space, time to talk, to be family again. Seeing them together felt right. For any stranger it would be hard to imagine that, with their age difference Aio could be Nana's son. But her story, the time she lived in the village, the years since she left, It all made sense to Serge: Norw, the stones, the bracelet, the pendants, the bonds ...

*　　*　　*

Aio was sleeping restfully, his injuries cleaned and bandaged. Nana came outside and found Serge sitting by the edge of the river, looking at the water, thinking about his own son. He longed for this, his other reality, his other life.

"Serge," Nana whispered.

He looked over his shoulder, stood up to greet her. She kissed him on the cheek.

"Thank you. Now you know, you see, you understand."

"Yes. It's magical there. You need to go back, get your family together."

"No, you need to go back, and take Aio with you. Norw will transfer his crystal to Aio, and life will go on there."

"Yes, but I have done what was needed, even though it was without knowing." He touched the pendant hanging from his neck, and held it out to her. "This belongs to you. You should go back."

Nana placed her hand on his. "No. The pendant and bracelet belong to you, and you to the crystal, until you die. My bond was broken when the crystal was stolen, when my bracelet was stolen. They are one again and you are part of it. San Luis is my life now. People depend on me here."

"But Aio ... Norw ..."

"They both know this is the way it should be now. The bond exists and the distance is short, but the void is now immense ... I failed and gave up years ago. I failed."

"You don't ..."

She placed her index finger on his lips and closed her eyes. Embracing Serge, she held both bracelet and pendant to her heart, and she and Serge immediately entered a meditative state. Serge witnessed, in what appeared to be a dream or a memory, Nana and Norw talking, holding hands, sharing tears, kissing, finding peace. In that state, in that suspended instant, both looked at him and smiled. Serge knew what he needed to do.

The way … finding the way

Two days had passed after their return to San Luis. Serge had left the police truck in a location convened with Ramos, then he ran through the jungle, his steps along the riverbank taking him back to San Ignacio at a fast pace. He remembered from years ago: "One two, breathe in, one two, breathe out …"

Minutes ago he had left Aio by one of the entrances to the main Cenote. Healthy and strong, Aio had said goodbye to his mother, perhaps not forever, but as it needed to be for now. Nana had given Serge the comfort of love and understanding and, the greatest gift of all, the gift of a meaningful life. He began to understand a new purpose for his life and the possibility of fulfillment of all his longing. He had been torn, wondering how to tie together both lives, both realities. He had struggled whether to be in a place he felt he belonged or to return to his son and his previous life. As he ran, his mind explored every direction, option, alternative; every way of solving this puzzle. "Steph, help me find my way …"

Serge was ashamed that during time in the village he had not thought more about Steph or his son. He felt selfish for desiring a reality that isolated him from his past and maybe from himself. He felt guilty for spending so much time on personal growth, on learning to be at peace. Now, outside that bubble, or existence, fantasy or reality, he could not say, now he needed to find a way to reconcile both worlds, to make up for lost time, to bring peace to his heart, an yet to move forward … He needed to learn how to keep moving, knowing now what seemed for him to be the best way.

"One two, breathe in, one two, breathe out …"

*   *   *

Max was studying for exams when a friend stormed into his dorm room and turned the TV on: "Max, you need to see this."

"Hey, don't people knock on doors anymore? I've got a final in two days!"

Max's friend switched between channels until he reached a news channel broadcasting an international feed. The screen showed images of a pier on a riverbank in a place Max recognized.

"Hey! That's San Ignacio, in Belize."

"Wait ... See? Here, look!"

The TV focused on a boat tied to the pier. A stack of cages could be discerned beneath a camouflaged canvas tarp. He recognized Captain Ramos and next to him a face he could never forget, though attached to a trimmer and stronger body than he could remember.

"Oh God ... Dad ..."

The phone rang, and Max and his friend jumped in surprise.

His friend took the phone while Max remained glued to the TV. "Hello?"

"Yes, one moment please ... " He held a hand over the mouthpiece. "Max, it's for you. It's Mr. Lightman."

Max took the phone, still watching the TV. "Hello? Yes. Yes, I'm seeing it. I just found out, though it's not confirmed. They're not saying anything ... But yes, that is definitely my father. Thank you."

Max heard his voice trembling, and he felt an urgent desire to go back to Belize. He was happy but also crying gentle tears of longing for his dad. "I understand, yes. A couple of weeks ago. No, I'm not sure. In fifteen minutes, thirty tops. I appreciate it, thank you again. I'll be waiting. Goodbye, Mr. Lightman."

"What was that all about?"

"I'm going to Belize. Someone will be picking me up in thirty or forty minutes. Come on, help me pack and make a few phone calls."

Alexa and Mama stood in Bob Lightman's office, listening as he ended his call to Max. Mama took Alexa's hands in her own. "He'll be ready. Let's give the Arizona office a call to get them started."

"Did he recognize him?" Alexa asked her father.

"Yes, he didn't hesitate. It was an absolute affirmation."

Alexa took a deep breath. The search for Serge had ended months ago; she had resumed her life. She had stayed in touch with Max after returning to Seattle, but the weekly phone calls had become biweekly then monthly. Her justification was the distance, work, family. Jimmy had stopped asking about Serge months ago, Sarah had focused on other things in her fast paced teenage life.

Alexa had been on a couple of dates. There had only been that one time in Belize when she and Serge had really connected, or felt something that was obvious but not expressed. But he had changed her life, helped her kids, touched them all. He had saved her life and Jimmy's. And now she was anxious, she needed to cry, to reach out for Serge, to be held in his arms. Alexa recalled the TV images; Serge's face resembled the man he had been, his expression was committed, concentrated; he looked healthy … Where had he been? What had happened to him? Why did he hide all these months? Too many questions.

Mr. Lightman put an arm around her. "He's fine, that's what counts. I can tell you're anxious." She knew he could read her well, so she did not try to pretend, but held his arm, embraced him, and cried softly on his shoulder. Mama hugged her from behind; she looked at Lightman and smiled.

* * *

Once again, Serge had followed the river downstream to San Ignacio, intending to track Dantz from his last known position. This was a loose end he needed to tie up, especially now that Dantz had recognized him. Spear in hand, he moved stealthily as the people in the village had taught him. He was not yet as successful as the most experienced hunters, but he could conceal his movement and monitor his surroundings without disturbing plants or animals.

Serge came upon a small wooden canoe paddled by two men who exchanged glances with one another, and pointing at the riverbank as if they had seen something. Serge followed them, and soon saw what they did: on a small sandy beach below the bank was the body of a man, motionless, face down, legs in the water. Serge watched as the canoe landed with a scratch of wood against sand, one of the men jumped out.

He approached the body and reached for the man's shoulder to see his face. A sudden violent push sent the man violently toward the water. The wet and exhausted Dantz brandished a handgun, he screamed at them to stay still. With a panicked look in his eyes the man still in the canoe shouted something first in French, then in Spanish trying to calm Dantz. Dantz shouted orders in English, indicating with gestures that they should carry the canoe up the bank and into the jungle. He looked in every direction to see if anyone else had seen him.

Dantz checked the contents of the canoe and found video equipment and two large backpacks. From the distance Serge recognized the men as the documentary filmmakers he had seen two days before when he arrived in San Ignacio with Aio. Knowing how desperate Dantz could be, Serge worried for their safety. He decided to act. He swam across the river, letting himself be carried downstream so that by the time he reached the other side he was a safe distance from Dantz. He crept through the jungle, working his way back upriver until he came to the sandy beach. Here he found a track from the dragged canoe and followed it to where the craft had been hidden, covered under a pile of brush. The video equipment was there but the backpacks were gone.

Serge heard noises from deeper in the jungle and followed them. He cautiously approached a small clearing where he saw the two French men, seated back to back on the ground and tied to a fallen log. Dantz knelt in front of them, gun at his side, going through the backpacks. A broad smile came over his face as he held up a leather sheath and slipped the large machete it held. Turning the blade in his hand he appraised its sharp edge and size with appreciation. "This would be handy," Serge heard him say.

Dantz stood up and struck a fierce blow to the fallen log, very near the French men. He shouted and teased. The blow had landed just a few inches from their hands, and although their faces were partially concealed by the gags of knotted shirt material across their mouths, Serge could see their fear. Serge he had to move fast.

Dantz picked up his gun and tucked it in his pants. He looked around: On a low branch of a nearby tree, a lazy boa was basking in the sunlight. Dantz smiled and stepped forward, machete in hand. Serge followed Dantz's eyes with his own and saw the yellow-green boa. He knew Dantz would take pleasure in killing the animal, if only to prove to his captives what he was capable of, or as a simple act of cruel entertainment with his newly acquired tool. Dantz raised the machete overhead, sent it swinging toward the boa.

There was a sudden and swift sound through the air across the clearing, an impact, and Dantz was screaming, his right hand pinned to the trunk of the tree by Serge's spear. Then with surprise Dantz realized that his wrist was trapped but not perforated or torn, held by the curved leading edge of a spear. The machete lay at his feet where he had dropped it and now could not reach down for it. With his left hand he tried to free himself but could not. Dantz looked in all directions, seeking an explanation for this change in fortunes.

His eyes came to rest on Serge who had emerged from cover and stood looking at him. Dantz reached for his gun, Serge noticed the movement and threw himself at Dantz. With a single motion Serge made a tiger jump across the clearing, rolled on the ground, and picked up a stone the size of his hand. He rolled to his feet and with the same momentum threw the stone, striking Dantz in the head. He fell to the ground, the weight of his body pulling the spear from the tree. He lost his grip on the gun, which fell to ground at the feet of the French men. The men stared in amazement at Serge as he gently picked up the boa and set it down outside the clearing, out of harms way. Serge made sure Dantz was immobilized, and untied the captives.

Captain Ramos finalized his last interview with witnesses to what had happened on the river. He repeated a few last instructions to his men regarding what to do with the poachers' boats. As he replaced the radio on his belt he turned toward a noise from the river, and saw a small canoe carrying three men, approaching the pier. The man in the front of the canoe shouted and waved. Ramos could not make out the words in a thick French accent, but clearly it was a plea for help. In the middle of the canoe a tied man was struggling. He caught a brief movement on the other side of the river and located the silhouette of a man, standing with spear in hand. The figure raised its arm in a familiar wave. Ramos and Serge nodded as old friends do when there are too many people around and you don't want to be noticed. The silhouette vanished in an instant, and Ramos smiled, wondering if he would ever see Serge again.

Leading Home

Months since the last news of Serge from Belize had become old news, deep in a rain forest, a group of explorers tried to move in a straight line. The trail had vanished, the jungle was thick again, humid and filled with the everyday life sounds that happen beyond human existence. In this sea of green only they were alien, the thing out of place.

Max stared quizzically at Professor Clark, the expedition leader. " I think we are lost," was his reply. He was a tall and broad shouldered professor of anthropology, a modern Indiana Jones leading this group of students on a field trip in Belize. Their purpose: to confirm and record the findings of a French film crew that claimed to have stumbled across a previously unknown tribe of people living in the deep rain forest out of reach of civilization. Their only clues were a GPS coordinate and the description of a weird animal-like pendant worn by one of the tribe's women.

With a GPS unit in one hand and a map in the other, Professor Clark led the search for other clues, and points of reference on his map. Now he and Max compared GPS readings and found a significant discrepancy; the difference from the reported location was at least of a couple of miles. Professor Clark shook the device and held it higher, trying to get better reception of the satellite signal. The humidity and heat had taken down most of the expedition's electronic equipment.

"We have to go back, trace our steps. I'm not getting a reading." Clark now wore a look of concern, of fear for his students, and frustration for chasing another ghost.

The rest of the party caught up with them. "Everyone, water and backpack break," he shouted. Men and women reached for their canteens and water bottles, unloaded the heavy weight of their backpacks onto the ground.

Max walked to the end of the line, and with his GPS unit and maps in hand approached the last man of the group who was seating by a small rock removing his hiking shoes. "Dad, we're lost. There's no reading and both GPS units are behaving strangely. If we don't find a place to make camp before it gets dark we'll be lost and the whole trip ..."

Serge winked at Max and stood up. He tied both shoes with the shoelaces and placed them on his shoulders. With his hand on his son's shoulder he walked to the front of the line.

"Don't worry, I know the way."